The Cornish Village School – Christmas Wishes

KITTY WILSON

The Cornish Village School

CHRISTMAS WISHES

CANELO

First published in the United Kingdom in 2019 by Canelo

This edition published in the United Kingdom in 2020 by

Canelo Digital Publishing Limited
31 Helen Road
Oxford OX2 0DF
United Kingdom

A CIP catalogue record for this book is available from the British Library.

Print ISBN 978 1 78863 977 4
Ebook ISBN 978 1 78863 335 2

This book is a work of fiction. Names, characters, businesses, organizations,
places and events are either the product of the author's imagination or are
used fictitiously. Any resemblance to actual persons, living or dead, events
or locales is entirely coincidental.

Look for more great books at www.canelo.co

Printed and bound in Great Britain by Clays Ltd, Elcograf S.p.A.

For my Dad, Jasper, Gemma and Stanley.

Love you all ♥

Chapter One

Alice loved the cosiness of autumn and winter: the scrunch of the leaves and the chance of snow; blankets and hot water bottles; cocoa; toast runny with butter, crammed into her mouth as she sat reading in front of a fire, its flames conjuring up images of sprites and fairy tales.

However, winter also meant she had to dry her hair properly, as she was now doing instead of letting the heat of the sun and the salt of the waves work their magic. Thick and long, it waved down her back and was a chore. She sat for what felt like aeons blowing hot air wildly around her head wanting nothing more than to be back in front of the fire, concentrating on her book.

Her phone started to vibrate on the dressing table, its gold casing jumping on the white wood. As she reached across and saw the display, a familiar pang of lust made her tummy pinch – her reaction every time she saw or thought of Dan, and just as inevitable (and irritating) even when she merely saw his name.

This crush had been going on for over a year now. She was hoping to grow out of it any day now.

'Dan, hello!'

'Help! Your mission, should you choose to accept it, is to rescue me and my dear friend whilst promising not to tell a soul about what you discover on the mission. Can you help?' Dan's voice whispered urgently in her ear and Alice could feel a smile spread across her face.

'How exciting. Will this phone self-destruct? It had better not. But, of course, I'll help. What do you need? You are in Cornwall, aren't you?' She wasn't sure – Dan might be Penmenna's vicar, but his mysterious behaviour implied he could be calling from anywhere.

'Oh yes, although maybe not a Cornwall you'd recognise.' Dan laughed and then lowered his voice to a whisper again. 'Or quite frankly ever want to think of again after tonight.'

'Will you stop teasing! Where are you?' She whisked her hair up and off her face with one hand, to its default setting perched at the back of her head as she spoke. It was her I'm-ready-for-anything move, hair up and ready to go.

'Ethel's.'

'Oh, for goodness' sake, I thought you were somewhere dreadful. I'll come over now.'

'Okay but this is the important bit: can you get yourself in the back door? It's open, and then as you head through the kitchen and come into the utility room you'll see steps down to the basement area with a door at the bottom. We're both locked in the basement and need you to try and free us from the other side. I'll explain how to once you're here.'

'I'll be there as soon as I can. I'll walk fast, promise!' she answered as she clattered down her stairs ready to grab her boots and winter coat.

'Brilliant, but Ethel says the important bit, and it really is important, is that you have to promise to keep schtum about tonight. She's dreadfully embarrassed, but I've promised her you're the most discreet and genuinely non-judgemental person I know, I'd trust you with my life and definitely Ethel's secret.'

Be still my beating heart. He'd trust her with his life.

'Of course I will,' came her more prosaic answer before hanging up and clasping the phone to her chest, wallowing in a five-second dreamy look – which involved leaning against the wall, rolling her eyes and sighing lightly à la every romantic heroine *ever* – before leaving her home.

She set a brisk pace as she headed to Ethel's house. Originally an old farmhouse, it was located on the other side of the village and would take just under ten minutes to get to. Her mind was alive with possibilities. What secrets could Ethel have? Was she keeping exotic animals in her basement? Did she have a white tiger tied to the radiator? Perhaps she was the leader of a cult; a cult that wore lace blouses, talked about maritime history and had a penchant for sherry and cards? This was too exciting. What *could* Ethel's secret be?

She wasn't particularly surprised that Dan was at Ethel's. He was so dedicated to his parishioners that he would spend all hours of the day and night nipping in for visits and helping them in different ways. Alice had witnessed him putting up shelves, digging a vegetable patch and pulling a carrier bag out of Mrs Talbot's collie's bottom – a sight she would happily never see again.

As she reached Ethel's house she crept around the side, checking to make sure no one saw her. She wasn't sure why she was doing this, but it seemed in keeping with the mystery that Dan had woven. Coast clear, she darted through the back gate and let herself in through

3

the kitchen door. The lights were all on, but it felt weird entering someone's house without them being present to let you in.

The house was much as she expected it to be, the décor reflecting Ethel's age and tastes. Prints of tall ships lined the lemon-painted walls and a jug of plastic irises decorated the windowsill. Alice manoeuvred herself past the small kitchen table, complete with a rather lonely lace place setting for one, and headed into the utility room. There, just the other side of the washing machine, was a doorframe with steps leading down and as she peered down them she saw what looked like the locked door that Dan had told her about.

Even though the steps were lit, there was something incredibly creepy about going down the stairs. The ominous door at the bottom didn't help. Alice didn't know if it was because she watched way too many horror movies, or just because any woman of sense steered well clear of a basement. It was Known Safety Tip #1.

She took a deep breath and headed down.

'Is that you, Alice?' Ethel's voice came from behind the door.

'Yep, here now. I'll have you out any second. No need to worry,' she called back, making her tone extra perky – both to calm Ethel and reassure her own brain that there was no serial killer with a sharp knife and evil intent lurking behind the door. Just a *very* dishy vicar.

There was a noisy flurry and whispered conversation coming from the basement as Alice reached out to the door handle. She wiggled the key in the heavy old lock.

'It will be fine, honestly,' she heard Dan reassure Ethel before raising his voice to address Alice, 'Ethel wants you to promise to not tell a soul about—'

'Not a soul!' Ethel's voice broke over the top of Dan's, loud and very firm.

'—yep, right, a *soul* about what you see down here once that door is open.'

'Promise!' Alice was now intrigued to the point of bursting. What *was* in there? She was going to be so disappointed if it was merely some washing baskets and wine bottles. 'This key isn't turning, is there a knack?' She wiggled the door, but she was convinced it would take a marauding army to break down. Heavy wood and metal brackets made it look as if it should be inside a castle somewhere on the continent – Transylvania perhaps – not in an elderly lady's house on the outskirts of Penmenna village.

'You have to pull it quite tight towards you whilst putting your foot on the bottom metal plate bit and pushing. That seemed to work,' Dan explained.

'It is a bit tricky,' his companion added.

'A bit tricky, Ethel? I'm beginning to think this is a plan to make me fall ars— um, fall over whilst you two have a good giggle. Hang on…'

With her top half pulling, her bottom half pushing and her hand doing a lot of wiggling, Alice managed to unlock the door and push it open, falling through red-faced and a little breathless. That had been some job.

'Keep your foot in the door! Or lean back against it so it doesn't slam shut again. That's how we both got locked in here. We'll run out of friends to call if you get trapped too.'

Alice rammed her back against the door to keep it wedged open and, taking a deep breath, exhaled in Dan and Ethel's direction before having a quick look at the room.

Oh wow!

She blinked – nope, still the same room. She tried blinking three times and taking another look. Still the same.

It would appear that the door to the room was a fair indicator of what was inside. For sweet octogenarian Ethel, currently standing beside her wearing a dainty white broderie anglaise blouse and a penitent smile, had a dungeon in her house.

Not a dungeon as in a cobbled room complete with a straw pallet and a chain hanging from the wall; that would have been less shocking. No, this was more of a S&M dungeon, complete with some kind of leather bed-bench – currently covered in various coloured strands of wool – and an array of paddles hanging on the walls. There was also a small basket beside the bench, full of knitting needles and crochet hooks. Alice didn't dare think what Ethel did with those.

'I know what you must be thinking, but it's not what you think. It's not perverted in *any* way.'

'Um… no… Ethel, its fine. I wasn't thinking that. Um… shall we go upstairs and have a cup of tea? You must be gag— um, sorry… desperate for one if you've been trapped down here. And I promise never to mention your basement, ever, to anyone. Promise.'

'Yes, tea, good idea! Ethel?' Dan didn't look at Alice as he spoke, of which she was glad because if she met his eye she'd lose all her composure.

'No, no I think I'll have something a little stronger, thank you. But it's important to me that you understand. It was my Derek's idea, we just liked to play old-fashioned type games, you know, brave knight rescuing the princess, villain and the train tracks, that sort of thing and now he's gone I use it as my craft room. It's great for organising the wools and the thread and that thing there' – she gestured at the bench – 'is perfect for ironing when I'm quilt-making. Look.' She indicated a sewing machine on the far side of the room, that Alice had failed to notice because of the dim lighting. 'We *were* married and it was never anything sleazy, more saucy, yes, just a little saucy—'

'Honestly, Ethel, it's fine. No explanation needed. Let's go find that sherry.'

Ethel still made no move to leave the room and Alice couldn't help but feel a smile twitch at the corner of her mouth when her eyes lit upon some kind of leather cuffs attached to one of the walls. She could never unsee this.

The trouble that vicar got her into!

'…not like that modern-day stuff, all that latex, ugh! *My* Derek was a romantic.'

Chapter Two

'Thank you so much for this, Alice. You were the only person I could trust to call,' Dan admitted as they marched back through the village, having left Ethel's being sworn to secrecy – the woman had actually pulled out her family Bible – and promising that they thought none the less of her.

'It's fine. I know I shouldn't giggle but it wasn't what I expected. Ethel and Derek, who knew?'

She looked up at him, matching stride for stride, as the street lamp lit his features. He was outstandingly handsome with sweeping high cheekbones seen more often on Parisian catwalks than in coastal villages and deep blue eyes the colour of a moonlit sea on a cloudless night. He didn't seem real enough for this world. More Fairy Emperor than Parish Vicar. As if he had been created to demonstrate male physical perfection.

'Derek was before my time. Are you suggesting that he didn't look the type?' Dan's smile was wide and generous as he spoke, but then it always was. Alice fought the urge to sigh again.

'I didn't know there is a type but he definitely didn't roam the streets in a gimp mask if that's what you mean. A nice navy blazer and life membership to Roscarrock Bowls Club was his look.'

'You are naughty.' Dan's laughter at her words warmed her. She loved their friendship. However, he wasn't getting away with calling *her* the naughty one, not tonight.

'Um, you invited me to a dungeon this evening, so I think today you probably get the most points for mischief.'

'Ha! True. If Ethel hadn't already made you promise not to tell a soul...'

'*A soul*,' Alice reinforced.

'Exactly, then *I* would have asked you to stay quiet. Imagine the damage to my reputation if it got out that I had invited Alice Pentire out for an evening in a S&M dungeon.'

'Shocking, I imagine church attendance would plummet.' Alice grinned at him whilst thinking that in fact it would probably go through the roof. There was no denying that his mere arrival in the village had boosted church numbers more than 400 per cent. Before there had only been eight regular parishioners and Alice, if you didn't count the bell-ringers. Twin the Reverend Dan Daniels with a hint of sexual danger and there wouldn't be room in the thirteenth-century church for the amount of women who would turn up. It would be more popular than the days *Poldark* filmed down the road. Even women with no children of their own would drag nieces and nephews to Sunday School in droves.

'I imagine it would. Do you want to come in for a coffee?' He nodded his head in the direction of The Vicarage.

'I'll have a cup of tea. If I have coffee now I'll never sleep. There was something I needed to ask you anyway.'

'So, it's not for the pleasure of my company you're coming in, you're agreeing because you want a favour.'

'You know me so well.' Alice smirked, wishing he knew her an awful lot better.

'Come on then, what sort of scrape are you trying to get me into this time?' he asked as he led her down the path and towards the bright red front door of The Vicarage.

'I'll tell you when you've made me that cup of tea, and um… I may need something sugary for the shock I've just had.'

'I don't believe you're shocked at all, not for a second, Miss Pentire.'

'Trust me, I am. Ethel, for goodness' sake! Have you got any of Denise's fruit cake?'

'I swear you're only friends with me to get hold of cake.'

'It's good every time, I'm no fool. So, have you?'

'Of course, and I shall cut you a hefty slice in return for keeping Ethel's secrets.'

They wandered into the old-fashioned farmhouse kitchen, complete with an Aga and a ginger cat keeping warm on a chair in front of it. Dan flicked the kettle on and reached for the cake tin.

'Make it a sliver and you're on. Hey, Butch Catsidy, all good?' Alice greeted the church cat, one who kept the mice down with a brutality that would have made Caligula flinch.

The cat stretched out a sleepy paw and licked the length of his leg slowly before making eye contact with Alice, eye contact that asked why she even bothered. Alice loved his bad-boy attitude. If only she could be more cat.

'I do love this room.' Alice pulled out a chair at the great big wooden table, which dominated the sizeable kitchen and had tiny little drawers all along the sides. She always imagined that the drawers had held the hopes, desires and secrets of people from bygone days. A heavy jumble of papers, a couple of hymn books, a bunch of dried lavender left over from the summer, a cake tin and Dan's laptop were all piled on the table. It felt homely.

Growing up, her mother's house had always been more of a show home with everything displayed to show how immaculate, how affluent, how very tasteful Mrs Pentire was. Figurines were set at precise angles, curtains were not to be drawn, merely hanging faultlessly, toys banished to the bedroom and then only allowed out between the hours of half past three to half past five.

Alice, rather like her father, much preferred a little bit of clutter. He had been husband number two and was the reason Alice lived in Penmenna. A gentle soul, with appalling taste in women, he was no match for her mother and spent most of his time hiding from his wife by heading to the church or lying low in his study, surrounded by books, papers, files, the very sort of thing that would make Alice's mum break out in hives if he were to bring them into any other room in their immaculate house.

Her mother's disinterest, in both of them, meant the two spent a lot of time together. It was he who had taught Alice how to swim, how to build a fire on the beach, how each headstone in the graveyard had a story and that sometimes slowing down and just being, that was when you really got to appreciate the joys life offered. It wasn't a lesson her mother had learnt. He had always bought her the best presents too, simple things: a kaleidoscope, a snow globe, a spirograph. To this day, Alice still loved toys like those.

Her mother had left him for husband number three when Alice was sixteen, and had put up no resistance when Alice elected to stay in Penmenna with her father. And she had lived in the village ever since, staying on when her father left, his affable naiveté taking him to France when he fell in love and married for a second time – to a woman remarkably like Alice's mother.

The warmth inside that she always had as she thought of her dad stayed with her now as she cleared some of Dan's clutter. As the kettle came to the boil, she popped down plates and mugs that she had taken from the dresser in the corner. 'It's so cosy and friendly in here, I do love it. Apart from Mr Clawsome in the corner there, there is nothing cosy about him.'

'He is a bit of an arse, but he must like you a bit now. He hasn't torn your arm to shreds today and you've been here a least five minutes. That's a good sign. Although, you know that's not his name.'

'And you know it should be. It's a good one. As to the arm, give him time. He's just lulling me into a false sense of security before he makes his move. I know how his sort work.' She arched her brow at the cat in the corner. 'Although more importantly, you do know that after this evening, we now have definitive proof.'

'Definitive proof of what?'

'Pippa said that she reckoned Ethel was the guerrilla yarn bomber. Do you remember all those knitted scenes popping up in the village over Feast Week last summer? There were beach scenes, knitted seashells, all that sort of thing and we could never work out who was behind it. Well, they were the same blues, yellows and greens as the wool that Ethel had in her dungeon. It had to be her! I can't wait to tell— oh, I can't, can I?'

'Best not, sorry.' Dan shrugged his shoulders and wrinkled his nose in a no-you-can't gesture as he handed her a mug of steaming tea.

'Grrr, I thought we had her banged to rights. I know Pippa is desperate for confirmation because she wants to ask if she can play too. It was funny though, Ethel's face as she tried to reassure me that her Derek was very romantic.' Alice shook her head as she grasped the mug with both hands, breathing in its warmth after their brief walk in the nippy winter air.

'Well, he clearly was. He built their very own role-play room.' Dan's grin took over the whole of his face, reflecting the same delight on Alice's.

'Oh don't! I think the most shocking thing about tonight was that you managed to get a signal from down there. How? How can you get signal in Ethel's damsel-in-distress bat-cave and not one on the top of Penmenna Hill?'

'Good point!'

'Right, and imagine if she hadn't, you'd still be in there, possibly starving to death with nothing but Ethel and some bits of wool to sustain you.'

'Would you not have tracked me down and rescued me?' Dan furrowed his brow as if he could not believe what he was hearing. Too cute.

'I don't think anyone could have tracked you down and rescued you. For a village with no secrets, we've clearly just uncovered its very best kept one.'

'You're not going to let this go, are you?' He placed a slice of cake in front of her which she immediately picked up and took a mouthful of before speaking again, the odd crumb falling as she did so. It seemed like ages since she had had a treat.

'I will, I promise never to mention it again after tonight but you have to let me enjoy it a little.' She took another bite and rolled her eyes skyward, intimating bliss. 'Oh yum, this cake is so good.'

'Denise is a marvel, as they say. I wouldn't be able to cope without her, the church may well fall down without her keeping on top of things and boy, can she can bake.' Denise was one of Dan's church wardens who not only helped keep things running super smoothly at all times but was also able to bung a cake in the oven at a moment's notice.

'We all need a Denise. Especially at school. Sheila almost deleted all the school data the other day. Matt had to bring some local computer whizz who works with him on *Green-fingered and Gorgeous* to get it all back. I don't know how that school stays running some days when Sheila's trying to organise things. In fact, it was school I needed to talk to you about.'

'Okay, how can I help?' Dan pulled out his own chair and sat down, taking a slurp of his tea and picking at the fruit cake he had cut for himself.

'It's okay, you don't have to put your concerned vicar face on, this is going to be fun.'

'See, you say "fun" and my heart begins to speed up, with panic.'

'Well you should have faith in me. I have been asked to take charge of the nativity play this year, it's supposed to be Amanda's turn...'

'That's the class teacher you work alongside?'

'Yup, that's the one, and I know I shouldn't speak ill but I'm going to. I'm secretly glad she's passed it over to me because she tends to be so strict she can sometimes steal all the joy from things and I think it's important that the kids have a good time with it. Obviously, with full respect for Jesus' birthday and everything, but still.'

'That's okay, you know you don't have to do that with me and it so happens I agree with you.'

'Which is exactly why I'm asking you to help me. Quite frankly I could do with all the help I can get. And it'll carry on building the strong ties with the school that you've started since you began here!'

'You know I'm not going to say no to you, Alice.'

She believed him. She also longed to move her hand to cover his on the table.

But she couldn't.

He held her gaze and she could feel a small flush flare up from her neck. She had to drag her eyes away before he could read too much into them. With eyes said to be the windows to the soul, they were something she'd rather he didn't concentrate on. He may not see her in quite the same way if he knew the thoughts that flooded her every time they were together.

She needed to stop all this nonsense. He was the vicar for goodness' sake, you didn't have crushes on the clergy! They were definitely out of bounds; she needed to exercise a little more self-control.

However, she really did need the help with the nativity. And it would be for the good of the children, *obviously*.

'I'm glad to hear that, thank you. It will be a giggle, I promise.'

'Good, although no one asked me to help last year if I remember rightly.' Dan quirked his brow.

Oh God, maybe this wasn't such a good idea, she thought as she willed her tummy to calm itself down. She'd be blushing and butterfly-tummying all around the school every time he came in. Although perhaps she could view it as some kind of aversion therapy? It was a known fact that no crush could ever survive the planning of a school play. She could well be over him by Christmas.

'Rosy likes each class to take turns so each year the responsibility falls on someone different. She says that it keeps it fresh, stops it becoming a burden for staff, children and parents and means everyone in the school who wants to can be involved every year without doing the same thing time and time again.'

'She's very switched on, that Rosy Winter. I like her a lot; she seems to be a very good headteacher.'

'She is, we're lucky to have her. But with it being Class Four's turn this year and Amanda busy doing her qualification to become a headteacher herself, it's fallen upon me and so that's why I wondered if you'd help.'

'So what did they do last year? Have they ever had the vicar help before?'

'Ah, um… well… your predecessor was a little fierce, very… um… stuck in his ways, quite rigid, didn't really work well with small children. It was Harmony Rivers' class's turn last year when you joined the parish, so she was in charge.'

'Ah, okay, she's always a bit odd when she sees me. I don't think she's managed to speak more than five words to me yet.'

Alice was surprised this wasn't a more regular occurrence for him. It had taken her three months before she could formulate a sensible sentence in the face of his beauty. She nearly changed church she was so tongue-tied around him in the beginning. It just wasn't fair that he was born looking like this and was such a decent, good man as well. Talk about being at the front of the queue when life chances were handed out. She was sure a flaw would reveal itself eventually, but it was taking a blooming long time.

'Hmm, she's not a big fan of the church, any organised religion really. But you should have seen her play. We've never had anything like it. I'm not sure Rosy is that keen on her repeating it in four years' time, so maybe it was all a cunning and very effective plan. She replaced the nativity with a winter solstice celebration, which was fine in theory, it's important for the kids to learn about different cultural celebrations...'

'I agree.'

'You might not, had you seen this. We had a mini stone circle where we witnessed the death of the sun followed by its re-birth, and I mean re-*birth*, complete with the universe panting and sweating and accompanied by the sacrifice of some of her class dressed as cattle. I was holding my breath the whole way through, which was more than the universe was doing. Let's just say as a school we have never received so many complaints, not even after the time that queen bee mum Marion Marksharp felt that it was her role to demonstrate safe sex to Class Four by putting a condom on a banana using her mouth.' Dan choked on the tea he'd just swallowed. 'It was something else, Rosy never let her anywhere near those classes again and I'm still traumatised. Harmony managed to top even that!'

Dan rubbed his sternum as his choking subsided. 'I thought this was a primary school.'

'Sorry, that may have been a story too far. Yes, it is a primary school, but one that has so far witnessed drama-based animal sacrifice and, well… don't make me tell you again.'

'They say never to work with children and animals, but they don't warn you it's the adults you need to be careful of.'

'Oh, it really is. The children are a dream in comparison. But if we can keep Marion *and* Harmony at an arm's length then I reckon we can make the most beautiful nativity this school has ever seen.'

'I don't think there's any doubt about it.'

'Is that a yes?'

And as he smiled, both of them knew it wouldn't be anything else.

Chapter Three

'Marksharp Boy Two, sit down now! Your brother should have warned you, this is not Ms Rivers' class, we don't sit and talk about our feelings here, you have had two years of that. And *you* have had half a term to learn to do as you're told and to do it immediately. Now sit!'

Alice, walking through the hall, didn't need to be inside Class Four to know that was exactly what every child would be doing right now. Amanda Adams had a very definite power to her and for the first few weeks of the academic year she would ensure there was not a single child in her class that didn't doubt that obedience was the key for an easy life. What they didn't always know was that Mrs Adams' fire-breathing, book-banging ways covered a heart that was as squidgy as freshly made fudge.

What many didn't see was the way she washed and combed through Abby's hair twice a week, every week that the child was in her class when her parents were struggling at home. That a couple of years ago she had been the anonymous stranger who had set up a GoFundMe page that got Lily's family to Florida before their mother passed away from cancer – Alice only knew because she had seen the admin page open on one of Amanda's browser tabs late one evening after school. People didn't know that when Keenan was off for two months last year because of a case of glandular fever, caught unusually young, Amanda would take an hour out of every day after school to go around to his home, to cover all the things he had missed and keep him up to date with the class gossip. He had been unwaveringly loyal ever since despite her brusque there's-no-need-to-tell-anyone-about-this attitude.

However, as Alice pushed the classroom door open she was fully aware that none of the children sitting in class there and then were thinking that Amanda Adams was some kind of nurturing angel. Instead they were looking at her as if she was Mrs Trunchbull and hoping that someone, anyone, might vanquish her soon.

'Ah, Miss Pentire. Good of you to join us.'

'Good morning, Mrs Adams, class. I was just checking that all was ready for assembly in a minute. We have a very special guest coming in today to talk about...' Alice hushed her tone and whispered, 'Christmas.' All the children let out an almighty cheer and then, remembering whose class they were in, quickly quietened down again.

'Now I know that it is ages away,' Alice continued, 'but this year it's our class's turn to do the nativity play. I know some of you were in charge last year as well when you were in Ms Rivers' class, but this year is going to be very different indeed and we're going to need your skills and experience. The rest of you won't have had a go at deciding what sort of nativity you want since you were in Class Two, so you've had so much growing up between then and now that I think you are going have the most amazing ideas. When we go into assembly in a minute, the Reverend Dan Daniels, you've all met Dan before, he's the new vicar—'

'New, Miss? He's been here ages.' Jordan, a child who had been selectively mute when he had joined the school and was initially responsible for Alice's teaching assistant post at Penmenna was now so settled and confident he didn't just speak voluntarily but also called out.

'True, he has been here for at least a year. I suppose it's because I'm so old I'll always think of him as new. That happens when you get old.'

'You're not old, Miss, not as old as… um… not old anyway.' Rupert, otherwise known as Marksharp Boy Two, had glanced at his class teacher Mrs Adams halfway through the sentence and, ever smart, decided to stop it there.

'Thank you, Ru. Always so charming. Anyway, Dan is coming in and is going to ask you all about Christmas and what we think should be in the nativity play. As the eldest in the school you may know some things about Christmas that the other children, particularly the younger ones, don't. If you know what I'm talking about, and I suspect you all do, then you have to remember it's your job *not* to go blurting anything out to spoil the magic for the little ones. Are you clear?'

'Got it, Miss. No telling the little ones that Santa is your mum and dad!'

'Or grandma or grandad.' Miles lived with his grand-parents.

'My mum jingles bells behind her back still and makes us look up at the sky. We all pretend to keep her happy, even the dog knows she's bonkers,' Emily said.

'Ha, mine too! My mum makes elf footprints up the stairs every year with glitter and we know it's her cos her wellies are all red and silver and sparkly for ages afterwards.

And she's so funny cos she won't lie so when we ask if it's her, she makes excuses to wander off and pretends not to hear,' Callum added.

'Right, yup. *That* secret. No upsetting the little ones, clear?'

'And no embarrassing me in front of the vicar.' Mrs Adams' head snapped up from the laptop she had been working on whilst Alice was speaking and gave the whole class A Very Firm Stare. She was the queen of those. Even Alice sometimes got freaked out. This time Mrs Adams had more to say though. 'Jake, Rupert and Betsy, *you* are the ones I am mainly talking to. Polite at all times. If Miss Pentire comes back and tells me any different you will not be helping with the school play. You will, however, be in charge of cleaning out the school hamster every week until you leave. Do you understand? Good.'

Alice led the class into the hall where Dan was now standing waiting for them. Most people were a bit nervous when taking assembly in school – a hundred plus children in front of a person could do that. But Dan seemed completely fine, excited even as he waved at Alice and the class.

The children sat down with crossed legs, in the grey and red school uniform, all ready and waiting, smiling a welcome at their friends or siblings as the other classes began to walk in. Alice surveyed her lot proudly. As a small village school there were only four classes in total and the one she was teaching assistant for, Class Four, was made up of the oldest children in the school, aged from nine to eleven and getting ready to face the behemoth that was secondary school. She had started as a special educational needs assistant to Jordan when he had come into the school and presented with speech and language difficulties. These had been resolved and the boy had grown in confidence until he no longer needed her. Luckily a vacancy had come up and Rosy had kept her on full-time as a classroom TA. Alice had an extra-special bond with the class, having been with most of them since they had started school. She felt maternal as she looked at them and a pang flooded her which, through habit and a strong dose of common sense, she dismissed as nonsense. She was still young, she still had time, plenty of time.

Her gaze swept up from the children and across to Dan, only to find his eyes upon her. She tried to kid herself she wasn't turning a mild pink. For goodness' sake! She was not going to get to have children with the vicar, she could get shot of that thought before her mind had a chance to develop it, grow it and give it wings.

Pippa, the teaching assistant for the youngest in the school, was right. She needed to stop being so shy and sign up for a dating app. Cast her net.

'Hello, everybody.' Dan's deep soothing voice – a kind of cross between the voices of George Clooney and Patrick Stewart – filled the room and Alice, who had sat herself next to the terrifying, inseparable trio of Rupert, Jake and Betsy, felt her eyes swivel back to him as his voice held her, and the entire school, enrapt. It was deep and mellifluous. Mellifluous – Alice loved words and this one was a particular favourite. It was the most fitting way she could find to describe Dan's voice; its literal meaning was formed from 'honey' and 'flow' – just perfect.

Clearly unaware of Alice's poetic turn of thought, Dan carried on using his voice as normal people do, without too much thought about the intricacies of it.

'So, Penmenna School, I'm here to talk about Christmas and specifically the Nativity. Now I know it's early in the year yet, only November, and in my house growing up my grandmother banned the C word until the start of December. But she didn't have to put on a play with four classes full of children. I think if she did we would have been planning since September, so I reckon it's okay to start now. Especially as we want lots of time to make it special.'

'We certainly do,' Marion Marksharp commented. Marion was a veritable force of nature, a tornado draped in a swathe of printed fabrics. A tornado with teeth, an iPad and impossibly high standards. For some reason that Alice couldn't fathom she was in school *again* – she seemed to spend more time here than the teachers – and was perched on a small plastic chair at the side of the hall, as the staff sat on the floor with their classes. 'We do like to do things properly here at Penmenna. I sure you too will have the same exacting standards, Vicar. We don't want a repeat of last year, do we?' She shot a look from up high at Harmony Rivers, the Class Three teacher who had been responsible for the previous year's travesty.

Alice was surprised to see Harmony screw up her mouth mulishly. Harmony had spent most of her career at Penmenna in abject fear of Marion and that expression was the very first overt indication of resentment. Bold.

'Thank you, Marion. Do carry on, Reverend Daniels.' Rosy encouraged things to move along from where she sat at the very front of the hall, before they got bogged down in a Marion-style confrontation. That woman did love a battle, her tongue far sharper than the deadliest of swords.

'I guess a good place to start would be to see how much you know about the Nativity. The story of Jesus' birth. But with many of you having so much knowledge I'm going to ask that you put your hands up if you want to share what you know with us and no one shout out. That way I can listen to as many of you as possible. Deal?'

The children nodded. Every single one of them knew the story of the Nativity inside out, having learnt it each year since pre-school.

'Right, who wants to start?' Arms shot up all over the hall and Dan chuckled. 'Oh, I can see I'm in good hands here. Go on then, um, you.' He pointed at Ellie sitting in the front row, her arm waving itself out of its socket.

'Jesus and Mary had to go to the stable and there were lots of animals and then people turned up for the birthday party. I like them. I've just had my sixth birthday party, and my daddy *still* hasn't got me an elephant. I bet Jesus would have gotten an elephant if he had asked for one.'

'Okay… um… more or less, you've got the nub of the idea. Although I don't think Jesus would have been given an elephant had he asked for one. I don't think they knew much about them in Galilee where Jesus' family was originally from. Does anyone want to add to Ellie's version? Yes, you.'

'Ellie is kind of right, but she's wrong.' The red-headed boy sitting with Ellie answered the question next, pausing to swing around and grin at her as she dug her fingers in his ribs, her face scrunched up in indignation. 'Mary went to the stable with Joseph, and Jesus was born there. It wasn't like a birthday party, but after he was born people turned up to see him and brought presents.'

'That's a very good retelling.'

'Sounds like a birthday party to me,' Ellie interjected.

'Yes it does, but this was slightly different to most birthday parties. Now does anyone know why they had to go into a stable?' Dan regained control.

'The king wanted them to?' Alex from Class Three piped up.

'It was the emperor, he wanted them to travel back to Bethlehem. The king was different, he was like the baddie of the story,' Chloe added.

'This is all fabulous, you know the story really well, I can tell this play is going to be awesome. You're right, it was the Roman emperor, the Caesar, who wanted everyone to return to the place they were born for something called a census, which was a way for Caesar to count everyone. So, Mary and Joseph had to leave Nazareth and go to a town called Bethlehem...' Dan retold the story and Alice let her eyes close as she listened to his voice wash over her. There was something about the story of the Nativity that made her feel all warm inside, like roast dinners, fires, mince pies and puppies. Proper comfort for the soul.

'So how do we make the story come to life? That's what I need you to go away and think about. What can we do to make our nativity really good fun, really tell the story well? I'll take a couple of suggestions but then when you're back in class have a think and when your teacher asks you' – Dan pointed at Kam Choudhury, Rosy Winters, Harmony and Alice – 'then you can let them know what you're thinking, what you want to be included. They'll pass them on to Miss Pentire, who is organising everything this year along with Class Four.'

He nodded to Alice and as their eyes met a frisson, a shudder of excitement – which the whole room must have seen – went through Alice. When she checked everyone's facial expressions, it didn't seem that anyone had noticed anything substantially unusual.

Just her then.

'We do like a play with panache. I'm sure, Vicar, you'll be very good at guiding Alice in this. You're clearly a man with great style.'

Dan looked at Marion as if she was completely bonkers – which was probably quite fair – before turning back to the children, his eyes wide.

'Right, ideas with panache then, c'mon, what have you got?' He pointed at the pupils with their hands up and they quick-fired ideas at him.

'We could have real animals.'

'I think we should have a spaceship for the shepherds to follow. It would shine loads brighter than a star.'

'Can we write all the songs ourselves? And make up dance routines, I'm really good at dance routines.'

'Can the gifts be something useful? I don't even know what myrrh and Frankie-says is, can we give them a PS4 or something?'

The assembly came to a close after the suggestions had flown left, right and centre, and Dan shot Alice a did-that-go-okay look, his vulnerability about talking in front of the school revealed in a flash after appearing so confident, so certain, and Alice felt her heart melt just a teeny bit more.

Chapter Four

Alice's phone rang as she raced to the staffroom at lunchtime to have a quick catch-up with her friends before heading out on break duty. Glancing at it she saw that it was her mother. If she answered she wouldn't be finished until well after the bell rang – her mother had no understanding of her work hours. Mind you, her mother had no understanding of anything much other than her own needs; Alice had always been the least important person in the room, her mother's friends, the hairdresser, the hairdresser's dog, all taking priority. On the upside it meant she only felt a smidge of guilt as she slid the phone back into her pocket and pushed open the staffroom door. Her fellow teaching assistants Pippa and Sylvie were sitting around the table, digging into the Tupperware box of biscuits that Pippa's mum had made them.

'Oh, they look good!' Alice swung in through the door.

'Mum's excelled herself this time, vanilla shortbread with strawberry filling. The kettle has just boiled, come and sit down. That vicar is rather handsome, you're so lucky to be working on the play with him. But you're quite good friends, aren't you?' Pippa asked, her sentences tumbling over each other at speed, in the manner they always did.

'We're *friends*, yes,' Alice answered, the emphasis clear in her tone whilst trying not to stare longingly at the biscuits. 'It will be nice to work on the play with him.'

'Anything would be better than Reverend Howells, oh my goodness. He was terrifying, gave me nightmares as a child,' Sylvie recalled.

'Not as much as he terrified poor Eric Gaskell. An out-and-out case of homophobia if there ever was one. It's a good thing he has gone, he was about a hundred years out of date. Completely out of touch with his parishioners and the twenty-first century, although he would have probably done quite well five hundred years or so ago. It meant that people couldn't go to him with real world problems; he had no understanding, no compassion.' Pippa's platinum blonde bob nodded furiously as she passed judgement on the last vicar Penmenna had had before Dan took up the parish.

'Why, what did he do to Eric Gaskell?' Sylvie was intrigued as Alice decided to keep schtum, as much as she happened to agree with Pippa's viewpoint.

'He created a really nasty atmosphere for him, delivered sermons on sin whilst casting stern looks in Eric's direction so much so that he ended up going to play the organ elsewhere. St Just, I think.'

'But if he was that much of a bigot, why did he have Gladys on the organ afterwards?'

'Because he didn't know, even though the rest of us did, that when Gladys kicked off her size ten kitten heels under the organ, that bias-cut skirt was hiding a lot more than a silken petticoat.'

Even Alice struggled to hold in a giggle at that; Pippa may well be a little too forthright for some, but Alice valued honesty and, in this case, she was right.

'Rev Howells didn't know?'

'Never. Not a clue. Well, not until just before his retirement. I think he suggested they have dinner once, but as Gladys told me, she explained that he really wasn't her type.'

'That's hilarious.' Sylvie chortled.

'Right!'

'Well, the new vicar should be fine, he seems to be. You know him best, Alice, is he anything like Rev Howells?'

'No, nothing at all, he has a very different style. Very inclusive, very approachable. I really like him.' Her two friends looked at her knowingly. Pippa raised an eyebrow.

'Oh dear, Alice. Have you got—' She didn't get a chance to finish before Sylvie jumped in.

'Gosh, Marion has seemed a little flat recently, hasn't she? I know she made her ridiculous comment about the nativity having panache, but otherwise she hasn't been quite right, something is just a little off, don't you think?' Before Sylvie had gone away to train as a ballet dancer, when they were children, she had often leapt in to help Alice out of situations with which she wasn't comfortable. It was clear that some things didn't change, no matter the decades that passed.

Alice shot Sylvie a grateful look. The last thing she needed was Pippa getting it into her head to interfere with her and Dan. After announcing her love for the new Class Two teacher in front of the entire village in the summer, Pippa seemed to be on a mission to bring romance to everyone and was not always willing to accept that not everyone was as confident or brave as she was. She had already bought a new hamster as a 'friend' for the school hamster and had been on a mission to find forever love for her flatmate, Lottie. Not a particularly easy task; Lottie's hobbies were somewhat niche.

Alice grabbed the chance to change the subject. 'I've been a bit worried about her to be honest, Sylvie. She's definitely not the Marion we all know and fear. Something is going on. Pippa? Any idea? You normally know everything that's happening in this village.'

Pippa gulped and looked a little shifty. 'Um, I know what you mean. Perhaps we should keep an eye on her. I had hoped the summer holidays would have perked her up a bit; she didn't attend Feast Week this year, unheard of. But yeah, she still hasn't been fully herself this last half term. Let's hope the run-up to Christmas will bring her back to us. Well, to you guys… I'm quite happy with her keeping her distance from me.'

'So you don't know anything specific that might help?' Sylvie pressed, obviously as unimpressed by the lack of detail in Pippa's answer as Alice was.

'Do you want another coffee?' Pippa bounded up and pressed the kettle back on again. Pippa had an inkling about something, Alice was sure of it, but there was no point pressing her. Pippa spoke her mind but was also unswervingly loyal. If she felt they needed to know what she did, she'd tell them when it was necessary. 'I tell you what though, from the looks of it, she may have competition. Have either of you come across Josie's mum from my class yet? She joined in September. Oh my word!' Pippa continued. 'Nursery warned me about her, she had only just moved into the area about a year ago, bought one of the houses on The Hill. I have a feeling she's going to be A Force. She may well be coming for Marion's crown.'

'Marion might be more interested in Roscarrock School now Rufus has moved up to secondary, so she may well be willing to hand the crown over,' Alice suggested, and then took a look at Sylvie and Pippa's face. 'Okay, maybe not.'

'Well, this new mum has already asked me about how she joins the board of governors. It is always good to have parents involved, and she could turn out to be a wonder. It's just that nursery did seem glad to be getting shot of her.'

'Hmm, that is a bit of a red flag. Ooh, changing the subject, you'll never guess what I've agreed to do next week.'

'Donate your body to medical science?'

'I don't think they'd want it.' Alice cast a despairing look at her tummy, her breasts and her thighs. She'd have blooming cankles next, she was sure of it.

'Um, sign up for Tinder or Bumble or Hinge, or anything that might get you a sex life?' Pippa nodded hopefully.

'Definitely not.'

'You know you want children, it might be a step towards getting some.'

Alice raised a brow at her friend that firmly indicated she did not agree.

Pippa lifted her eyes heavenward before saying, 'Go on then, what?'

'I've promised to help Mr Byatt by being a Christmas elf for a week.'

'No!' Sylvie's delicate eyes were round with surprise. 'Why? How will you fit it in?'

'Hahaha! Please, please promise me you'll have plaits.' Pippa giggled.

Alice stuck her tongue out at her before turning to Sylvie. 'Well, I've got the costume already cos of school and I thought it would be Christmassy. All those excited little faces, it could be fun. And Bernie who usually does it has had to book a week off to see her mum in Darlington, minor operation or something. When she gets back she'll take over again.'

'Maybe you'll meet a Mr Elf,' Pippa suggested, practically bouncing out of her chair with enthusiasm. 'You never know.'

'I don't think that I can be trusted to pick a partner from the elf pool. You know my appalling taste, I'm guaranteed to find the one elf most likely to burn down the workshop.'

'Do you have appalling taste?' Sylvie asked. It was only in the last year that they had made friends again since Sylvie had started working at the school, so she wasn't as aware of Alice's dating history as Pippa was.

'Oh my goodness, yes,' Pippa answered, quickly selling Alice down the river. 'Just dreadful. Alice tends to rescue Lost Boys. She falls in love with potential rather than reality and then tries to heal them and put them on the path to good, but it never quite pans out.'

Alice nodded. 'That's true, harsh but true.'

'There was that Alan, wasn't there? He had all those news stories about missing cats printed out and stuck to his wall. Alice had wondered why she was never allowed around his house and one day she called in unannounced and saw the living room walls. It wouldn't have surprised me if he had the real things in zip-lock bags in the attic. Just not normal. Urgh!' Pippa was clearly enjoying recounting Alice's relationship history to an open-mouthed Sylvie. 'Then there was Tim, he was a bit odd wasn't he?'

'He was, and I let him move in, we got engaged. I thought he was the one. I wasn't even suspicious when he was walking his dogs for three hours every evening. He ended up running off with that woman who crocheted birthing blankets from yak hair for a living, insisted on feeding the seagulls and did all that chanting up and down Fore Street every full moon.'

'Wasn't she friends with Harmony?'

'Are you trying to rub it in?' Alice asked as the three of them giggled. 'Oh, and then there was that man who I met a couple of times and thought we were going somewhere. He seemed so normal, no mother issues and he actually went to work rather than just sitting around all day shouting at the TV. That was going so well, Chris he was called. Do you remember Chris, Pips?'

'Ha, ha. Oh yes.'

'What was wrong with him? He sounds all right so far,' Sylvie queried.

'He was a jam fetishist.'

'A what? Are you serious. He wanted you to what? Smear yourself with jam?'

'Do you know, I may be a girl with traditional values, and I'm proud of them, but I like to think I'm open-minded enough to give pretty much anything a shot. But it was more specific than that.'

'Oh, go on, you have to give me the details now.' Sylvie was agog whilst Pippa was practically wetting herself at the memory as she lifted her foot up and waggled her shoe in the air.

'Uh? Pips, I don't get it.'

'He was a jam-in-shoes fetishist. Apparently, it's a thing. He didn't want me to smear myself in jam and have sex with me. He wanted me to smear jam in all my shoes, walk around squidging it in between my toes and then upload videos for all his fellow fetishists to have a look at on a WhatsApp group,' Alice explained, a tear of laughter falling down her face.

'Did you?'

'No! I can wash the sheets; there is no getting jam off suede. And if he was asking me to do that two weeks in, what was two months going to bring? There's being non-judgemental and then there's downright common sense.'

'Fair point. Although that vicar is gorgeous and doesn't appear to fit your usual pattern; perhaps you could try it on with him.'

'I don't think so! I'd be mortified. I can't even think about that. That would be ridiculous. And most unfair on Dan. He's a professional, he's meant to tend to my *spiritual* wellbeing. So, no, a big, big no! I mean it, Pippa, I love you but no. No!'

'Okay, okay.' Pippa held both hands up in defeat. 'He is a bit lovely though. So gorgeous. If you like striking blond good looks and cheekbones supermodels would die for. Obviously, that's not my own personal taste.' They all smiled, knowing Pippa was fully loved-up these days with Kam Choudhury. 'Anyway, you know I would never do anything to make you feel uncomfortable.' She proffered the Tupperware container with her mum's biscuits in it. 'Jammie Dodger?'

Chapter Five

This was the hardest bit of Dan's job, even with faith as strong as his: watching someone prepare to pass from this life to the next and providing as much comfort as he could was a privilege, but it was tough. He was as human as the next guy and he had found it difficult sitting with Carol today, holding her hand, her skin so thin, and trying to reassure her that there was nothing to be scared of. Not because he was uncomfortable with what she was saying or the answers he was giving but because this was his first visit to see her in here and he was shocked to see how gaunt she had become in such a short space of time. He suspected this was the last time she'd ask him such questions, about faith, the existence of an afterlife, Hell. The next time he saw her she would probably be at that stage where she just didn't have the energy to care any more.

It was not uncommon for people to question their faith at this point of life; he questioned his own on a fairly frequent basis and he wasn't staring death in the face. But he did believe with every atom of his being in a higher power, responsible for the miracle of life and the world in which they all lived. And he did believe that when you died you went to a better place, a place free of pain. But whilst the Christian faith stayed the same, perceptions across the generations differed. Carol had been born into a generation and a family that was true Cornish Methodist, weaned on tales of fire and brimstone. That which we learn in childhood has a habit of rearing its head at the end as well.

He had sat with Carol and answered her questions to the best of his ability and then stayed a little longer, holding her hand, stroking it gently and murmuring encouragement – *I'm here, you're doing so well* – until she began to nod off, her face relaxing as sleep curled around her.

But now he was running a little late and as important as this had been, and it was, he did not want to keep Annie Bolton waiting. His grandma was the person on this earth dearest to his heart, the one he would willingly give his life for and the one he respected above all others. He hadn't seen her for a fortnight and was itching to catch up with all her news.

It took him just over an hour to get from the hospice in Roscarrock to Plymouth and another ten minutes of driving around the grid-like streets trying to find himself a parking space. He knew she wouldn't be cross that he was late and would welcome him with wide open arms and her customary sparkle but still, he felt bad. As he approached her house he saw her car parked outside, one she had covered in ladybird spots to bring a smile to people's lips as she drove past.

Running up the stone steps, he turned his key in the lock and let himself in.

'Hey, I'm here.'

'Come in, come in.' Annie bustled out of the kitchen, her apron tied around her waist, raising a hand to keep him at arm's length as she said, 'Let me look at you, yup, still handsome,' before letting herself be wrapped up in a giant bear hug that told her exactly how much her grandson loved her.

'Now I've made you a lovely steak pie and some roast potatoes, it'll be ready in a bit. You come and sit down in the kitchen and I'll make you a drink.'

'I'll make us both a cup of tea and then you can tell me all about your holiday. Was it amazing?'

'It was. Quite spectacular, I made some lovely friends. I do love that about a coach trip, they're always so sociable. Although there was one man I could have done without being there, so rude. He didn't think much of women, that's for sure. He turned his back on me the very first night when we had dinner and if ever any of us women spoke he'd make a harrumph noise' – Annie drew herself to her full height to demonstrate and made a noise, along with an action that looked like the Big Bad Wolf with a frog stuck in his throat – 'every time a woman had something to say.'

'I bet he learnt his lesson quick.'

'Oh he did, I was very polite and pointed out that it was a pity he wasn't. I explained that I quite understood and was sure it was simply generational differences. His face was like thunder. He made that noise again, quite a few times actually and then hmphed on out of the restaurant.'

'Oh dear, I expect he was a bit nicer the next day. But enough of rude men, tell me about your holiday.'

'Well, I don't mind a rude man. It's the impolite ones I don't like.' She winked at him before turning to get the pie out of the oven and his heart swelled with love. This woman was wonderful. She had had her fair share of troubles in her life, had raised him from the age of six onwards, and not once, never, did she complain about her lot. Merely filled this life and the lives of people who knew her with joy. Most of them anyway. Maybe not Grumpy Man so much.

'You are naughty.'

'I know but I like it. And you're very good so you make up for me. Very pretty, that part of the Spanish coast, you know, sandy beaches and cobbled streets, lots of bars and restaurants when you need a quick blast of cool air and a sit-down. And I met this woman, she's my age so we had a lovely time, fabulous. She lived in London when I did so we enjoyed having a good old trip down memory lane. Sally she's called. She was there with her husband, but she didn't like him much. So we left him with Mr Grumpy, sat together and did all the excursions. We had a whale of a time. Mind you she can't half knock back a drink or two. No flies on her. Welsh.' Annie gave her grandson a knowing look.

'I don't think you're allowed to say that sort of thing any more.'

'I can say what I like. I'm seventy-eight years old, if I can't say it now I don't know when I can.'

'Well, there is that. But it's also why I should be cooking for you and not the other way around.'

'Being seventy-eight doesn't mean my arms don't work. I like having something to do. It's been dull as ditchwater since I've been home. As well as Sally there was a lovely couple, young men a bit older than you. One of them had the bushiest moustache which he said was ironic; I don't know what that's supposed to mean but I do know I'd never seen anything like it. Victorian. Anyway, they were lovely. Helped me get Sally to bed more than once.' She motioned at him to stop faffing by the kettle and sit down. She didn't need to say the words; the two of them were so close they could probably have whole conversations just using their eyebrows.

As they ate she told him all about the beaches she had seen, the shops she and Sally had visited and the bars — apparently a lot of bars. How Kevin and Martyn were so helpful she didn't have to lift even a teacup the whole time she was there and she didn't have the heart to tell them she would rather do it all herself.

'You don't seem to have any problem telling me,' Dan remarked as she batted him around the head.

'Was it nice to come home though?'

'It's always nice to come home but I do have some news to tell you. It was a bit of a shock at first and I expect you're going to be cross at me for not saying before now but I think the time has come to tell you.'

Dan's heart suddenly stopped, or at the very least felt like it might. It had certainly leapt up into his throat and was stuck there. His grandmother may be straight-talking but she was never really shocked by anything much. He prayed it wasn't health related as his mind flitted back to Carol from earlier. Annie's passing would be the one death he wasn't in the slightest bit able to deal with.

'Oh, look at you, you've gone as white as a sheet. Eat up.'

'What sort of a news? You are okay, aren't you?' He could hear the panic in his tone. He should be better at this. It was his job to help people in times of need, not get all flustered.

But it was Annie.

'Oh of course I am, you silly boy. Fit as a fiddle, well most of me anyway. My hips aren't quite as convinced, and I had the one night where I didn't think I'd be able to do the macarena, but no, it's not me. It's the house.'

'What's wrong with it? Can I take a look? Have you told Arnold?'

Arnold was his grandmother's landlord. She had worked hard all her life but with her husband sodding off when she was quite young she was left bringing up Dan's mum, Laura, all by herself and had always lived in rented accommodation, battling to keep the house warm and food in the fridge whilst working incredibly long days as a carer.

'It was Arnold that gave me the shock.'

'No, he didn't! What do you mean? Is he in the country? Do I need to go and have a little chat?'

'Ha, you sound more like the Krays than the Krays. You're a vicar, I don't know that you'd have quite the same effect!'

'Are you suggesting I can't be menacing?' Dan raised an eyebrow and then brought his arm up, flexing his muscle at her as he had when he was a little boy and giving her his very best strongman look, complete with quirked brow.

'Not really. Certainly not scaring me, I'm afraid. For me you'll always be my little freckle. But no, don't be silly, Arnold hasn't done anything wrong. He's just getting older like all of us and had decided he wants to move back to England from Spain and preferably by Christmas.'

'He can't do that, it's November. Doesn't he have to give you several months' notice? I'm sure it's three months.' With all the work he did within the community Dan was fairly au fait with this sort of thing.

'He does, and he has. I just haven't told you. I've been speaking to the council, they know... I can't believe I'm having to say this, but they know I'm going to be homeless from the first of December. Homeless! What has the world come to? Mind, I've always known that this house wouldn't be forever, and truth is many more years and I'm going to struggle with these stairs, so I was always going to have to think of finding somewhere soon. Even just getting up those front steps is a chore. Like I say, I've been in touch with the council and they say if I satisfy the requirements they might be able to help, and whilst I won't be out on the street they may have to put me in temporary housing for a bit. There's some kind of shortage of housing. I did toy with not telling you, and I decided to go on my holiday and enjoy myself before I dealt with it, but you're going to find out sooner rather than later. So, there it is.'

She sat opposite him at her kitchen table, her posture daring him to challenge her but her eyes a little watery. He couldn't believe she had been going through all of this on her own and hadn't said anything to him. To be carrying the burden by herself, to have this hanging over her and not saying a word. Protecting him as she always had when he was a child. However, he was no longer a child; he was a thirty-year-old man and it was his turn to hold her up, to support her. He just had to make her see that.

'I'm so sorry you've had this to worry about, and I can only imagine how daunting it must feel, but there's only one solution that I can see. I have a vicarage that I'm rattling around in: come and live with me.'

'You're a good boy.' She leant forward and chucked him under the chin and then sat back again in her chair and stared at him for a while, not saying a word. He knew this meant she was building up for a fight, just working out how to get her own way in a manner that wouldn't upset anybody.

'Come on, it's a great idea,' he encouraged. 'We'd have so much fun.'

'No, no. Absolutely not.'

'Why not? We know we can live together.' He really meant it; they had done so contentedly for most of his life.

'Yes, yes we can. But we're not going to now.' She really was as stubborn as a goat.

'I know you love living here, but it's not far, you can pop up on the train whenever you want.'

'Oh, it's not the same here since Coleen went.'

'Ah exactly, Coleen went to live with her son, didn't she? And this area is very studenty now.'

'I like students, I like seeing the young live their lives, all full of optimism and hope. It gladdens my heart.'

'That's not what you said about them the last time I saw you.'

'Well, some nights there's that awful noise they make, they say it's music but it thuds through the walls like thunder. Boom, boom, boom. It's not like any music I know.'

'So you want to stay because you like being kept awake by drum and bass? Okay then.'

'You are a monkey.'

'I might be a monkey but you're a mule. You can't go and live in temporary accommodation until the council find you a home!'

'I'm not going in a home. They'll find me a nice flat somewhere.'

'You might have to go in a home. Or, you could come and live in The Vicarage with me.'

'It's not right, you can't have your grandma knocking around your house. Look at you. The most handsome man in the world. What if you want to bring a young lady back home?'

'Gran!'

'Daniel!' She made her eyes as wide as his.

'You do know what I do for a living.' He pointed at his dog collar as a visual reminder.

'Yes I do, and I'm proud of your calling. But you can still have a woman back. It's not like you're a Catholic priest. Vicars get married, and they don't get married if they don't start off with a nice girl popping over now and again. Oh, take that stupid expression off your face, I did have three kids myself. I know how it works. You can believe in God and still enjoy a bit of nooky.'

'Gran!'

'Yep, and you know I think you should be out there getting some. You need to settle down and look to your future, young man, instead of harking back to the past. It's been long enough now, love; Sophie would want you to have moved on now. You know she would.'

'We're not discussing my personal life, we're talking about you moving in with me. I could do with the company, and you could do with a roof over your head where you don't have to share a bathroom and a kitchen with a whole host of families that you've never met before. Have you ever visited temporary accommodation? It's far from ideal.'

'I didn't bring you up to be a snob.'

'It's hardly being a snob, just stating the facts. Help me out here, I'm not going to sleep easy knowing you're sharing with strangers all the way up here. Come stay with me, just until the council find you a decent place. Please.'

'I don't know, love. I want you to be independent. I don't want to be a burden.'

'Aha.' Dan raised both hands in triumph as she admitted the truth. 'There we are, that's the nub. Oh, Gran.' He took both of her hands in his and pulled her forward a little across the table where he planted a great big kiss on her forehead. 'You could never be a burden. Not even vaguely possible. It's coming up to Christmas, it's my busiest time of year. I'm having to help with the school nativity, organise the food and gift packages for vulnerable families to try and make sure they have a little bit of Christmas cheer, not to mention the Christmas dinner for the homeless, which, without being a snob, I would prefer you weren't part of unless it's helping. You could help me with some of my community work. Move in, see it as doing me a favour and we can use my house as a base to find you somewhere after Christmas, somewhere more permanent, that you like and that you aren't rushed into choosing. Please.' He gave her his very best puppy dog eyes. They worked a treat when he was little and he wasn't averse to using whatever it took to get his own way in this particular battle.

Annie sat there, with that look on her face she had had all throughout his childhood. The look he knew meant that she was so proud she could burst. He offered up a quick prayer that she wouldn't be stubborn, that she'd see the merit in his suggestion. She really was managing to drag the silence out.

'You're a good boy.'

'Is that a yes?'

'I love you very much.'

'Gah, is that a yes?'

'Will I be able to look for a nice woman that you can settle down with?'

'Absolutely not.'

'Oh well, in that case.'

'You're such a rat.'

'And you, my dear, dear boy, are an angel.'

'But am I one with a house guest?'

Annie Bolton, his grandmother and official Force Majeure, gave him a brisk pat on his hand and winked. He'd take that as a yes.

Chapter Six

Alice was excited about the afternoon. It was going to be the first serious session of nativity prep, with Class Four managing the organisation of the nativity themselves and her merely providing a guiding hand. A firm guiding hand – spaceships would not be likely to be included regardless of demand – but the children would write the play, choose the songs and maybe even compose some, plan the staging and finally, the most nerve-wracking bit for the kids, assign the director and cast roles. There were two performances scheduled to ensure all the parents got an opportunity to come along but the nativity was often a logistical nightmare. Alice had enough faith in her pupils and really did believe they were old enough and more than capable. She had no doubt that her class were going to smash it.

First, she had to attend a quick PTA meeting during lunch break. Despite being neither a parent nor a teacher, she was the member of staff who liaised with the PTA and attended all their meetings. Although Marion, who was in charge of the association, could be an absolute monster – she was often referred to as Monster Marksharp – Alice was quite fond of her in her own way. Yes, the woman said and did the most atrocious things but when you peeled back the layers there was a woman utterly devoted to her family and consequently Penmenna School. Yes, she was a nightmare, but she was a very effective one. Fundraising at the school had reached stratospheric heights since Marion had been in charge and her presence did unite the majority of the parents, even if it were in shared dislike.

Pushing open the staffroom door, she headed over to join the circle of PTA members already sitting on the far side of the room. Alice bagged herself a seat and peeled back the lid of her lunchbox to reveal the salad she had prepped this morning – leaves, edamame beans, beetroot and feta nestled together in the tub – and she braced herself to eat it, trying to tell herself how much she loved salad.

She didn't. She loved cake. And in winter she loved deep rich stews with huge hunks of bread slathered with butter, and golden syrup sponges drowned in custard with a splodge of clotted cream on top. Not salad.

However, she also loved the beach, and knew she should be empowered and bold enough to enjoy it regardless of what she looked like. It was the twenty-first century and fat-shaming was no longer acceptable. She knew she should be embracing who she was and not what she looked like, but being aware of how you should feel and feeling it were two different things.

And what she actually felt every spring was that it would be a really good idea if Victorian bathing machines were re-introduced. A little wooden hut on great big wheels that would carry her from sand to sea and from which she could descend into the waves – preferably wearing one of those all-in-one Victorian bathing dresses complete with ruffles – hence avoiding anyone having to see her waddle across the beach before she ran into the freezing cold water. And she did run, not out of any particular bravery but because she was afraid if she didn't get her body under the water quickly, someone might mistakenly harpoon her. Not for her the luxury of tiptoeing in as did those bikini-clad women who could potter around the edge of the sea, delicately shrieking at the cold and drawing attention to themselves as they entered slowly, slowly, step at a time.

Yep, salad it was. She was a strong believer in the change or accept principle and if she didn't like being big then she needed to take steps to change it, not keep putting it off. That being said, she had promised herself a week off this diet over Christmas so only a few more weeks to wait before she too could treat herself to yummy-yummy nice things. Like that carrot cake currently sitting on the staffroom table and calling to her. All rich and dense with sultanas and that cream cheese icing and… she shifted her chair a little and lifted a fork full of green goodness to her mouth instead.

Meh.

'Right, hello, everyone. How are we all?' Marion came flying through the door, trusty tablet in hand and failing to wait for a response. 'Excellent. Busy, busy, busy then. This is such a magical time of year we will need to get everything running smoothly so chop chop, let's really focus today. Oh, glad to see you eating salad, Alice. Very sensible, you're trying so hard. I'm sure you'll be a normal size in no time at all. Don't forget you can also join me at my weekly Pilates, we could be gym buddies, wouldn't that be fun?'

Alice gave her a look; she appreciated this was Marion being nice but sometimes less definitely was more and when it came to Marion's opinions it was very much the case. In Marion's defence she hadn't been quite so bad recently, her worst excesses toned down. Alice (and the rest of the school community) weren't sure if it was because she had had a mother publicly turn on her at the Summer Fayre earlier in the year or because of rumours that her marriage seemed to be dragging out through a long, slow and painful collapse.

'You would do well to take a leaf out of Alice's book, dear.' Marion turned to Jane, one of the newer parents. 'A little less cake and a little more exercise and you'd be setting a much better example for your son.' She adopted a simpering look on her face as she said it, in that majestic, bestowing-words-of-wisdom way that she had.

Alice shot a look of sympathy at Jane – who had put her cake plate on the floor and looked as if she might begin to well up – and was just about to reprimand Marion when one of the new mums spoke up.

'Don't you worry about what she says, Jane is it? Everyone knows that bullies behave the way they do because they're deeply unhappy. You enjoy your cake; better to enjoy life than to try and make everyone as sour and miserable as those that don't.'

The whole room went silent, even the teachers and teaching assistants who had, up until now, been ignoring the PTA meeting in the corner. Alice wondered if she should do something.

As if by magic, Marion seemed to grow taller as she looked directly at the mother who had defended Jane. The woman opposite her didn't flinch. She was polished: long glossy hair an expensive shade of honey blonde, immac-ulate nude nails and was dressed far more casually than

Marion in a pair of skinny jeans and boatneck striped Breton top, complete with external label letting everyone know it was ethically sourced and the price of most normal families' weekly grocery bill. She held Marion's gaze.

'And your name is?'

It would take more than courage and an accusation of bullying to make Marion back down. No one had challenged her in the seven years that Alice had worked in Penmenna and succeeded. Alice doubted that anyone in the room expected the new woman to successfully do so. But it would be interesting to watch.

Alice glanced around the staffroom to see if Rosy was present. With the headteacher not here, she figured it would be down to her, along with Pippa and Kam and Amanda, to step in if things became physical. Marion always relied on her sharp tongue and unflinching aim in battle but Alice wouldn't put it past her to pull hair if she deemed it absolutely necessary.

'My name is Serena Burchill-Whyte, I'm Josie's mum in Class One. I was very active in playgroup and was excited to get involved with Penmenna's PTA. I'm aware of its reputation and was looking forward to taking part' – Marion's shoulder relaxed a millimetre or so while offering a tiny regal smile in acknowledgement, before Serena, a smirk playing at the corners of her mouth as she held the pause, continued – 'and reshaping it, taking it forward in the future. It's so important, don't you think, to remain relevant, not getting stuck in a rut.' She flashed a grin at Marion, its insincerity as glaring as the lighthouse at Penderry Point.

No one moved.

There was not a rustle of a crisp packet, a bite of a sandwich or the teensiest sip of water taken as the whole staffroom waited to see how long it would take for Marion to wrestle Serena Burchill-Whyte to the floor and carve her heart out with a teaspoon.

'Quite. Well, dear, we're always happy to take those who begin at our school and train them up to be useful. I'm sure time will just fly by very quickly and it won't take long at all for you to be able to make a *meaningful* contribution. We're very understanding here at Penmenna, very inclusive, we do know everyone needs to start somewhere.' She gave Serena her most understanding look as she said all this, the one she usually reserved for the elderly and children whose fathers she quite fancied. 'Now, let's not spend any more time on this than we need to, after all this is about community and not an opportunity for self-promotion. So now you're quite au fait with that, Selina' – Marion accentuated the l, drawing out the ee sound afterwards, the glee glinting in her eye as she did so – 'perhaps we can move on to the purpose of the meeting and you won't hold us back any further. Is that okay?'

Serena looked like she didn't believe the mispronouncement was an accident for a moment whilst Jane had gone back to looking at the floor, sucking what was left of her cake so it didn't make any noise or draw attention to herself.

'The term in the run-up to Christmas is one of our busiest times of the year; as per usual we shall have a special and extended Christmas Fayre planning meeting in a couple of weeks' time and just use today to get some of the other—'

'Christmas Fayre? How delightfully archaic. Have you ever considered changing the name to something, I don't know, more modern and inclusive?' Serena sat forward in her chair as she spoke, with a look that nearly rivalled Marion in the patronising stakes. 'In London these days, we have moved on a lot and like to make our celebrations a lot more forward-thinking. Perhaps we should have a Winter Celebration instead? It would be a shame not to move with the times, don't you think?'

Alice thought Marion might send sharp scarlet lasers shooting from her eyes any minute.

'Or a Solstice Celebration, in keeping with the true roots of Cornwall,' Harmony contributed from the doorway. Alice wasn't sure what was happening – had she by some chance woken up in an alternate universe today? Harmony Rivers was the teacher most scared of Marion, reluctant to even be in a room with her and certainly never daring to make eye contact and yet here she was practically in the room and challenging her. This was madness.

She caught Serena slip a smile and a nod at Harmony. Aha, intrigue was afoot.

'Oh dear, Selina, you do think a lot of yourself don't you. Pushy doesn't do very well here but I'm sure you'll learn in time. We like to do our own thing in Penmenna rather than emulate life in the capital; after all we don't all want to be deluged in transport strikes and crystal meth, do we, dear?' Marion looked amused as she stared back at the thorn in her side, whose eyes were huge with indignation, before turning to Harmony. 'And Ms Rivers, how lovely of you to join us, perhaps you'd like to come and pull up a chair? Some of the more delicate mothers haven't quite recovered from your input at Christmastime last year but I'm sure those of us with a stronger stomach could brace ourselves for any more ideas that you may have. No? Such a shame. Best get back to the classroom then.'

Alice sent Harmony a sympathetic look, even though the woman really did have no one to blame but herself; she made herself so unlikeable with the constant ramming of her beliefs down everyone else's throats that it could be hard for most to feel much compassion. She certainly didn't show any to the rest of the staff as she lectured them on their sugar intake or the bathing products they used. It wasn't Harmony's message that annoyed people, but her delivery.

'We did consider changing the name to Winter Wonderland, Selina. We did an extensive poll of staff and parents to see which people preferred or indeed if there was any parent that felt excluded by the existing nomenclature. That's "name", by the way, would hate for you not to feel included. But the overwhelming majority was for us to stick with Christmas. So we shall do so, if majority rule is acceptable to you. Let no one say this is a dictatorship.' Marion tinkled her trademark tinkle but this time didn't even try to mask her insincerity. 'Now, time is slipping away and Alice will have to get back to class so perhaps if we have no more interruptions we could get back to the business at hand?'

That was the first time in living memory that Marion had given a sod about how important Alice's time was, but nonetheless it didn't make it any less true so Alice found herself nodding in support.

They raced through – or rather Marion, true to form, told everyone else what to do – in quick-fire fashion and doled out some of the jobs that would be undertaken in the run-up to Christmas. Serena, seeing as she was so keen, was given charge of the Parent's Pasty and Christmas Bingo night, a job that had been known to turn many mothers' hair grey and leave them smelling like a Cornish bakery for several days afterwards. Alice flashed Serena a glance and felt bad for feeling thankful that she was off the hook for that one this year.

Chapter Seven

Alice hotfooted it back to the classroom before the afternoon bell rang, in the hope of spending a few minutes with Dan before the children came in from the playground. He had offered to come in and help her and with Mrs Adams being out of the classroom this afternoon, Alice was only too happy to say yes.

Although truth be told, if he had suggested they spend five minutes in an abattoir or a Slimming World class she would have still said yes and turned up looking willing. Pippa's advice about firming up her boundaries was something she really needed to start working on.

As she approached the classroom she felt her heart speed up. It didn't do this when she knew that Amanda would be in there. She hoped the afternoon would go smoothly and that she wouldn't blush beet-red every time Dan breathed. At church, it was either so blooming cold that everyone else was too busy praying to not get hypothermia to notice, or it was so hot that the entire congregation resembled a lobster straight out of the pot and she blended right in.

School would not be so easy. There was nothing as sharp-eyed as a roomful of children, especially a roomful of children that spotted any kind of discomfort or a budding unrequited crush. They may only be nine, ten or eleven, but collectively they made a powerful force, didn't miss a trick and could possibly be MI5's sharpest weapon.

Entering the classroom, she saw Dan standing there browsing the bookcase, relaxed and presumably completely unaware of the fact she was only ten heartbeats away from tachycardia. Letting her breath splay out slowly over her lip she managed a cheery 'Hello' as she wandered over to him.

He immediately turned and his eyes, deep blue in colour, sparkled at her. She hoped he didn't hear her involuntary sigh, quickly covering it up with a 'Thank you so much for coming, I know how busy you are.'

'Oh, it's a pleasure. I've been really looking forward to this afternoon. I like working alongside kids; no one is quite as fresh or honest.'

'Isn't that so true? They're excited to be working with you too. It should be an enjoyable afternoon. Mrs Adams won't be with us, so it's just you and me.'

'Perfect,' Dan answered.

One simple word, completely free from subtext – but a girl could dream, couldn't she?

She was quite relieved as the school bell rang out, forcing her to break away from staring adoringly and trying not to dribble, instead presenting herself at the play-ground door and rocking the consummate educational professional look. Much more dignified.

'In you come, onto the carpet and remember to welcome Dan, who's come in to work with us today.' She ushered the children through as they came bowling in, cheeks ruddy from the blustery autumn afternoon air. Checking everyone was present took a matter of seconds and once the hellos to Dan had been said, Alice launched into business proper. 'Right, you lot, I am so excited about this. Today is the day we take charge of our Penmenna nativity and what's more it's going to be designed and implemented by you. I'm here to oversee but not to take the lead once we've got the first steps in place. So, Class Four, I have one question for you. Are you ready?'

'Born ready!' the class chanted back as Alice exchanged a smile with Dan. They were such a lively engaged lot, and with Mrs Adams out of the classroom, they let it shine through even more.

'Glad to hear it. So where do you want to start?'

'I reckon—' Rupert started to say.

'I reckon that we don't have shouting out. You're not so big that you don't have to put your hand up. Otherwise only the nosiest get heard,' Alice countered before he got any further.

Rupert put his hand up.

'Thank you, go on then.' Alice nodded at him. Rupert Marksharp was an exceptionally bright boy, but like his two brothers tended to do exactly what he wanted in school, and life generally. With no fear of his mother Marion, who terrorised everyone else in the community so successfully but was a shocking pushover when it came to the pleading eyes of her offspring, he was used to getting away with murder. His father had more of an authority but seemed to be permanently absent these days, off doing terribly important things in The City. The only person that seemed able to contain him was Mrs Adams – and that was by virtually tethering him to her foot and shutting him down if he looked like he might speak or move. Even then Alice couldn't put her hand on heart and be convinced he wasn't playing a long game with Mrs Adams too.

'All the big parts always go to the same people, the goody-two-shoes of the class that can sing a tune and do as they're told and everyone else will have to be an angel or a shepherd. And if the whole school's going to be in it, eighty angels won't all fit on a stage at once. But if we have different cast members for the two nights, then the odds, umm... I mean, chances of people getting a better role are doubled. People who might not get a turn at doing what they want to will be in with a shot.'

The whole class mumbled support.

'Ru for president!' Betsy shouted and Alice looked at Dan, who nodded as if he may agree. Knowing Rupert as she did Alice couldn't help but think he may indeed be qualified for political office.

'Anyone else got something to add or a different view? It's okay if you do, there's no right or wrong answer here.' Everyone shook their heads. 'Really, no one? Okay then, let's take a vote. Firstly, who wants to keep to the same cast both nights and involve the whole school in each performance?' She deliberately offered this option first but no one budged. 'And who wants to split the performance in two so we have less children on stage at once and two sets of main characters?' The whole class raised their hands.

'Democracy in action.' Dan nodded and beamed in approval at the whole class.

'Excellent, so we'll do that. Now, what do you think we need to do next? Hands up.'

'We should decide who is being who,' Rupert said.

'Yep, cast it,' Miles agreed. 'Can I be the innkeeper?'

'Easy, we need Joseph and Mary, and three shepherds, three wise men...' Emily looked thoughtful. 'Do you think we need jingly bells like I said about the other day, for when the angel descends from heaven? I think that would be pretty cool.'

Alice caught Dan looking a little confused. 'Emily's mum makes them look at the sky whilst she rings bells and pretends it's Santa on Christmas Eve.'

'Um... can I be the innkeeper?' Miles said again, but a little louder this time.

Alice sent the children to form small groups, draw up cast lists and make notes of anything they felt it was important to do. She wandered from group to group chatting to the children and seeing what they were thinking of. Dan followed her lead and she couldn't help but smile as his blond head bent when he chatted to the children. He spent a lot of time with Rupert, the two of them getting very animated and both waving their arms about, bursting into laughter at one point and then checking to see if they had disturbed anyone. Out of all the children in the class with whom she had thought Dan may bond, Rupert was not one of them. The middle Marksharp boy had been the number one suspect when Dan had first moved to Penmenna and his shed had been burnt down. Yet it seemed Dan believed in innocent until proven guilty, and was now happily chuckling away with Rupert and sketching something for him on paper.

She called them back together and asked what they wanted to do and was besieged with answers.

'We need a Caesar.'

'And an innkeeper is very important. I think I'd be quite good. I know the words.' Miles was certainly determined.

'Can we use my nan's donkey? He's very well behaved,' Tom asked.

'No!' said Alice. She was all for the democracy in action thing, but she was here for a reason and that was to say no to ideas like this.

'I think we should have snow,' Rupert said in a loud but considered manner. 'I think snow would make it awesome.'

The class, as one, nodded.

'We do have to remember that this will be performed in the hall,' Alice reminded them, picturing Betsy hurling buckets of polystyrene as she hung off the climbing bars whilst dressed as a snow cloud.

'Hmmm,' Rupert said.

'I think we should elect a directorial team, maybe three people who could oversee the whole thing. Three would be best,' Adele said before swinging herself around and giving her two friends a smug look. Adele was very good at smug looks and as one of Ms Adams' favourites was well versed in them. 'People who have a good track record in getting things done and who can be relied upon,' she continued.

'That is a good point. Who'd like to nominate people?'

'I'd like to nominate myself and Giselle and Issy,' Adele suggested, saccharin literally pouring from her face and onto the carpet. Alice fought not to roll her eyes.

'And I'd like to nominate myself, Jake and' – Betsy grinned widely – 'and Rupert.'

Alice muttered a little prayer. Amanda Adams would have her guts for garters when she found out about this as a possibility. Adele, Isabelle and Giselle had experience of dominating their year group in every possible manner and had done since they were four. With these three in charge then the nativity would promise to be a polished and respectful retelling, with all the joy sucked out. Ms Adams would love it.

Alice took a deep breath and said, 'Good idea, so hands up if you want Rupert, Betsy and Jake to be your team of directors.'

Yet again every hand, bar three, went up. And very quickly too.

Chapter Eight

Dan was walking home as quickly as he could. It was so cold, the wind particularly biting today. He could feel it nipping at his cheeks no matter how deeply he tried to bury his face in his scarf. He had come out to feed Mrs Williams' cat whilst she was away and as he had to fumble with Mrs Williams' keys, he had visions of his fingers snapping off and falling to the icy ground beneath him.

This winter had been harsher than any he remembered and the lashing rain of the past week was now solidifying into ice underfoot. This was a concern for a lot of his parishioners and would mean he would have to ring around tomorrow and make sure everybody was okay and see if anyone needed groceries delivered or pathways gritted.

The other reason for his speed was that his grandmother was back at The Vicarage, and he didn't want to leave her alone for too long. Today was the one day of the year they always spent together, a special if sad anniversary that they commemorated. She was also on the verge of agreeing to move in with him on a temporary basis, or at least he hoped she was. With the council having come up with no tenable alternative as yet, and the date of her eviction looming ever closer, he had a feeling he was about to seal the deal.

As long as nothing horrendous happened in the mean-time to put her off.

There were a couple of parishioners he could do without turning up and every minute he was away from her and The Vicarage was a window of opportunity for Mr Greenleaf to arrive and complain endlessly about how he didn't understand why he wasn't allowed to shoot teenagers that congregated outside his house, or Mrs Wavering nipping around to ask why in the world Jesus thought she should be plagued with bunions when she hadn't done anything wrong in her life *ever*. Dan had found gentle words about pride fell on distinctly unwilling ears. As yet she hadn't pulled her socks off and demanded he sorted them out, but he had a feeling it was only a matter of time.

As he turned the corner on the final stretch home he saw someone walking gingerly in front of him. He was sure it was Alice. He hadn't seen her at all this week and he had noticed the absence. She had this way of making everything right in the world, quite effortlessly, unaware of the effect she had. Having her in church lifted everyone's spirits – she pulled the average age down to just under sixty for a start – and she had been missed on Sunday when she had texted him to say she was suffering from a horrible cold and didn't want to risk making the others ill.

Her neck was huddled down into a scarf as his was and she had a bizarre-looking hat rammed tightly on her head, a hat a little reminiscent of Noddy's and with what looked like, the closer he got, an actual bell on top. He also spotted two long plaits peeking out. Despite the warm coat covering her body she seemed to only have tights on her legs, which unless they were hand-knitted out of the wool from Highland cattle, he couldn't see keeping her very warm. As he got closer he realised that his initial instinct had been right.

It *was* Alice.

What on earth was she doing outside in this freezing cold, especially if she had been poorly only a few days ago?

He picked up his pace in the hope of catching her when, to his horror, he saw her lose her footing and heard a scream pierce the air as the bundle in front of him flew up and forward, landing with a loud thud and an even louder 'ouch', followed by a curse. Definitely Alice, although he had never heard her swear before. It was still milder than what he imagined would come out of his mouth in similar circumstances. He raced to her side and as he got to her, he held out his arm to steady her and used the other to winch her up.

'Are you okay? Oh my goodness, you're frozen through.' The concern in his voice was clear – that had been one great big wallop.

'Oh, thank you. Yes, I'm okay. I'll be fine.' She tentatively got herself steady and glanced at the palms of her hands. 'I knew I should have looked harder to find my gloves.' She held up scratched palms then bent over to rub her knees. Dan hovered, feeling a bit useless, and as he glanced down at her legs saw, thanks to the orange glow of a nearby street light, that one knee was scuffed and the other was streaming with blood.

'Fine? Hmm, that doesn't look fine. Come on, let's get home and we'll get you all cleaned up.'

'Oh no, don't be daft.'

'I'm not being daft, come on. I feel bad I didn't get to you in time to save you from going fully over; the least you can do is let me help clean it up.' Dan was half holding his breath as Alice stood in front of him, her thickly lashed eyes half closed for a second before she looked up at him, her eyes, dark brown and rich, holding his as she nodded her head. He could feel the smile cross his face as he came around to her side and offered his arm to help her limp towards his house and down the path.

Once the door was unlocked, he pushed it wide open so he could help her through.

'We've got a patient!' he shouted to Annie as he felt Alice pause at his side. 'It's okay, it's my grandmother, she's spent the day here and' – he lowered his voice to a whisper – 'I'm trying to get her to move in. You can be my secret weapon, she'll love you.'

'As much as I love a mission, and we do seem to be good at them, I don't know that I'm full weapons grade right at this moment,' Alice responded, glancing down at her knee.

'I think the knees give you an edge.'

'I've never been told my knees might hold the key to winning a secret assignment before.'

'They're very winning knees,' Dan shot back and then realised that might be a little inappropriate, but Alice just giggled and he reminded himself that as much as he used his dog collar as a bit of a wall, she was his friend, a proper friend, as well as a parishioner. Even if she was dressed as an elf. 'Come on, you know you only fell over to get your hands on a bit more of Denise's fruit cake. This one is crammed with cherries and soused with brandy. It's a winner.'

'Well, hang on a minute, let me whack my elbow against the wall to see if I can get two bits.'

The two of them wandered into the kitchen, laughing between them with her still leaning on his arm. Sitting in the rocking chair by the Aga was Annie, stroking the cat, who looked ridiculously content on her lap, all curled up and purring loudly enough for the humming to be echoing around in the silence as they entered. A quiet soon broken.

'Hello, you went to feed someone's cat and you've brought a Christmas elf back with you. How fabulous. Oh, you poor thing, what has happened to your knees? Those tights need to go straight in the bin. It's treacherous out there.'

'Hello, lovely to meet you. I'm Alice. Isn't it toasty in here? You're right about it being treacherous. I slipped because I was so busy rushing to get home and warm. Luckily Dan was out and saw me tumble and has been kind enough to bring me in. He didn't tell me until a minute ago he had a guest. I'm so sorry. I would never have intruded, had I known.'

Dan looked at Alice askance; she was hardly an intrusion. He liked it when she nipped in – surely she knew she was always welcome? He didn't get the chance to reassure her though before Annie jumped in.

'Not a guest, I'm this poor child's grandmother, we always spend every November twenty-second together. And it's lovely to see you, far from an intrusion and I suspect, from looking at you in that get-up, that you may be a breath of fresh air. Come in, come in and get warm by the Aga and tell me why you're dressed as an elf in sub-zero temperatures. Hang on, let me just pop the kettle

68

on.' She leant forward, her hand holding onto the cat as she lifted the metal hob lid and moved the kettle on to it. 'Stand here and you'll be warm in no time. And Dan can get you cleaned up. Quickly, love, the poor child has blood pouring down her knee, it's—'

'It's all right, it's stopped now. And I'm dressed this way because I was helping a friend out. I've had so much fun – the kids' little faces as they wait for Father Christmas are magical, it really makes you appreciate the season, get into the spirit of things. One little girl burst into tears this evening because she was so happy to see Santa. Please don't worry about my knee though, it looks far messier than it is, it's just a scrape. I'll be fine, honestly.'

'Nonsense. We can't have a bleeding elf on our watch, it's not very Christmassy is it? Here you are, pull up that chair.' Annie motioned to the low-slung, battered dusky pink velvet one opposite her – Alice's favourite – and then turned to her grandson. 'Dan, have you got that water yet? How long does it take?'

Dan, who was at the sink filling up a bowl of warm water, rolled his eyes in exaggerated exasperation at his Gran's bossiness. 'I am, honestly! Alice, get yourself comfy, don't let The Original G in the rocking chair there scare you and I'll be with you in a second.'

'Aye, right away, Cap'n. The Original G, do you mind him calling you that?' Alice asked Annie. 'I'm not sure I'm safe sitting that close to The Great Catsby; honestly, Annie, I know he looks sweet all curled up like that but I'm amazed he hasn't pounced yet. I think he may be playing a long game today. He likes to see how much blood he can get out of me in a limited time frame. He's a thug, he's taken out the entire bird and mouse population of Penmenna and can sniff out vulnerability a mile off.'

'The Great Catsby, I like that. But Dan said he was called Dave.'

'He is, and it's a crime. He may not be the gentlest beast in the world but he is quite magnificent. Cruel but magnificent. Dave doesn't cut it, so I've mounted a campaign to see which name, any better name, sticks.'

'His name is Dave!' Dan called from the direction of the sink.

'I think I'm on your team there. But as to him being a bit of a thug, I don't doubt it. He's not fooling me for a minute. But he did whisper as you came in that he didn't much care for elf blood and he hoped you didn't drip all over the floor. Apparently, the fun is the chase.'

Dan turned to see Alice's mouth fall open as Annie teased her, before she chuckled and responded.

'I shall do my best to reign any bleeding in. I know from past experience not to upset Ghengis Cat. Oh, that's got to be it, surely?'

'No!' was the single-word response from Dan, now making his way towards them.

'I like that one too,' Annie chipped in.

'No!'

'As to the bleeding, I think that wise, dear; he's a very clever beast, best heeded.'

'He's not the only one,' Dan muttered as he popped the bowl on the floor next to Alice. 'Give me a minute, I'm not using kitchen roll on those knees and I think there's some cotton wool in the bathroom.'

'Honestly, I'm fine with kitchen roll. I'm not so sure I'm comfy with my vicar on his knees washing my legs down. It doesn't seem very respectful.'

'I think if the disciples accepted it, you can manage to suck it up. And *your* vicar, hey? Now, hush up and I'll be back in a minute.' Dan hotfooted it upstairs, although it hadn't escaped his attention that Annie had remained in her seat, which was most out of character. When he used to come home with scuffed knees she would have been up like a shot, and he'd assumed she still would. She was not the sedentary sort, no matter how many times he suggested she practised!

He could hear them talking in the kitchen below as the kettle whistled.

'Here, let me get that. You stay with the cat, you seem to have some wonderful soothing, soporific effect on him. It's nice to be here and not be scratched within an inch of my life,' Alice said. 'I am sorry to have disturbed your evening.'

'Absolute nonsense, my dear. You're not a disturbance, I can tell you're going to be a joy. I feel very lucky to meet you. We do try not to let November the twenty-second become a sombre day but sometimes it can be hard. We think it's right, important, to honour Laura – that's Dan's mum and my daughter – every year. Or before you know it memories slip. So it's nice to have you here bringing Christmas cheer in your elf hat and its jangly bell, brightening the evening up.'

'Oh. I'm sorry, I had no idea. I knew Dan had experienced some tragedy in his life with his—' They both stopped speaking as he re-entered the kitchen.

'You can keep talking, I don't mind,' he said to a very flushed Alice, who was now standing by the kitchen table pouring the boiled water into mugs, the tea caddy next to her.

'No, I'm sorry. I didn't mean to talk behind your back.'

'You weren't, and I really don't mind. I don't talk about my history much because quite frankly, it's not that interesting and because I don't need to. If you encourage Annie she'll be showing you my school reports and a collection of my baby teeth – which I know for a fact haven't been thrown out yet – before you've had time to drink your tea.'

'True, I still have them, would you like to see them?' His grandmother turned with a wink to Alice. 'If you just pass me my bag, I'm sure they're in there somewhere.' Dan's face fell as Annie looked back up at him and laughed. 'As if I carry your teeth around, I know you think I'm a little bit potty but even I draw the line at that.'

'I wasn't sure. It was possible. Here, come and sit down, bring your tea. It shouldn't take long to clean you up and then I'll grab you some cake.'

Dan motioned back to the chair and knelt down on the floor, dipping the cotton wool into the warm water, whirling it around and squeezing it out before gently dabbing at Alice's knees, trying to clean any grit out of the wound without hurting her.

'You might need to get out of those tights for me to clean this properly.' He looked up at her and she flushed again, making him realise that actually sitting here on the ground with her and her tights off – the elf skirt was pretty short – might be well over the line of what was comfortable. 'Sorry, scratch that. I'll just do the best I can as is.'

He hadn't meant to embarrass her. He'd had so much practice over the years at putting his feelings into a box and burying them – and not infrequently those that popped up whenever he spent time with this woman – that he forgot that other people had different ways of reacting to things. Often reactions that were more honest and far more open then he was able to be.

Dan was just giving her knee one more swirl with the cotton wool when there was a ring at the door. It was a big old-fashioned bell that made a good old-fashioned ring, one that spoke of bronze and weight and tradition.

'Ooh, this is exciting. I had no idea you get so many guests.' Annie enthusiastically nodded her head towards the door. 'Who do you think it is?'

'I don't know, not this time of night. Could be anybody. I'll go and check. Alice, I think that's pretty clean now, if you let me see to this then I'll come back for your hands and pop a plaster or two on.'

She looked down at her knee to check out his work. 'Thank you so much, you really didn't need to do this.'

He liked to. He enjoyed his parish responsibilities, but being able to look after Alice a little was completely different to that. She was so lovely, the way she always had her eye out for others, always went the extra mile for everyone within the community and anyone else she came across. She was a bit of an inspiration to him, reminding him how important it was to be cheerful, how it impacted so positively on those around you. He found that he could hear her voice in his head some days, the days the pain popped out of his carefully constructed box, reassuring him that the world was a fundamentally good place.

'It was a pleasure.' He stood before her and held her eyes with his so she knew how much he meant it. He thought that adding that he sometimes heard her talking to him even when she was physically absent may be a step too far. Then he scooted out into the hallway to answer the door as he realised Annie was watching him and he could practically feel the mischief, the questions, radiating from her.

Squinting through the coloured glass of the door he couldn't work out who was there. Pulling the door open, best vicar face on, his heart dipped a bit as he realised that underneath the huge woolly hat and winter coat and scarf it was Bill Meacher. Bill tended to go on. What would take most people a sentence to say could take Bill a good fifteen minutes. It didn't help that he was going deaf so thus struggled to hear what you might say in return. Not that he was ever interested anyway.

He supposed that, on the upside, Alice's knees would have scabbed over by the time he returned to the kitchen. Although it was also possible that by the time Bill had finished talking, Dave would have eaten both women and he'd be greeted with a pile of stripped bones and an elf hat in front of the Aga.

He didn't say any of this to the man in front of him. And, as vicars most definitely weren't meant to swear, instead he put on his most professional face and asked how he could help.

Chapter Nine

'I've got to nip out quickly. Bill has seen someone trying to break into the church, or at the very least being very suspicious. I'll check and then be back in a jiffy. Don't you dare go anywhere.' Dan had returned to the kitchen to update his two guests and directed the last part of his sentence at Alice, who immediately heard herself retort, 'Bossy!'

But the truth was she was quite happy to stay. She had a feeling Annie was going to be a hoot, and all that was waiting at home this evening were chores. She could easily skip those for cake and a chat with Annie. It was better to be polite and eat what she was given than worry about her diet. The cake was virtually all fruit anyway, so it should be allowed, right?

Plus, she wasn't sure if she'd actually walk home right now or float – although that would definitely stop her falling over again – so staying would be the sensible thing. Just while her heart slowed down from its frenetic pitter-patter that had resulted from Dan kneeling at her feet and tending to her knee.

The minute his hand had dipped the cotton wool in the water she had felt her heart speed up, the anticipation of his fingers on her skin making her zing merely from the thought of it. She had been terrified she would flinch when Dan had actually touched her and it had taken all of her self-control to hold herself taut and make sure that didn't happen. His touch had been so gentle but deliberate, in control. It was a heady mix. She had tingled literally all the way up her leg, through her whole body to the tip of her head and back down again. But she figured she had managed to get away without letting on. At least she hoped so; she didn't think Dan knew she was harbouring a crush the size of the *Titanic*, and just as deadly.

Her crush was now so monumental that it wasn't even based on the superficial things any more, like the ridiculous set of cheekbones he had, the twinkle in those deep blue eyes that suggested all manner of naughty things, that wonderful blond head of hair or the fact that he was tall and with such broad shoulders that he couldn't fail to make anyone safe; although the thought of those arms wrapping themselves around her was enough to make her hyperventilate. But it was more the way he behaved, his character in the true sense of the word, that meant she was sighing from afar – apart from tonight where she was trying very hard not to sigh visibly, being so close.

'So, shall we have some cake then. I know where he keeps it and he's promised me a slice; would you like one with me? Then you can be my partner in crime and I won't get the blame solely by myself.' Alice tried to get Annie to collaborate.

'Ah, I'm not so sure if I go along with that, that I won't be the one to be blamed as ringleader.'

'See how clever I was, not only do I get free cake but I can shift the blame onto you. He's definitely not going to get cross at his grandma.'

'With that boy, I think we could rob the whole house and he still wouldn't raise his voice. He's always been a love.'

'Were you close to him as a child then? I bet he was adorable,' Alice asked as she went to grab the cake tin from the shelf. Perhaps she shouldn't have added that last bit – it might well have just given her crush away – but she'd learnt long ago to shut up when she had said something stupid. To try and explain often made it so much worse.

And yet the words, the lie, *I don't fancy him or anything* were burbling over the top of her lips, desperate for escape.

Thankfully she contained them.

'That I was, I brought him up. Such a sweet, sweet boy. You know about his mum and dad, of course?' Annie asked, her hand still stroking the cat but her gaze directly on Alice as she asked this question.

'No, he's never mentioned them. He's quite private, always there to support everyone else but he rarely talks about himself. So, I don't know anything about his mum and dad.' Alice shook her head to confirm what she said. 'Your mention of your daughter, Laura, was the first I had heard.'

But now of course, she was wondering what had happened to his parents. Why did his grandma bring him up? Did that make her madly nosy or just friendly and concerned? Arghh! This wasn't about her at all, when would she learn? It didn't matter what she was thinking; how did it all, how had it all, impacted on Dan?

'He's always been that way. Brilliant in looking after others – and trust me I count myself among that group – but quiet about his own things. I don't blame him, he's had more than his fair share to deal with. Although, when he was upstairs you said you knew about something, but then he interrupted us— ooh, cut me a large wedge if that's fruit cake, that looks amazing!'

'It is, shall I cut a piece for Dan as well? It seems rude to wolf down his cake and not cut some for him.'

'Good point, we best had.'

'I tell you what, let's see if I can get it into a Dan shape for him, something to make him giggle when he comes back in.'

'How on earth are you going to do that?'

'Aha, I work in a primary school, I can shape anything out of anything if you give me a second.' She started work on the cake in front of her before changing her tone and talking more softly. 'When Dan first came to the parish there was a bad habit amongst the locals of drinking and driving. Now, I have never known Dan to be judgemental about anything, but a couple of weeks in, when he realised how bad things were, how normalised it was, he delivered a sermon about it. It was just as the church was beginning to fill up; people are always curious about the new here, so with a new vicar in town people wanted to see what he was like. Then The Dan Effect swiftly followed.'

'The what?' Annie queried. She had finally ditched the cat from her lap, who, now he was awake, had attacked the back of Alice's leg half-heartedly and then scooted out of the cat flap in the back door, no doubt to terrorise and plunder the flora and fauna of Penmenna.

'The Dan Effect. Having been seen around the village... well, your grandson *is* quite good-looking...'

'Oh, I know.' Annie stopped fiddling with the fruit cake alongside Alice, having both been using their fingers to push the slice into a circular shape for the face. 'He has been batting off both boys and girls for years. He was never interested in any of them, apart from Sophie, of course.'

'Right, well it's Sophie that I know about. So, The Dan Effect, that means that the church was full, people had turned up to test our new vicar, see if he had any horrendous habits – our last one was quite fearsome – and women had come in from miles around, I mean miles, to check out the new hot vicar. Oh, sorry, not hot... um...'

Annie waved her hand and grinned in acknowledgement that Alice was fine.

'Okay, sorry... honestly we had never been so busy. Anyway, unlike Reverend Howells ranting and wailing about the evils of the world from the pulpit, Dan had a chair at the front and quietly and openly told us the story of Sophie, of how a drunk driver had taken her from this world when they were both eighteen and the ensuing impact it had had on him and all those involved in her life. He spoke so quietly, and so openly that the whole church was silent, everyone leaning in to hear what he had to say. He wasn't fooled that the huge amount of people in church that day had suddenly found God, and he didn't mind that in the slightest – he added that in every action we make, we must try and put others above us, and by doing that we'll be living a good and supportive life and that is as important, if not more so, than faith. He pointed out what if that person hadn't got behind the wheel that night and listed the possible positives that could have occurred, from a local taxi driver having another fare to the obvious, to Sophie being alive today and impacting her good on the world around her.'

'Shall I take these two cherries out and use them for eyes, do you think?' asked Annie, apparently far more intrigued in the shaping of the cake into her grandson's face than she was moved by Alice's retelling.

'Yes, that would work. Anyway, point is the church was awash with tears that day, most of us learnt about Sophie, felt trusted by him and thus were happy to trust him and most importantly, as the news flew around Penmenna, as it does, people thought twice about getting behind the wheel. He's never shared as much since. So yes, I knew about Sophie and that's what I was referring to earlier, but it sounds like there is even more tragedy in his life… Oh, that looks great, I love how you've put a sultana on the cherry to give him pupils. You should come into school.'

'I'd love to, but I don't know how much I'll be around. Although Dan is pushing me to move in.'

'Oh that's a great idea! Why would you not?'

Annie ignored the question but did open up about her grandson. 'The loss of Sophie hit him hard; you could say, after his parents, it finished him off. Or I worried it did. He lost all faith for a bit, faith in humanity, his faith in God, his hopes of ever being happy. But I'm saying too much, he always tells me off for oversharing his things, but part of it is my story too.'

'I don't want you to say anything that he wouldn't want you to, but he lost his parents too? Your daughter? They're both dead?'

'Not exactly, but yes in a manner. I brought him up from the age of six, saw him through primary school, secondary school and the time of losing Sophie, when he changed trajectory completely. Ultimately, he ended up in the church, which none of us saw coming even though he had been brought up by me as a Christian. But you're right, I probably shouldn't say more. He'll tell you when the time is right for him, I know he will.'

Alice wasn't so sure. There was no reason for Dan to tell her anything and there was no way she was going to push. For such a lovely man to have been through even worse than that which she already knew about was a bit hard to compute. But maybe that was why he was so kind, maybe he had learnt such harsh lessons at such a young age they had shaped how he had behaved ever since. Her daydreams of him wrapping his arms around her and making her feel safe changed; suddenly she wanted to be the one comforting him, keeping *him* safe, not letting any more wolves come to the door.

'I think you're right not to tell me, but I do hate the thought of him suffering so much.'

'Ah, you're a pet but don't worry about him, honestly, that's my job. You just help me find something to make his dog collar on this here, so he knows what we've done. Otherwise he's just going to think we've pulled his cake to bits and not know why. We need to finish it off beautifully.'

'Icing, I know he has some in here somewhere, we bought loads of ready-rolled when we made Dalmatian cupcakes for a fundraiser, he may well still have some left. Hang on, let me check.'

'You'd better hurry up, he'll be back any minute.'

'Not if he's with Bill he won't be. Once he's chased off anyone hovering around the church that shouldn't be, then he'll be subjected to a twenty-five-minute talk on the state of Bill's onions. Honestly, your grandson is a saint. We'll have time to make a Catpernicus – no? Not so good? – as well out of these ginger nuts if you wanted to, although that may be a step too far.' She held up a packet of biscuits briefly for Annie to see and then replaced them in the cupboard, shrieking with triumph as she pulled out pots of icing and some almonds as well. 'Look, a nose and a dog collar, and oh my goodness, he's got some strawberry laces. This is going to be a work of art!'

Chapter Ten

'I'm so sorry. That took a while.'

'We thought the burglars might have carried you off!' Annie joked.

'As usual, there wasn't a whisper when I got there. It must have been kids but I walked all around the church with Bill and we double-checked everything.'

'Oh well, that's good.' Alice smiled.

'Yes, it is, but Bill told me he's withdrawing from choir, which isn't so good. He says with his voice changing he doesn't really feel it's for him any more. It may actually sound the choir's death knell. I tried to talk him out of it but as we all know, Bill is… um…'

'Great at talking and not so good at listening. There you go, I've said it so you don't have to.'

Dan crinkled his eyes at her – the crinkle enhancing the sparkle rather than diminishing it – and Alice was ridiculously glad she was sitting down.

'Look, I've managed to keep Alice here, she tried to sneak home but I reminded her you had found her a plaster and everything, plus we've been creating art.' Annie interrupted them, and stood aside to reveal his piece of cake, now less a neat slice and more a hotchpotch topped with white and black icing, a whole almond and half a strawberry lace. 'Ta-daa!'

'Oh wow, what is that? Oh gosh, sorry. Is that… is that meant to be *me*?' Dan started to laugh so hard that he had to put his hands out to steady himself on the table, and then he carried on laughing, clenching the table to prevent it wobbling. Alice and Annie both stood watching him, a grin on both their faces as they exchanged a look of pride that they had reduced him to tears. For he was currently wiping at his eye with his sleeve. 'Oh that's brilliant. No one has ever turned a piece of cake into me before.'

'Have they not? How could you not have done?' Alice turned to Annie and teased her about her failing. Alice was definitely comfortable in her company now; they had had so much fun this evening that it had been worth getting a scabbed knee, or two. Alice really hoped she did decide to move to Penmenna.

'Are you saying I have a cakey face?' Dan asked with a chuckle as he rammed a bit of his 'cheek' into his mouth.

Alice giggled and turned back to Dan, who had made short work of that piece and was now eating a bit of strawberry shoelace. 'You said that Bill was dropping out of choir. I'm sure he elaborated on his reasons?'

'He felt he was letting the choir down what with his age and his voice not being what it has been. I pointed out that without him, especially with Carol so poorly, that we were bound to fold. You can't really have a choir with only four people. But he wasn't budging.'

'Might we really lose the choir?'

'I'm afraid so, fancy joining?'

'I'm not a particularly confident singer, I don't think I'm good enough for a choir but of course, I'll give it a shot if it helps.'

'What about The Dan Effect?' Annie asked before Dan had a chance to answer. 'I thought you had lots of people turning up to church now?'

'The Dan Effect? What on earth?' Dan's eyebrows shot up so hard and so far that they practically bounced off the top of his head.

'Alice was telling me' – Alice wished the ground would open up and swallow her right now – 'that half the women in a five-mile radius turned up to church when you took over from, what was his name again?'

'Um, Rev Howells,' Alice muttered, eyes on her stripy toes. She was still in the ripped elf tights and was currently concentrating on counting the stripes from her toes to the first rip. Anything had to be better than looking up at Dan right now.

'That's right, apparently Rev Howells was a bit of an old bast— um, not very nice but Alice said that when people saw how good-looking you were they flocked to church, isn't that right, Alice? I'm sure some of them would come to choir.'

Alice knew that now her face, neck and probably arms were fully fledged scarlet and wondered how she was going to make a quick exit before Annie ratted her out any further. She was relieved she hadn't got so comfortable that she had mentioned her all-consuming crush on Annie's grandson. That would have been one way to ensure this evening became even more mortifying. She avoided Dan's eye even though he looked directly at her as Annie was speaking.

'Okay, well I'm obviously not going to comment on my predecessor but yes there was a spike in attendance once I had been in the village a couple of weeks.' Alice dared to peek up and was met with him winking at her; great, that would help stop the mad blushing. 'However I'm afraid my magnetic good looks weren't enough to guarantee they all came back every week. Although there has been a definite increase, I'm going to carry on thinking it's because of my hypnotic sermons and hymn choices rather than my biceps.'

'Ha, I think it might be those biceps.' His grandma cackled.

'I love your sermons, they always resonate with me. You're very... well, you just say what needs to be said and make me reflect upon the way I'm doing and looking at things.'

'That's very nice to hear. I'm glad it's more than my handsome face that pulls you in every Sunday.'

'To be fair, I did attend before, so you know...' Alice teased, her flushing a little more under control and her courage back.

'I'm going to take you up on your offer of joining the choir you know.'

'Well, you're desperate. I'm sure you'll change your mind after you hear me sing.'

'You've managed not to shatter the stained glass so far. I did ask last week if anyone was interested but you know what it's like, people suddenly get very interested in their hymn sheets or what's in their handbags.'

'I tell you what, seeing as you're helping me with the nativity play... which is going amazingly well by the way, Rupert and his group are so creative. Amanda was furious when she heard him, Betsy and Jake were in charge and told me she wasn't prepared to share any of the responsibility when they burn the whole of Penmenna School down. I'm getting sidetracked, although I can't wait for you to see it so far. Anyway, seeing as you're helping with the nativity I shall be chief rounder-upper and see if I can get you some more numbers for choir, if not permanently then definitely in time for the main Christmas services. How does that sound?'

'That sounds awesome. Are you sure?'

'Yes, had I known you were worrying about it I would have done so earlier. I can't promise I'll succeed but I'll give it a jolly good shot.'

'Atta girl.' Granny Annie high-fived her.

'Excellent, and then if you could just get this monster of mine to agree to come and live with me then you really will be a miracle worker.'

'I'll see what I can do.' This time it was Alice's turn to wink, but at Annie, who was still standing up and shaking her head.

'If anyone could do it, it will be you. Now are you going to let me put this plaster on for you?'

Alice would rather have let the air dry out the wounds on her knee, but it was almost Christmas. Everyone was allowed the odd treat. Was she going to let Dan touch her legs again with that oh-so-gentle but firm touch? Hmmm. She pulled her elf skirt down a little further and held her leg out and wondered if he'd think she was really weird if she just closed her eyes for a bit.

Chapter Eleven

Alice had been busy since that night at The Vicarage, chasing up everyone in the village who she knew could sing, and a few that couldn't, in an attempt to get them together for the choir. So far, she had been amazed at the response, but then she had always known that people were fundamentally good. Most were happy to commit over the Christmas period but were unwilling at the moment to sign up to more and Alice quite understood. Life was increasingly secular these days, had been for decades, and for people who didn't have faith they didn't want to commit themselves to the church. She was secretly hoping that even if just a couple of people enjoyed the community aspect enough then they might be able to make it last longer than the seasonal period, but she wasn't counting her chickens.

So far, from school, Rosy had committed to helping out over Christmas and Lynne had offered up her husband, Dave, who had a taste for medieval music which she thought would translate to singing in a choir pretty well. Lynne and Dave had a new baby, Piran, who was just over six months now, and it meant Dave was clucking around the house constantly and driving her bonkers. She practically begged Alice to take him and suggested if there was any way they could find of locking him in the vestry for a couple of days then she would be endlessly grateful.

Harmony and Amanda weren't so willing; in fact, they weren't willing at all, and both had looked at her as if she had grown five heads and sprouted a wagging tail when she suggested that they join the choir on a temporary basis. As Harmony began one of her favourite speeches on the evils of organised religion, Alice rather wished she did have multiple heads and a tail with which to defend herself. Thwack, snap, snap.

Rosy had added that she would ask Matt, her partner, to put feelers out to Chase, his sister's boyfriend, who was apparently so talented at everything he was bound to be able to sing and added that she would drag Matt along, unwilling or not. She also suggested reaching out to Sarah Fielding, who had retired from Penmenna school in the September, suggesting it would be a nice way for her to remain involved with the Penmenna community. Alice had scheduled in a visit after school today to see if it was something Sarah might be keen on.

Pippa had laughed a lot when Alice asked her and pointed out that she had done her fair share of publicly embarrassing singing in the summer but added that she knew her mum would be quite keen. Polly, her younger sister, was due back from university soon and had a fab voice, making a fortune busking in Edinburgh, so Pippa was fairly sure that her mother would be able to bring her along, especially if Alice could fix it with the vicar to save her mischievous soul. Alice suggested that she wasn't sure that it worked like that, or that Dan had superhero powers, but she'd ask, just in case. One more person was one more person to make Dan happy as a newly invigorated, thoroughly rehearsed choir marched into the chancel for the Christmas carol service. It would be the best Christmas gift ever.

Her next stop was today's Christmas Fayre planning meeting with the PTA. She was not looking forward to it. It was no secret that Serena Burchill-Whyte had begun a whispering campaign about Marion and practically had an alternative PTA up and running. Harmony was very keen to support her as was Alison, one of the mums who had had a fair few run-ins with Marion in the summer, culminating in a drunken rant at last year's Summer Fayre. Whether it would find legs and Penmenna School would be split into civil war with two battling factions remained to be seen but Alice knew it could get nasty, and she hated confrontation of any sort – would rather curl up into a ball and roll away than have to watch others say or do things that may cause hurt.

However, she needed numbers for the choir and she had a responsibility to turn up at this planning meeting where she would pitch her Christmas Choir plan. Marion would have everything under control and all in order, so the fayre would progress smoothly and without mishap. As it was one of the PTA's big events of the year, the rest of the staff would be present at this meeting too – theoretically so everyone knew what role would be assigned to them – which was a bit of a relief from Alice's point of view with the advent of this Serena woman, to help diffuse any tension.

Alice left the classroom as the children did for lunch – Amanda calling after her that she had too much work to do and to let Marion know that she'd do the toy stall again – and headed straight for the staffroom. Alice wanted to get there early so she could write a big colourful notice on the board about choir participation before she brought it up verbally. As she walked through the hall she saw that signs for the Winter Fayre had gone up already. Wow, that was on the ball even for Marion. Normally she waited to get this meeting out of the way before they were finalised and popped all over the village. Alice suddenly had that feeling, a niggle, she was missing something but wasn't sure what it was. She headed to the staffroom, sure that it was nothing important and whatever it was would come to her in a bit.

As she entered the communal area she drew a sharp breath, for there at the head of the table and in the seat Marion always occupied for this sort of thing was Serena, flanked by Harmony and Alison. Behind them were a flurry of mums, largely new ones from Class One but some who had had run-ins with Marion in the past.

Talk about 'Winter is Coming'; *Game of Thrones* had nothing on this. They may as well have built an Iron Throne in place of a padded metal chair and hired some dragons to fly around their heads. They were certainly throwing out enough menace to warrant it.

Alice poured herself a coffee and took a seat, her cup shaky in her hands, and she felt cross at herself for being such a wuss. Should she say something? Was it really her place? She was the first member of staff here, bar Harmony, whose colours were clearly pinned to the mast. Wasn't practically anyone else better placed to pass comment? Her heart sped up, not in the nice way it did when Dan was around but in that 'your mother has just come in the door early and you've drunk a lot of her gin and stolen her best dress' vibe. Which Alice had only done once at fourteen and had never, ever, ever repeated. Even to this day she couldn't drink gin, such was the guilt.

'Um, hello everyone. Shouldn't we save that one for Marion?' Alice dug deep and asked. All the eyes in the room stared her down.

Deep breath and try again.

'Normally Marion sits there, always has.' She beamed as she said it so everyone knew she wasn't attacking.

'Yes, Miss Pentire. But we thought we'd bring in some—' Serena's expression virtuous, benevolent as she started to answer.

'Hey, isn't that Marion's seat?' Lynne, who job-shared Class One with Rosy, and didn't mind the odd showdown – indeed seemed quite fond of them – wandered in. 'Oh, Rosy will be late I'm afraid, if she gets here at all. She's had to nip out with Kam for an emergency child protection conference. She'll be back as soon as she can, but you know how these things are.'

'I was just saying to Miss Pentire that we were hoping to shake things up a little within the PTA and thought this meeting about the Winter Fayre was the perfect time to instigate some change.'

Lynne looked at Serena and then gleefully rubbed her hands together as she pulled up a chair. 'Oh goody, I can see this meeting has just got about five hundred per cent more interesting.' She shot Alice a look of unabashed joy, whereas Alice's tummy was swirling. Ahhh, this didn't bode well, and now she knew she couldn't count on Lynne for support. In fact, she was surprised that the teacher hadn't pulled popcorn out of her bag and sat back with her feet up. Mind you, Lynne had always been very outspoken about how much she disliked Monster

92

Marksharp, never having warmed to her in the same way Rosy, Alice and Sylvie had.

Alice was worried, without Amanda here and with Rosy and Kam called away, there might not be a teacher present prepared to take Marion's side. Marion was rude, she insulted everyone who came into contact with her and stripped the parents of all self-esteem before building them back into little Marion clones in matching printed dresses and fuchsia lipstick. Alice knew there was no excusing her behaviour. But her love for her family, her commitment to community and her sheer iron will elicited respect in Alice, as she could see that Marion's ends were purely good, even if her means were somewhat suspect. The woman did seem to end up more than most in Alice's prayers. And Alice was convinced that a new nice Marion was just around the corner and could appear at any minute.

New nice Marion however wasn't the one standing in the doorway right now. Terrifying, slightly possessed-looking Marion was. The staffroom had filled up now and every head turned as people cottoned onto her presence in the doorway. Alice flashed a look at Serena, who was smiling the smile of the innocent although her eyes didn't reflect the same welcoming sentiment. Her eyes looked like they were revelling in the upcoming explosion. Harmony on the other hand looked like she regretted her boldness and Alice half expected her to bolt under the table any second now.

Whilst her hair, make-up and dress were immaculate, Marion's face looked like she was about to bring Dante's seven circles of Hell into the staffroom. In her hand, originally down at her side but now brought up and waving in the air, was a ripped-down piece of paper.

Trembling, her eyes narrowed and her mouth pursed, she spat, 'What. Is. This?' Each word staccato and filled with fury. It was only then that she saw where Serena was sitting, and she increased in size, hissing and inflating herself like a poisonous puff adder.

'Hello, do come in.' Serena carried on smirking at her. 'We've been expecting you.' Alice bet there wasn't a single person in that room right now who wasn't reminded of a Bond villain. 'We popped some posters up. You've been looking so overworked we thought we'd help out. Do say if there's anything not quite right with them, but I think we listed all the main attractions, didn't we, ladies? There's Santa Claus obviously, then the Christmas tombola and the jar stand. Mince pies and mulled wine, I've popped Alison in charge of that, I understand she did very well on the Pimm's stall in the summer. Guess the weight of the Christmas cake. I did speak to the vicar about the church choir coming in and singing some carols but he said unfortunately that the choir may not be available...'

This was Alice's chance. 'About that, I did want to talk—'

It was like getting caught between two rutting stags. Marion shot red-hot lasers out of her eyes at her – Alice could practically feel her face melting such was the power of Marion's looks – and Serena leant forward and patted her hand patronisingly without actually slowing her speech.

'—I *am* speaking, just a minute. Choir not available so perhaps we could table that for discussion.'

She flashed an I'm-so-inclusive-and-can-be-relied-on-to-fight-for-my-followers'-dreams look at Alice before continuing. 'A Christmas cards and tea-towels stall. And, of course, the reindeer food, although I've insisted that we remove the glitter from that. In London we haven't used glitter for years, everyone knows how much damage it does to the habitat and small creatures who live amongst us.' Harmony appeared to have recovered from her fear and nodded supportively, if a little smugly at this. 'Then I have a—'

'Stop. Just stop. This is ridiculous.'

Alice couldn't help but nod in agreement, although she was with Serena on stripping out the glitter.

'You're in my chair, you've advertised the Christmas Fayre as a Winter Fayre and—'

'And I've distributed the jobs in a fair and democratic fashion, Mrs Marksharp. Something I understand you never really did. I haven't barked orders at people and then belittled them when they have failed to do exactly as you wished. People aren't telepathic and neither are the parents at Penmenna your slaves, here to do your bidding.' Harmony and Alison were nodding furiously by now whilst Alice found herself exchanging uncomfortable looks with both Sylvie and Pippa.

'How dare you, I have run—' Marion responded in a pitch that was only a whisker away from a shout.

'If part of why you are red and spitting right now is because *we've*' – Serena glanced around at those standing with her; Alison looked so happy that she might explode like a piñata of rainbows and sparkles – 'found that despite your extensive poll, people were happy with the change in nomenclature.' She paused. 'That's *name*, by the way.'

She nodded to reinforce her last couple of words. Smug victory seeped out of every pore, coating the women standing close by and even part of the staffroom table.

Alice no longer felt merely uncomfortable but pretty ashamed of the whole scene unfolding in front of them all. But like the rest of the staff – excluding Harmony grinning with the taste of victory and Lynne beaming as if the greatest soap opera in the world had just pitched up in Penmenna School – she was almost frozen, catatonic with shock at the unpleasantness unfolding.

Serena continued as her foe also seemed felled into defeat, standing but comatose, unable to respond. 'The trouble is, Mrs Marksharp, that you only have a handful of support and that's really only a few members of staff and a couple of acolytes. People don't like you. You don't let them close and see the real you. You just bark commands and wave that stupid iPad about. I find that a more approachable manner is helpful when seeking and retaining pow— approval of others to foster a collaborative and productive working relationship.'

Marion jiggled herself back into her body and snorted. 'Who on earth speaks like that? I don't think anyone in Penmenna is going to respond well to your city-like nonsense speak. Ridiculous.'

'Who speaks like me? I think you'll find your husband does, oh but you wouldn't know that any more, would you?'

Boom!

Alice had had enough; she stood to her feet at the same time as Pippa banged the table.

'Stop this now!' The words were out of her mouth before she knew what she was doing. But she didn't care.

This was unacceptable and she wasn't going to sit by and continue to let Marion be torn apart. If change was needed there were better ways of doing it.

'Yes, this is not okay. Marion, come and sit down. Mrs Burchill–Whyte, this is not how we do things here. Sylvie, can you make Marion some tea and I think everyone can go somewhere else for ten minutes and then come back.' Pippa took control of the staffroom, exchanging a look with Alice as Lynne initially shrugged her shoulders and then realised she should have perhaps stood up earlier. 'Yes, ten minutes and then we'll see if we can salvage some kind of plan for the Christmas, or Winter, Fayre.'

Chapter Twelve

Alice put on a long-sleeved top, a thin woollen cardigan buttoned up to the neck and then added a thick woolly jumper on top before heading out to church that morning. It was such a cold winter – she had never known cold like it – so she was taking no risks today. She was wearing her wellies as they had the firmest grip of all her shoes and there was no way she was falling arse-over-tit again. There was a casserole on the side in the slow cooker and she'd made some soda bread earlier ready for the next couple of days so when she came home, after church and lunch in the pub, she'd be chore free and could indulge in an Audrey Hepburn movie marathon *and* then start her new book as she sat in front of the fire.

She was in two minds as to whether to tell Dan about the choir that was beginning to shape up rather nicely; she was so excited she wanted to share it. She also wanted to accomplish a giant 'wow' on Christingle day – which happened to fall on Christmas Eve this year – and giving him an inkling of what she had achieved so far would spoil the surprise.

She was torn between the two options, to tell or not, and tried to decide which was the kindest thing to do. Was it to put him out of his misery and let him know everything was fine? Or was it to defer her own gratification and give him the big surprise? She'd see if an answer revealed itself during the service this morning; failing that she'd run it past Rosy, Sylvie and Pippa as they met for their once-a-month-girls'-Sunday-roast lunch in the pub and see what they thought.

Despite the horrendously awkward planning meeting a couple of days ago, things had worked out relatively well in the PTA, although everyone knew that would only be a temporary state. The school was officially riven into two warring factions as Alice had feared, with two very strict teams. Without a doubt, Alice was on Team Marion and she didn't like the way this new mum had come in and tried to set fire to everything. Neither did she quite trust her constant love-life-laugh nature. Alice absolutely supported it as a sentiment, she just didn't believe Serena embodied it.

Once Lynne had remembered to be a professional, dampening down her glee at Marion's downfall and restoring order, things had worked out. Marion was handed back overarching control of the PTA but had to accept Serena as her new joint deputy alongside Jenny, who was already well-established in the role. Most of the stalls had been looked after by the same people for years, and then any that were undecided were taken from the list Serena had organised. The Winter Fayre posters were already up so Lynne suggested they leave them. Fundamentally, they had just treated the warring women as if they were five years old and used practised conflict resolution techniques on them. Alice wouldn't be surprised if a behaviour rainbow chart was put up in the staffroom for the PTA. It was all a bit ridiculous.

With that ironed out and the mood in the staffroom temporarily subdued, Alice had been able to ask about the choir and Jane and Jenny had volunteered. But the real win had been Marion's suggestion – happy to have her crown back even if it might only be temporary – that Alice use a children's choir filched from the nativity play. She pointed out that the beauty of carols was that many people knew them having sung them for years and children were no exception. If Alice were to include a rendition of 'Away in a Manger', which they were already practising for the play, it would be a really simple solution and have massive cute appeal.

When she had put it to the class that afternoon they responded extremely positively so Alice had managed to write a couple of sentences of a letter and whack out a quick note to parents and children so they could talk over the weekend about whether they would be up for it, available on the days needed and willing to audition first thing next week.

Discussing it later with Sylvie and Pippa over a cup of tea at the end of the day, they had clapped their hands excitedly. Pippa immediately volunteered to lead the children down the aisle and mouth the words as they did in school once they were sitting at the front. She had so wanted to be part of the choir and was over-joyed to now have a role in it that didn't include singing. Whereas Sylvie suggested she gave all the kids a quick lesson in walking solemnly, which wasn't something Alice would have considered necessary, but seeing Sylvie's wink realised it was for Pippa rather than the pupils. Pippa was rather like a puppy – one that had just eaten its weight in sugar, or whatever the doggy equivalent was.

Wrapped up in all her layers, she walked through the lychgate up to the porch and once again felt her heart leap as she saw Dan standing there welcoming his congregation. He was chatting to someone as he glanced up and, with a light in his eyes, he nodded a welcome at her. She walked towards him, her focus on him and his on her.

She had thought about telling him about her crush several times, but every scenario that played out in her mind, even with her in full control of what was unfolding, ended in him giving her a look full of pity and her moving out of the village, mortified. As she walked towards him today, though, she wondered if that was really the case. Was he really *just* a friend? Right now, he looked how she knew she felt.

This was a classic case of wishful transference and she need to stop it immediately. She knew he had suffered loss, knew from that sermon he had delivered in the early days, knew from what Annie had confided. When he had initially come up to Penmenna, rumours had abounded: so good-looking and no wife in tow. Was he gay? Asexual? Why would such a decent man, drop-dead stunning and with a sound set of morals – and a free house – not be in a relationship? Alice didn't believe in putting people into boxes and felt life and identity was a little more complex than the questions that had been asked.

That sermon had answered all their queries. He was single because he had suffered catastrophic, romantic loss. He was single because he was still hurting.

She walked up the granite steps of the church into the porch and Dan greeted her with open arms, arms that she knew were all muscular at the top and sinewy at the bottom, sprinkled in thick golden hair just peeking out the end of his purple robe, worn as it was the Advent Sunday, arms right now wrapping them around her in greeting.

Catastrophic romantic loss, she reminded herself. *This is a minister tending to his flock. A slightly lost sheep, but very definitely a member of the flock.*

He gave her a strong squeeze and then took a step back, squeezing her arms and looking at her with love. She wanted to look back properly, hold his gaze with boldness, a declaration.

Sudden Catastrophic Romantic Loss. And his parents possibly as well; this man has so much healing to do. This is nothing but a friendly hug, she told herself, *and you are a gross, sexually frustrated old spinster who needs to stop harbouring inappropriate thoughts of the clergy on a Sunday. And a Monday, a Tuesday, a Wednesday...*

'So good to see you, look at that smile! What's prompted that?'

You.

'Um, I'm just pleased to be here, it's a fabulous day.' She waved her hand out to the graveyard, the wide-open skies which, although bitingly cold, were clear and crisp.

'Uh-huh.' He didn't look convinced. She tried her best believe-me-I'm-a-good-girl face. He arched his eyebrow.

Oh dear.

He let her off the hook and continued to speak to her, his arms no longer around her, one down by his side and the other gesturing towards the pews of the church. 'Look over there, isn't it wonderful? I'm ridiculously happy with this new development.'

Alice looked at him quizzically and then followed the direction his finger was pointing in. Oh fabulous!

'Annie moved in yesterday. She's nowhere near as chuffed about it as I am, but she *will* be pleased to see you.'

'Oh, this is such good news, no wonder you're pleased. It must be so good to have her near.'

'It is. I feel if I can just give her a smidgen of the care she gave me as a child, then there may be some justice in the world.'

'There's lots of it, but I know what you're saying.'

'There is, you're right.'

'Hello, Vicar!' Mrs Talbot, standing behind Alice, was clearly getting impatient and wanted to get into church, or at the very least her own snippet of dashingly-handsome-vicar time. Alice wanted to step to one side and see if Dan gave Mrs Talbot the same intensity of hug as she had received but knew that she was better off if she just went to say hello to Annie.

Alice nodded a hello as she walked down the aisle past Gladys, who played the organ and who was standing and chatting with Denise Williams, before sliding into the pew next to Annie.

'Hello, you!' she whispered as she sat down.

'Alice! How perfect. I'd hoped you'd be here this morning. Let me give you a hug.' Annie immediately squished the younger woman up into the tightest hug, a hug that spewed life-affirming love and affection. That was were Dan got it from.

'So I've heard the wonderful news, I'm so pleased you're now in Penmenna.'

'It's not wonderful, it's blasted inconvenient and not what I wanted. Of course, it's lovely to see you, darling girl, but really I wanted to be living independently from

Dan. I don't believe in becoming burdensome and stopping your children or grandchildren from living their lives. You don't teach them to be independent to then become dependent upon them.'

'I think sometimes, and certainly with Dan, people are happy to give back. They love you and they want to support you, and even more importantly spend time with you. So, it's not always a selfish act to take them up on their offers of help rather than, often incorrectly, assuming you're a burden. Just saying.'

'Okay, noted. You have a good heart. But also, I want him to have a private life, which is hard when you have your grandmother in the next bedroom. Oh my, what on earth was that?' Annie startled as a ghostly drawn-out noise rang out through the church.

'Ha, please don't panic. It's the organ. The keys get stuck from time to time and when they release they let out the ghastliest sound, like a baby banshee. It drives Gladys potty. Sometimes she has to skip a note in the hymns because the sticky key will not budge until it's ready. She gets rather cross, even though we're all quite used to it and don't blame her. It makes it very difficult to play. Dan said he'd try and get it sorted. That's all it is, promise.' She rubbed Annie's shoulder to reassure her. 'So, what were you saying?'

'It sounded pretty spooky. But... oh yes... I was saying that boy needs a private life and let's not forget, I might want to get lucky too!' She winked at Alice, and Alice couldn't help but think how very lucky the person would be who caught Annie's eye.

'But honestly, all that aside, you should have seen the place the council offered me. I think I can turn down two before they kick me out the door and leave me on the streets, so I had to say a definite no to this one and, consequently, suck it up and come and crash with my grandson.'

'What did they offer you?'

'It was a third floor flat, the lift was broken, there were needles in the stairwell, and the whole place smelt of wee. Someone offered me weed within five minutes of walking onto the estate and there were two teenagers fornicating by the bins.'

'Oh dear.'

'I'm openminded and some of that I don't object to, but I'm not stupid.'

'Quite, but you are now here and I am very pleased.'

'Only temporarily, I'll get Christmas out the way and then we'll see what the council offer next. I guess this makes me a silver sofa surfer.' Annie grinned at Alice and Alice couldn't help but grin back.

'I guess it does. Here, whisk out your phone, I'll pop my number in and whilst you're here we can do fun things together. You can help me with a mysterious vestry mission in a bit if you want. But you have to keep it top secret, kind of "if I tell, I die" status. What do you think?'

Annie handed Alice her phone. 'I think that sounds right up my street. Dan loves a good secret mission as well, you know?'

'Yes, yes I did as it happens. He has got me into some scrapes with his "secret missions". One time he had the both of us stealing Carol's hanging baskets – it was to do nice things.' Alice realised she needed to clarify this. 'We returned them, obviously, all planted and pretty-looking just as she was starting to get ill, but you should have seen us. To make it fun we both dressed all in black and then a police car came haring through the village, lights and sirens blazing – you know how rare that is – and we pinned ourselves against a wall by The Smuggler's Curse, clutching the baskets quite desperately and looking very suspicious. I closed my eyes until they passed, I was that scared. Honestly, I nearly wet myself with fear. And then again, laughing afterwards. Your grandson is a rascal. And don't get me started on the time he had me capturing fornicating frogs in the churchyard and – Ooh look, there's Ethel, hang on a minute. I think you two are going to get on like a house on fire. Ethel, over here!' Alice waved the woman over – these two were a best friendship waiting to happen.

Chapter Thirteen

Alice couldn't believe her luck as child after child, of all ages, came back into school after the weekend with permission slips and a desire to join the choir for Christmas. Whether it would last beyond that, at this point she didn't know. But she did know that she would have at least twenty children alongside the adults that had volunteered. The adults were all coming to the school hall tomorrow night at six, after one of Sylvie's dance classes, to see what their voices sounded like and how they would all work together. This afternoon she would gather the children together for the last half an hour of the day and do the same with them.

Being the first week of December meant that the school was looking Christmassy; some of the staff had been in yesterday to decorate the classrooms, and the great big tree had been put up in the hall by Matt and Rosy over the weekend. Each class took turns to decorate it and as morning break approached there were children from Class One draping strands of threaded popcorn, interspersed with oranges and cranberries, through the branches under Pippa's direction. Music was playing and as 'Jingle Bells' blared out, the children and Pippa happily singing along, Alice was beginning to feel remarkably festive.

As the music changed into 'All I Want for Christmas Is You' she began to feel both festive and a little teenage. The music seemed to be highlighting the desire to tell Pippa about how Dan consumed her thoughts almost every minute of the day and night. It was there, balancing on the tip of her lips, the compulsion to tell her friend how excited she was for Christmas this year, for making it special for Dan. But she knew that Pippa would never let this go, would jump in and try to help, and Pippa's way of dealing with things was not Alice's. Still the temptation to spill to her friend was almost unbearable.

'Mum's excited for tonight, although she says to let you know that Polly won't be back for another couple of weeks.' Pippa caught her eye as she stopped decorating to have a little dance with some of the children. Alice felt a wave of relief wash over her. *Phew, that was close.* She had been so near to confiding in her friend, vocalising her crush. But vocalising it would give it a power that Alice was too scared to witness. Plus, Pippa would have probably scrawled *Alice 4 Dan* on every tree and gatepost from here to the beach. It would not have ended well.

'That's fine. How are you doing?'

'Okay, had a great weekend. Kam and I went down west but I think I'm coming down with that cold that's been doing the rounds. Not madly happy about that, but I guess it's the time of year for it. Could be worse. How are things going in there?' Pippa nodded towards the classroom. Being the first week of December meant that all the data, so much data, had to be in this week, which often led to things getting a little bit frantic, no matter how organised the teacher was.

'Fine, we're just a couple of assessments down, Keenan has been absent until today so I need to do that this afternoon, but once that's sorted we should be done and ready. You know Amanda. Military precision. Right, don't let me get caught up in your festive madness, I must get to the stationery cupboard or Amanda will have my— ahem, Mrs Adams will worry. That looks great by the way, really effective.'

'Thanks. The popcorn was Rosy's idea but it's great for fine motor control and also learning about history, so a bit of a win really. I miss the tinsel, although I've gone a bit wild in the classroom to compensate.' Alice imagined that *a bit wild* could easily be an understatement. She did love Pippa's joie de vivre.

She opened the door to the stationery cupboard – a bit of a misnomer really as it was more room than cupboard, which Alice absolutely loved. It was one of her favourite places in the school. Who wouldn't love a room filled wall-to-wall with pens and pencils of every colour of the rainbow, art and craft supplies with which you could make anything your heart and brain could conceive and paper in so many sizes, colours and shapes? The endless possibilities made Alice happy. On top of which it was always empty, so was a great place to sneak into if you needed to make a phone call privately or just shove chocolate in your mouth and catch your breath for a second.

What she didn't expect to see in there was Marion. Marion sobbing and sitting on a small stool with tears running down her face.

Alice came in and shut the door behind her quietly.

'Hey.' She tentatively took a step closer to the woman and tapped her gently on the shoulder. 'Marion, whatever is the matter?'

'It's nothing.' The woman sniffed before shaking her head and attempting to pull herself together. 'Really, I'm fine.'

Alice could tell the woman was embarrassed, she also knew Marion wouldn't be crying if it weren't for a very good reason. She hoped it wasn't the stress of this new woman and the PTA causing this. She walked around and knelt down in front of her.

'I'll grab what I need and leave you on your own and promise not to let anyone know that I've seen you in here, but before I go and leave you in peace, I know I'll worry like crazy if I don't just check if there's anything I can help you with? There's nothing wrong with the boys is there?' Marion was known for her lioness-like tendencies when it came to mothering. Although sobbing would not be considered her normal M.O. Snarling and ripping heads would have been far more par for the course.

'No, the boys are okay. They're doing well, dear Rafe has settled beautifully into Roscarrock School.' Marion named the local secondary school that her eldest boy had started at in September. 'Rufus is still so cute and *so* gifted and I'm sure darling Rupert will be the star of the nativity.'

'He's certainly doing an amazing job as director. He could well have a career in that field, he seems to have a natural good eye.'

'He could have a career *anywhere* he wanted. There's nothing those boys can't do.'

Alice knew it, but she also knew her interpretation may not be quite the same as Marion's.

'I don't doubt it. So, if it's not the boys, please tell me it's not this nonsense with the PTA.'

Marion snorted so hard, Alice was surprised half a lung didn't fly across the stationery cupboard and land in the batik wax.

'It would take more than that imposter, stupid woman to make me cry. Imagine! She's got Hippy-Dippy Harmony and No-Knickers Alison on her team as her deputies. My Jenny could take them down with a mere look.' Alice didn't doubt it but was fairly sure that this wasn't how PTAs were meant to be run, and neither was she sure what exactly had caused Alison to be gifted such a horrid nickname. Harmony's needed no explanation. 'Of course, *they* wouldn't make me cry. That Serena has a lot to learn before she'll win this war. Stupid women. I'm made of far stronger stuff!'

Alice couldn't argue with that.

'Okay, well if you need a willing ear, then I'm here. And you know I'm very good at keeping secrets.'

'Why? What secrets do you have?' Marion's head shot up with the speed of a whippet after a rabbit.

'Um, well I can't tell you, Marion. They're secrets.'

'Hmmm.' Marion didn't look convinced. 'Well, I can't imagine what you might know or be doing that I wouldn't know about.' Even though Alice was still perched on the floor, Marion managed to give her one of those up-and-down looks that certain women are so very skilled at. Alice had been on the receiving end of such looks for a lifetime; if anyone had had a mother anything like hers, they too would have stopped responding to them somewhere around the age of six. Marion's bounced off her as if she were brand new Teflon. 'Oh, unless you've actually managed to shag that dishy vicar? No, of course not.'

'Shall I get you a cup of tea, at the least?' Alice offered, managing not to respond to Marion's catty words, although *No, of course not* with a touch of defeated resignation would have been her call on that question as well.

'I'll have Lady Grey.'

'Oh, okay, I'll go and see if we have any in the staffroom.'

'There is. Jenny makes sure of it. And there should be some quinoa and kale crackers in the biscuit cupboard, I should probably have one of those as well. Chop chop.'

Alice shook her head, got up and went to get Marion what she had asked for, relieved that the mask seemed fully back in place.

Except it wasn't. As Alice smuggled the tea and crackers into the stationery cupboard Marion was crying again. The mask, one that Alice and the rest of the school had always thought was impenetrable, was so flimsy right now it hadn't lasted more than a minute.

'Here you are,' Alice said brightly. 'Look, are you sure there's nothing I can do?'

Marion didn't attempt to bring the mask back out, but neither did she answer. Alice had brought a box of tissues from the staffroom as well and offered the tautly stretched woman them.

'Do you... do you promise not to say a word?'

'I promise.'

'Swear on the Bible?' Marion looked up at her, head cocked and glare shooting from under one eyelid. Quite an impressive element of menace encapsulated for someone whose heart had been breaking but a few seconds ago.

'I don't have a Bible on me, Marion, but I do give you my word.'

'Hmmph,' was Marion's response – luckily Alice had had training in non-verbal communication and took this as an intimation that she could be trusted. She slipped to the floor once again. Amanda was going to send out a search party if she didn't get back soon.

Marion opened her handbag, a great big slouchy leather affair with which she could clearly run the world and handed her a small white envelope, about the size and shape of a birthday card. It had been ripped open and Marion nodded as Alice looked up at her tentatively, assuming she was supposed to pull out the letter that was inside.

The envelope itself was marked Roscarrock so the letter had been sent from close by, any one of the neighbouring villages if not the town itself. Alice could feel herself being nervous; whatever was it going to say? It wasn't an official-looking envelope so she hoped that meant it wasn't a medical diagnosis or something equally worrying. She pulled out the A4 sheet inside and opened it out.

What she saw shocked her to her core.

'Oh my. Oh, um… Marion, I'm so sorry. This is dreadful, no wonder you're upset. You mustn't pay any attention to it, it's obviously a mean-spirited, cowardly bully who doesn't know what they are talking about. Have you… um… have you taken it to the police? Maybe you should do that.'

The two women both sat there looking at the letter Marion had received that morning, a letter made out of letters cut from newspapers and glued down to spell out a message. A missive like the old-fashioned poison pen letters that Agatha Christie used to write about. An old-fashioned method of creating fear and tension and hatred completely anonymously and with evil intent.

The letters on the piece of paper in Alice's hand spelt out the phrase 'Your husband doesn't come home for a reason'. And as Marion glanced at it again, the tears began to roll down her cheeks once more.

Chapter Fourteen

Marion's poison pen letter played on Alice's mind for the rest of the day, all through choir practice and even as she opened her front door it was still spooling over and over as she was trying to work out the best way to support her. Marion had sworn her to secrecy but Alice really felt that it should be reported; she also knew that she wouldn't do anything behind Marion's back. Whilst the woman may have no qualms about doing exactly that sort of thing herself, Alice knew it would be wrong. She did plan to talk to Marion about it again though, maybe ask her to involve their mutual friend, the head Rosy Winters, and the three of them could work out the best way forward. For now, she'd wait and see what happened, see if Marion received any more and keep a jolly good eye on her.

It had been a long day and her tummy was growling. She needed to find something quick and easy to eat and then she'd light the fire and curl up with her book. She popped the kettle on and pulled the hairband out of her hair. It was a silly thing but whenever she felt her hair ripple over her shoulders she could finally relax. It took away any formality left in the day, a physical symbol that all she had to do was done and now was her time. It was always accompanied by a deep sigh as she did so.

With her hair rippling down her back, she peeked in the fridge and realised there was still some leftover stew from yesterday and if she pinged it in the microwave it would take no time at all. She was just taking it out when her phone buzzed in her back pocket.

The number that came up wasn't one she recognised, so with a deep breath she answered it.

'Hello.'

'Hello, Alice?'

'Yes, is that…?'

'It's Annie. I've called you as you said I could call anytime and I'm in a bit of a pickle.'

'Okay, how can I help?'

'Thing is, I've got a bit stuck at Ethel's and I wondered…'

'If I could come and get you out? Ha! This is obviously a family trait. Of course, I can. Don't you worry, I'll be there in a minute.'

'Family trait? How come?'

'Never mind, hang fast and I'll be there in a flash.'

Alice grabbed her coat and shrugged it back on; the casserole could wait. She headed quickly to Ethel's. How on earth had she managed to convince Annie down into the dungeon? How had she decided to confide in her so quickly that it even existed, especially seeing as it had taken Alice thirty years of living in the village to discover it?

Just as she was turning down the side path she heard a noise ahead of her and wondered if it were perhaps a badger or a fox. She liked both but knew she'd scream if anything ran past her in the dark, whether she wanted to or not. Screaming would bring the village to their front doors and she imagined Ethel, and presumably Annie, would not be grateful for that.

Turning the corner, she realised that it wasn't an animal at all, but a rather tall vicar that had been making the scrabbling sounds. He made a triumphant 'aha' noise as he lifted up a key from underneath a flowerpot by the door.

'Oh hello,' he said, 'how come you're here?'

'Your grandma called me. Did she call you too?'

'No. No she didn't. How odd. I had a call from Ethel, her voice was really tremulous and she said I'd have to let myself in the back door. It's unusual for her to lock it. I was worried for her.'

'Well, my understanding is Annie is in there as well. What on earth are they both doing?'

The two of them exchanged a look and started laughing: a smirk turned into a giggle which with no further words spoken led to the both of them laughing so hard that Alice had to steady herself with her hand against the wall.

'No, not that, surely not,' Dan managed to splutter out.

'Both over the age of consent,' Alice noted as she wiped a tear from her eye.

'I don't know if I want to go in there now.'

'They might be in dire peril, wasting away and cuffed to the wall. Come on, get that door open and we'll get it over with.'

'Fair point. No more laughing though. They've called us because they trust us. Your hair looks nice by the way.' Dan took a deep breath and unlocked the door.

'Thank you and I'll do my best,' said Alice with a very stoic lift of her shoulders and firm tone, whilst surreptitiously fiddling for her hair band on her wrist. She didn't want Dan to think she was making an effort to be attractive for him. That would be way too embarrassing and she had hardly expected him to be here on the doorstep with her. She smiled wanly at him whilst realising her band was on the kitchen table. Rats!

Dan pushed the door open.

'Ethel!' he called.

'Annie?' Alice called at the same time. They were standing in the doorway of the kitchen, presumably both wondering what to do next, whether they should brave the stairs to the cellar, when Alice took in the scene in front of them.

'Um, I think they may not be locked in the basement at all. There seems to be some mischief afoot.' She nodded at the room and its furniture.

There on Ethel's table was no longer a place setting for one but two candles, lit and flickering, casting a glow over the room. The lights themselves were dimmed and there were two places set at the table, with what she guessed was Ethel's very best silver and a single red rose in a vase placed between the candles.

Alice looked across at Dan to see how he was reacting. He arched his eyebrows in return and wiggled them a bit, breaking the tension and Alice's embarrassment.

'Are those letters addressed to us?' he asked, gesturing to two envelopes, one in between each knife and fork.

'I guess we should take a look and see, it's all a bit odd but I feel distinctly like we're being set up here. Annie?' Alice called out again and there was a muffled sound from down the hall, accompanied by some giggling before the soulful sound of Teddy Pendergrass came out from speakers located on the windowsill and the front door was slammed shut.

'Yep, I think that is exactly what has just happened. Looks like one of them is pretty good with Bluetooth.' Dan nodded at the windowsill. The music wasn't loud and was pitched at the perfect volume for a romantic evening.

Alice felt like dying.

Dan apparently didn't and added, 'I vote we sit down, read the letters and see what those two are up to.'

'Why on earth would—' Alice stopped as Dan quirked his brow at her and she didn't feel brave enough to go any further. Okay, she knew everyone thought she had a crush on him, but she didn't realise he knew as well. She nodded instead; it couldn't do any harm and she couldn't be more embarrassed than she already was.

They walked to the table and Dan pulled out the chair for her with a flourish.

'I feel we should do this properly.'

Alice smiled up at him, too shy to actually form words and wondering why he was teasing her, playing the part of romantic lead when this evening couldn't lead to romance. Even if her own views on sex before marriage were a little slacker than even the most liberal of churches, she knew – no, assumed – that Dan's were not. He pushed her chair under the table and then rested his hand lightly on her shoulder before going to sit opposite her.

'On three?' he asked as he picked up his envelope. She nodded and picked up hers. He ripped his open and scanned it quickly. She scrutinised him through her eyelashes, her eyes seemingly downcast. She watched him read his note, his lips twitching in wry amusement as he put it back into his envelope and placed it down by the side of his table mat.

She opened hers, her heart beating, and scanned it quickly.

Oh! She wasn't expecting that. Um, *wow*. The writer may be spot on but there was no way she was sharing that with Dan. Not in a million years. Even if she agreed with it. She just couldn't, she'd be mortified.

Dan caught her eyes and grinned. 'I'll tell you mine if you tell me yours.'

Oh shit.

She really didn't want to read this out. She could feel the colour rising in her cheeks.

Dan didn't seem to notice and, still holding her eyes with his, held his paper up. 'Mine says, "*Tell her about yourself*". A bit near the knuckle, that one. I do keep it a little locked up. Go on, what have they got to say to you?'

'Um...' If he could read his message out then she could, she should, but his was about *him* not about *them*, that made it easier, didn't it? Mind you, his was implied criticism alongside advice whereas hers was quite sweet and very complimentary. If he had been brave enough to reveal his, and what his grandmother, or Ethel, thought he needed to do more of, then surely she could read a very flattering statement out, even if it was also putting her own feelings on the line?

'Okay.' She smiled at him, knowing it looked nervous and not even attempting to hide it. She opened up the piece of paper again. 'Mine says... it's a bit embarrassing...'

'Yeah, I think that's their skill.'

'Uh-hmm, mine says "*You're perfect*".' She realised she was whispering it as Dan leaned across the table. He nodded. And she indulged herself in a split-second fantasy where she had been able to say that phrase to him, about him.

'You are.' His answer was said matter-of-factly, as if it were a truth no one doubted, taking her completely by surprise. Still half in her fantasy, she realised that now maybe the reality was even better. Had he just said that he thought she was perfect? *Deep breaths and try not to leap around the room like an over-eager jack-in-the-box*, she told herself.

'Um, thank you, if I wasn't red enough!' She thought she may as well acknowledge she knew she was now the colour of Rudolph's nose. 'But, um that's not quite all of it.'

'Okay. Go on then.'

'All right, can I remind you that I didn't write this.'

'Haha, no need. I am pretty clear on that.' He laughed and reached across and squeezed her arm, presumably reminding her they were both in this together but actually just sending electricity straight up her arm and mainlining into her brain, making her more than a bit fuzzy.

She centred herself back at the table and hoped there had been no physical indication that she had just had jagged spikes of lust run through her.

'Okay, mine says "*You're perfect for each other*".'

Dan's mouth dropped open, which didn't indicate whether he agreed or not. Alice's heart had been in her mouth as she had read it out, but he didn't throw his chair back and storm out, outraged. Nor did he laugh and say 'as if'. He merely chuckled as he shook his head.

'They're good,' he said.

'No, they are *so* bad!' Alice retorted, laughing at the expression on his face.

'Yeah, they are. But you know what, this is quite—'

They were interrupted by the doorbell. Both looked at each other with alarm.

'What are we going to do?' Alice asked, whilst wishing he had finished his sentence. This was quite what? Horrifying? Endearing? What he had always wanted? Wouldn't that be something.

'Well, we're not breaking and entering. Ethel didn't just give us permission to be here, she did actively trick us into it. Although I'm quite glad she did.' He flashed her a look, one that almost seemed to be seeking affirmation, an indication that she was too. It surprised Alice as she found herself nodding. His face relaxed, returning to normal at her nod and he continued, 'I'll go. It seems to me that they've planned this evening rather meticulously; we should perhaps see who it is and what is coming next.'

Alice sat back for a second. He was quite pleased to have been tricked into this situation. That's what he had said. And he had wanted confirmation that she was too. That had to say something didn't it? Then she realised she was missing out on whatever excitement was happening at the front door, so scooted out of her chair at speed and raced into the hallway to see who was there.

It could be anything, there could be a full mariachi band on the doorstep for all she knew.

There wasn't, but Dan was in the process of taking stylish-looking paper bags from a teen when he heard Alice behind him.

'Looks like they've delivered us dinner from The Bay.' He named a restaurant in the neighbouring village, a chi-chi seafood restaurant that people drove from miles to visit. 'How awesome is that?'

'Wow. I guess I'm staying for supper then. That is so much better than casserole.'

'Huh?'

'Never mind.'

'I think we're going to enjoy this evening.'

'I think we are too.' She moved forward to help him grab the bags. 'It looks like they've ordered a feast.'

They carried the bags through to the kitchen and unpacked what had been ordered.

'Oh my goodness, oysters to start.'

'Hmm, they clearly have a very definite agenda.'

'Yeah, I think they may have.' Alice wondered whether she could suck her starter down and look oh-so-cool, sophisticated and irresistibly sexy. She knew she should try, but she *really* didn't like oysters. Was she brave enough to reveal that she was as unsophisticated as they came?

She could imagine everyone else in school getting really excited about this. Sylvie would eat them like a little pixie queen, Rosy would be remarkably sophisticated and Pippa would be gung-ho. Last time Alice had tried to eat one at Falmouth's Oyster Festival she had ended up surreptitiously spitting it into a nearby plant pot when no one was looking. At least she had thought no one was looking until she caught sight of herself on the local news, tucked away in the corner but nonetheless recorded. Thankfully no one else had ever noticed or at the least said anything about it. She couldn't do that here, even with the complete absence of cameras. Ethel would be mortified, both at spat-up oyster amongst her spider plants but also because their intention – although a little obvious – was sweet. Spat-out oyster would be a very definite rejection of all they had arranged.

As they moved to the table, Dan didn't seem to have any trouble at all, squeezing lemon and eating them at a rate of knots. Alice supposed he might not object to more. She pushed the long plate sitting in the middle of the table filled with four more oysters towards him and explained the plant pot fiasco. He paused his eating and burst out laughing.

'Will you eat mine for me? I'd hate Ethel or Annie to think I wasn't grateful for all they have done.'

'Of course I will.' He pulled the plate towards him and picked up another shell, gulping it down with relish. Alice knew she shouldn't sit staring across from him. But it felt like a sexual act, watching him throw his head back as the seafood slid down his throat. He was enjoying the oysters to the full, which added to the sensuality of the scene being played out in front of her. On top of which if he had eaten two portions, maybe they would have double the aphrodisiac effect. She realised she had shaken her hair and shimmied her shoulders as she thought of the word 'aphrodisiac'. God help her, she'd be pinching her elbows into her chest and leaning forward to maximise and flash cleavage if she didn't control herself – and she had a lot of cleavage to flash.

She hadn't even had the oysters and she was already thinking filthy thoughts and was a bit squirmy in her seat. Mind you, Dan had come out this evening without his dog collar, and somehow the lack of that visual reminder made him even more man than usual, taking all aspects of untouchable vicar away. Tonight, he was an ordinary man – a man that she had a ginormous crush on – sitting across from her at a candlelit table and sharing a meal. A meal she suspected had been designed to be as romantic as possible. She had no idea when the day had started that this was how her evening was going to unfold. But she was going to enjoy every minute of it.

Chapter Fifteen

Dan held the plate out to Alice to check she didn't want the last oyster before he finished the lot. She shook her head and he swallowed it down. He felt a little rude eating them all, but Alice had been quite clear in her dislike for them and he did love oysters. Annie used to take him down to Bigbury in Devon when he was little in the holidays and after splashing in the waves all day she'd stop at The Oyster Shack on the way home where they would shuck and gulp with glee.

Mind you, he hadn't eaten them with a woman since Sophie, and that was at Bigbury – unless you counted Carol Roberts and Mrs Talbot at Feast Week in the summer. But here, tonight, sitting opposite Alice he felt both at peace, and thoroughly grateful to Annie and Ethel for setting this up.

Alice was something else. He had been drawn to her from the moment he saw her in church in his very first week in the parish, just under two years ago. It had been that instant feeling you get when you meet someone and know you're going to get along. Instinctive. She was such fun and easy company, he felt as if he could tell her anything and her unique goodness would mean that she responded to everything without judgement.

His grandmother had been bang on the money in the note. He did keep everything closed up and tightly hidden and he *should* talk about things; he knew it was part of the process of healing, moving on but he thought he did a pretty good job at life, despite the constant nagging self-doubt, but didn't everyone have that?

He knew he hadn't talked about certain things enough, because he had never found a person whom he wanted to hear him. Annie was too close and he was aware that because their lives were inextricably linked he couldn't be completely honest and open with her without feeling burdensome as he did so. She had done so much for him, he didn't want to sit down and dissect his demons with her. He needed her to know that he appreciated all of her nurturing and love over the years, not be told where he saw himself failing.

He knew as well that part of him hadn't been ready to talk, hadn't been ready to heal, not ready to be separate from the familiar pain and fault he had felt from the age of five onwards. A burden he hadn't been able to define until he was much older, one that he had felt like lead around his shoulders. But with Alice – he looked at her across the table, smile on her face, thick chestnut tresses falling across her shoulders – he felt that Annie had been right, he could tell her anything. And what's more, he wondered if he wanted to, and wanted her to know who he was a little better.

The answer was yes and he realised it had been for some time. The wish to confide, to share who he *was* not who he presented as, was something he hadn't felt in, well, who knew how long? Until Alice.

At the moment he felt a bit of a fraud. He wasn't sure who she saw exactly when she looked at him, but he knew he wanted her to know the real him. See if she would be so willing to accept him then? The odd thing was, he thought she would.

His grandmother had also been spot on in her note to Alice. She *was* perfect and he had had moments when he really had considered whether they could be together. But the truth was that whilst Alice may indeed be perfect for him, she could definitely do better and he didn't want to stand in her way when it came to finding the right person.

He wasn't sure he had ever met anybody like her. Honest, without artifice and always welcoming, always seeing solutions never problems. And the night she had grazed her knee, as she sat in front of him, he had a sense of her vulnerability that hadn't been so obvious before. A vulnerability that he was surprised this beautiful, good, gentle-hearted woman felt. But then he knew better than most that what we projected and how we felt were two completely different things. He also knew that how one looked was in no way a reflection of who they were.

He wanted to say all of this to the woman in front of him, a woman who spat oysters into plant pots and was watching him eat these with unmitigated joy, her face flickering in the candlelight looking like she was as pleased as he was with the way tonight had turned out.

Instead he said, 'So, what's going on in your world at the moment? How's school and high-level elf duties?'

'Ha, I'm relieved of elf duties for the time being, until the Christmas Fayre at least. I was only standing in for a week. I had to help out a friendly Santa Claus whose chief elf had to go up north and help their mum out after an operation. I happened to have an elf costume hanging in my wardrobe.'

'Of course you did.'

'But look!' She poked her leg out from under the table, waving it at the side before leaning over, her hair falling over her face as she did so, and rolling up her trouser leg to show him her knee. 'Look how beautifully it's healed.'

'It has healed beautifully.' Dan could hear the amusement in his voice. 'Oh wow, look, you've got a freckle. There, just in the middle of your knee. How did I not see that the other night?'

Alice pulled her leg back sharply and rolled her jeans down again. 'I do, I have a freckle on each knee, it's a bit embarrassing. And sorry, I have no clue as to why I decided to show you my knee whilst you were eating.'

Dan laughed. 'It was a perfect knee, and I think a freckle on each sounds adorable rather than embarrassing.'

'My mother used to scrub them with lemon when I was little and insist they looked like dirt specks. She was not a fan. You probably didn't notice them the other night because they, the knees, were kind of gritty and bloody.'

'True. I'm glad they're better. Your mum scrubbed them with lemon! Really?'

'Oh yeah, and then she'd rub the lemon juice all in my hair as well whilst squawking, "You'll never get anywhere in life with dark hair, darling, you've got to be blonde, everyone knows that. Oh dear, there's no hope for you is there?" You know, that sort of thing.' She smiled as she said this but also looked a little embarrassed, as if she had overshared. Before Dan could interject she continued, her tone bright. 'So school, um yes. It's been a bit stressful really. I'm not good at confrontation, and there seems to be a civil war brewing.'

'Really?' Dan's eyebrows shot up. 'I can't imagine Rosy allowing that.'

'No, normally she wouldn't but she seems a bit preoccupied at the moment, then so is Marion. I think that's how it's happened. We've a new mum, absolutely lovely, always friendly to everyone, appears willing to help anyone out and has her eye sharply on Marion's crown. There's just something about her that makes me prickle, you know, tingle.' Dan felt his eyebrow arch up and then tried to lower it before Alice noticed. Too late; she laughed and tapped him on the arm. 'Not like that!' Dan snickered in return as she continued, 'You know, like when you have no reason to mistrust somebody but your instinct is to not believe a word they say, and definitely never get into a car with them, do you know what I mean?'

'You're saying that Marion has a rival who you suspect may be capable of murder just to take over Penmenna's PTA.'

'No!' Alice's word was emphatic although a hint of teasing played at the corners of her mouth. 'Well, maybe a little. I don't know. I could be off and really regret saying this, but there's just something, you know, something I can't put my finger on, but my instinct says stay away.'

'Yeah, I know exactly what you mean. And I would argue that you should trust it. We have instincts for a reason and it's very easy to let rational behaviour take over and we ignore them. We shouldn't. So yeah, don't get in a car with her.' Dan winked at Alice. 'You haven't eaten yet. Shall we see what else is in the bags?'

'Ha, I already have, so I know.'

'When?'

'You were so busy salivating over the oysters you missed me taking a peek. We've got what looks like a lobster risotto to me. I could smell the tarragon and I think I picked up a smidge of cognac.'

'You smelt it! And I didn't notice?'

'You were preoccupied and I was stealthy. But yeah, let's eat. I'm so keen for this.'

'So, you've been sitting there knowing what is next and excited about it whilst I stuff myself full of oysters.'

'Yep.'

'You should have eaten it when you were stealth sniffing.'

'Ha no, it's fine. I was happy to wait.' And she looked like she genuinely was.

'Was it part of a cunning plan?'

'Rumbled.' She held both hands up. 'I was hoping you'd be so full on oysters I'd get your risotto.'

'Do you want it? You can have it.'

'No. I'm teasing. Come on, let's get it into bowls.'

'Deal. Did you peek at pudding too?'

'Nah, a girl has to keep some things a surprise or life gets very dull.'

'Well, tonight is far from dull for me.'

'Tonight is beyond spontaneous, I can't believe those two, but you know what, I am very grateful to them.' She had taken the risotto out of the special bag, checked it was still warm and tumbled it into two shallow bowls that Ethel had left on the side. She passed one to him. 'Here. Doesn't it smell good?'

It did, Dan had to admit it. His nose might not be as sensitive as Alice's, from what he understood she was a real foodie, but he could tell by the scent rising from the dish that he was going to enjoy this.

'Oh my G-goodness,' Alice said after she took her first mouthful, the fork paused just by her lips and her eyes rolling in delight before her lids lowered a little as she fully appreciated the moment. 'That is so good.'

Dan found it hard to take his eyes off her, which was a little awkward as she opened hers again and found him staring. Luckily, she didn't flinch; maybe she hadn't even noticed as she dipped her fork in her bowl for more. 'You must try it, honestly.'

That was a good suggestion; he was beginning to feel distinctly more than friendly towards Alice in this moment and that was not a good look for a parish priest. Platonic and protective, yes. Predatory or even mildly appreciative, probably not. He decided he'd be best off concentrating on his risotto.

'So anything else apart from imminent civil war amongst the parents?'

'Yes, the nativity is coming along brilliantly. They are all working together so collaboratively and Team Naughty, although obviously I don't call them that in front of the children, or the adults actually…'

'Just me then?' Dan grinned and she grinned straight back.

'Just you.' The smile reached her eyes, lit them up. It was intimate and just for him. 'Anyway they seem to be doing so well, having responsibility is good for them. And the way the c— um… the singing is coming along is great too, I think we'll have a real treat in store.'

'Better than last year's?' Dan said with a wink.

'You have no idea. I am still traumatised. Shall we have pudding? Help me think of nice things, I really don't want to have to go to sleep tonight thinking of Harmony's universe giving birth again.'

'I think we can do better than that and pudding is a good place to start, it's always a lovely thing. Actually, this whole evening is pretty awesome, isn't it?'

'It is.' She held his eyes as she had a minute ago and he held hers right back, feeling a powerful hit of lust for the first time in, well, years. He wanted to reach across the table, just to rest his hand on her arm. Physical contact. But he knew he wouldn't be doing it in such a friendly fashion as usual and it wasn't fair to try and start anything with Alice.

'Pudding?' he repeated.

'Let's.' They jumped up and as Alice rinsed the bowls under the tap he rifled in the bags and brought out two boxes for dessert. This shared domesticity was nice, even if it would only last a minute or two. As he pulled the boxes out of the bags he noticed that one of them had a large, bright pink Post-it note on it.

'It seems like we have another message. They're good at this.'

Alice came and stood by him, just slightly behind and leant into him, peering over his shoulder. He could feel his heart pick up and start beating far faster than he thought it should. It wouldn't take much, he could just turn a smidge, angle his head and they would be so close.

But he didn't.

Neither did he move away.

He knew he should put a little physical distance between them but he really didn't want to. He wanted to savour this moment a little longer, for who knew when two elderly ladies would abandon a house, order dinner in for them and force them to spend an intimate evening together again? He was fairly sure this was a one off.

'What does it say?'

He could feel her as she raised her body onto tiptoes to take a look, her words causing her breath to be warm on his ear. He pulled the Post-it note off the box and held it up so they could both read it.

We hope you've had the perfect evening but ask just one thing: would you mind lighting the fire for me so the house is warm for later? Love Ethel. And then scrawled below were the words *and Annie*, which she signed off with a little heart.

'Oh, of course we can,' Alice immediately answered. 'Light a fire in return for secretly planning such an awesome evening? I think we can manage that. Don't you?'

'Have you had an awesome evening?' He moved his head a smidge so he could see her entire face. That face full of generosity. That face he wanted to take in both hands and kiss.

'Of course I have. I had such a long day and thought all I wanted tonight was to curl up and rest but I was wrong. This is far better. Absolutely perfect. Perfect food and' – she paused and he saw her gulp, just briefly but gulp nonetheless – 'perfect company.'

'I'm glad. I feel the same. I could do this every night.' He knew his words were true. He couldn't think of anything better than being able to engage in such domestic intimacy with Alice. To have her there in the morning when he woke up, to bring her a coffee in bed and look at her with that gorgeous, thick hair all mussed up and a sleepy smile on her face. To know that when he came home she would be there, that he could provide a shoulder for her to lean on, to care for her. This really wasn't helping. Perhaps he should imagine something else quickly. Maybe recite the Apostles' Creed or perhaps the Lord's Prayer. Something that would remind him of his role, his proper and appropriate role in Alice's life.

'Me too, and I don't think it would stop feeling special. We've been really lucky.'

'We have.' He felt he needed to change the energy here. What should be an evening between two friends was quickly morphing into something else and the compulsion to take her in his arms, wrap her up, keep her safe and show her how he felt was becoming far too strong. Professionalism here was key. He was her vicar. The safe spot she could turn to for support both in everyday life and in times of crisis. He could not change that. Apart from anything else, she was his favourite parishioner and contributed so much to the church community. One false, misguided move and it wouldn't be just him that lost her.

A part of him whispered, like the archetypal cartoon devil on his shoulder, *but what if you didn't lose her? What if she wants this? Shouldn't she be given the chance to say yay or nay? Doesn't making these decisions for her make you paternalistic and controlling? She has a voice, she's a smart woman, she can say no if she's not interested in a way that doesn't make her hightail it from St Blaise's.*

Currently Alice, unaware of the battle taking place within his head, stood taller and leant over him to open the boxes. He could feel the curves of her body leaning against his back. Just for a second, he let himself lean back into her, enjoy the moment. Just for a second.

'Oh, chocolate and cherry cheesecake. Yum. These two are not thinking of my diet. Let's go make the fire and then we can eat pudding and give them a call to let Ethel have her house back.'

'Okay, good plan. Although I don't think you should worry about a diet. Let's just enjoy what we have this evening,' he answered her. And although he had agreed to the plan, half of him (more than half, most of him) was desperate for the evening to never end. He didn't want to pick the phone up and then, swoosh, go straight back to their normal lives, with the barrier of their roles between them once more.

'I'll grab some forks.' She moved her body away and over to where the cutlery was kept and he felt the loss of her proximity. He wanted so much to pull her back and keep her there, but as he reminded himself at this moment in time she wasn't fully informed, she didn't know the facts. She just thought she did. Annie was right. He needed to talk to her.

Chapter Sixteen

Alice ensconced herself on the sofa, with cake plate and fork in hand as he set his down on the hearth and started to make a fire. He enjoyed this; he wasn't a fan of house-work and was very grateful to Denise, who cleaned The Vicarage once a week and stopped it looking like it was a student squat, which was the state he suspected it may descend into if he were left solely in charge, but fire building was a task he loved.

During his years in school the whole forest school ethos was beginning and he was considered to be one of those children that needed extra pastoral support because of his situation at home. The fact that he was very happy with Annie and much more settled than he had been before wasn't taken into account. And it seemed that nearly every year when forest school came around, both in primary school and secondary, his name would be put forward. It was meant to make him feel special, valued and for many children it worked, was a really useful way to connect with school, but for him it often felt like he was the one that was singled out for being different. A difference he wasn't really struggling with until it was brought to the attention of all his classmates every bloody summer. That micro-expression of pity, sympathy, that the adults always showed. That made him want to hit out at them, because how dare they say, imply, that his life wasn't perfect with their unasked-for sympathy. He was happy, he didn't like change. He just wanted to be treated like everybody else.

However, the upside of this was that he could start a fire with practically anything, and that included Tampax and Vaseline, an unusual skill within the clergy. Oh, and he could whittle, whittle creatures out of sticks at a drop of a hat. That, his ability to mask his true feelings and his fondness for toasted marshmallows, could all be tracked back to forest school.

Which meant right now as his heart was beating out of his chest and he was torn in two by his overactive head, veering off at one point about how much he wanted to take Alice in his arms and veering back to how it was important to behave in a proper way, he could still light the fire and look perfectly normal.

'Oh look, she's got a copy of *It's a Wonderful Life*, I've never seen that. My mother wouldn't have old movies in the house, not even on the television. She said there was no time in the world for things that had been and gone, we had to have new everything. Wow, you know what you're doing,' Alice finished, forkful of cheesecake to her mouth as the orange, red and yellow of the flames rose up, making the room cosy and casting an even more romantic glow over the evening.

The music had stopped just as he lit the fire, the playlist presumably over now, and the only sound left in the room was the sound of the two of them breathing. He stood up, saying, 'I'm a man of many talents.'

'I don't doubt it. I'm now adding firestarter to the list.'

'Twisted Firestarter' was the immediate thought in his head which then skipped his thoughts to his parents. They had started their journey together as rave culture was exploding. Unfortunately, it hadn't been the brief youthful foray into happy highs as it had for many but became an extended exploration into dark, nasty. He'd have to talk to Alice. He'd have to explain. He picked up his cake and approached the armchair.

'Oh come sit with me here, we can both watch the flames then.'

She was not making this distance thing easy. But he was determined. Until she knew who he was, all the time she was labouring under this false illusion of him being the fit vicar – he knew what people said even if he didn't see it himself – then she was seeing things through rose-coloured glasses and that wasn't fair.

However, if Ethel and Annie were about to come powering back in then maybe tonight was not the right time.

Maybe he should stop being such a coward.

'Oh, this cheesecake is good. I was going to offer you mine to make up for eating all the oysters, but I don't think I can bear to.'

'I'd rather you didn't.'

'Just as well. Shall I text Ethel and let her know the fire's lit? Then we'd better wash these bowls and give her the house back.' He could see from Alice's face that she was as keen on this plan as he was, although being Alice her disappointment was only on her face for a split second before she replaced it with her usual cheery expression. But he didn't feel he had a choice. They couldn't just steal Ethel's home and play pretend house forever. Well, they could, he would love to, but they'd get kicked out at some point.

He sent a message to Ethel, sharing a sad look as he tapped the words out, only to have a message ping back immediately.

You two are so lovely. I'm really sorry but Annie and I have just started Gone with the Wind, *Matt — you know that jolly, good-looking one from the TV — mentioned it to me the other day and we realised neither of us had seen it in years. I'm going to be hours, please feel free to stay and enjoy the fire. It would be a shame to waste it. ;-)*

He read it out loud, feeling the grin take over his face as he did so.

'They are so naughty, and that winking face. Do you think this was their intention all along?' Alice slid herself off the sofa and plopped herself onto the floor with her back resting against the couch and her toes wiggling out near the front of the fire.

'A romantic dinner for two, followed by some time in front of the fire. I think they may have done. We need to watch out in case a burly opera singer bursts through the door in a minute with a flower in between his teeth. It wouldn't surprise me.'

'Nope, in fact I'm going to be disappointed if it doesn't happen.'

'O Sole Mioooo,' Dan started to sing.

'Not really burly enough, distinctly lacking a beard and a pot belly and you don't have a rose in your mouth, so nope, no good I'm afraid.' Alice laughed at his attempt.

'Ouch, it's hard to find a rose at this time of year.'

'I imagine it is, especially as you haven't moved an inch from the fire to even look. Where is your commitment to the cause?'

'Haha. Fair point, although still a little mean. Although talking of meanies, I can't believe your mother wouldn't let you watch old movies. What was that about?'

'I have no idea. Although to be fair to her she did take me to the cinema every Christmas to see the new ones. I remember being completely bedazzled by *The Grinch*. But I sometimes wonder if she just did it so she could tell everyone what an outstanding mother she was.' Alice's hand flew to her mouth, an age-old gesture but one she looked genuinely surprised by. 'Ooh, I don't know why I said that. I'm sorry. I take it back.' She spoke heavenwards, lifting her eyes skywards to reinforce her apology.

'Oh, my condolences, I didn't realise. Is she um… has she…?' He was a vicar for goodness' sake, he should be able to speak about death. Especially bearing in mind his own circumstances.

'Oh gosh no, oh that's worse now, isn't it? She's still alive, very happy in Dubai with husband number four. I don't know why I did that.' She pointed with one finger up to the sky. 'I guess I always feel so guilty if I talk ill of anyone, especially my mother. I should have more respect. She did give birth to me and then bring me up.'

'And she did an outstanding job, you're pretty awesome. Did you say fourth husband?'

Alice flicked a glance at him as she answered, clearly trying to ignore the fact that she was blushing slightly. Was that because he had called her awesome? He knew she was prone to the odd blush now and again and he thought it was quite cute, but it could easily be the warmth of the

141

fire. With the flames jumping and swirling it was kicking out a fair whack of heat. 'Yes, she's… um, very popular. You know what, seeing as Annie and Ethel are going to be busy for hours, maybe we should take them up on their offer and enjoy the fire, just for a little bit longer.' She put her plate down and Dan shuffled over towards her so they were both sitting facing the fire, their backs against the sofa.

'I think that's a really good idea. And we can watch *It's a Wonderful Life*.'

'Oh yes, let's do that.' Alice held his eye and he had a feeling something else was coming, something not related to a black and white movie. 'Although, it seems to me that Ethel and Annie, and let's assume it was Annie, were very keen to put us here together, create this magical evening and get you to talk to me about something. I don't want to push you, you know what you are and aren't comfortable with but if there was something you wanted to tell me about, I'm a really good listener and it seems to me that this is the perfect set-up. Us, a fire, no one else to interrupt and you know you can be sure in the knowledge that anything you said, anything at all, would never be shared by me. I have a mouth like a trap, nothing is getting out.' She flushed a little again and Dan smiled at her.

Sitting here, with the firelight flickering off her hair, and knowing that she was who she was, that she would listen without judgement and hear without telling, made it a very appealing prospect. Maybe he could just start, see what came naturally, what he felt free to say in the moment and what he chose to hold back. Apart from anything else if she was as attracted to him as he was to her, if she was one tenth as attracted to him as he was to her, then he owed it to her to put her straight. However, right now he wasn't sure where to start so he nodded instead, hoping that she accepted that it meant that he would try.

She seemed to and leant over, resting her arm on his and nodding back. As electricity coursed through him, a sexual chemistry he hadn't experienced for so many years, he felt he should move away but noticed her eyes weren't on him any more but fixed in the distance.

'Are you okay?' he asked and she turned to him with the cutest expression as she extended her arm to point towards the window.

'Look, it's snowing. How perfect is that? It's December, we've got a fire and it's snowing outside. My tummy is full and I'm all warm and spending the evening with someone I really like.' She smiled bashfully, and rested her head on his shoulder. Dan knew in that moment, as the snow flurried down past the window and the flames licked the fireplace, that he was as happy as he had felt in years.

Chapter Seventeen

They sat there for a while in silence, staring at the snow as it fell. Dan had no intention of moving an inch, he was so happy right now. He couldn't remember the last time he had shared such intimacy with someone. Of course, he was always there for Annie, his friends, his parishioners, but none of them tended to cuddle in and snuggle up. If he had been a cat, like Dave, he would be purring so loudly right now – okay maybe not Dave, he only purred as he was planning an attack, but a normal, less blood-obsessed cat would be purring so loudly that they would hear it all the way back to The Vicarage.

Alice said something to break the spell, but it was so quiet he wasn't sure what she said.

'What did you say?' The only sensible way to find out was ask.

'Just that this is the first snow of the season and… and I like to cast a wish when I see the first snow. I used to have the prettiest snow globe, it had Truro Cathedral inside and I thought if I shook it I would have a wish each time. I shook it a lot. I always figured with wishes and prayer I had all my bases covered.'

'That's sweet. "Used to have" – what happened to it?'

Alice shrugged and sat silently for a few seconds, as if she was weighing up telling him. 'My dad bought it for me, he was the one who used to take me to church every week as a child. When Mum left him the snow globe disappeared. I'm still not convinced that it was an accident, that it was lost in the move as she claimed. But hey, could be a lot worse. It was only a snow globe. Although talking of family, what does Annie think you need to tell me? Obviously if you're not ready, or don't want to share then that's fine but if you want to, I'm here right now. We're cosy and I'm told I'm a good listener.'

He thought about it. He did want to talk to Alice, he wanted to lay himself bare, show who he was and see how she'd react but... but what? He had been carrying around guilt for an age, Annie had been quite clear that she thought it was time to move on and he knew, on one level, she was right. But this wasn't that. Annie wasn't asking him to do anything he didn't want to, and he had such respect for Alice, he did want her to know.

'Annie worries about me.' He started to speak and then found himself stopping; what on earth could he say next? For a man used to writing sermons and using words to articulate comfort he shouldn't be finding this so difficult. He took a slug of wine and waited to see what Alice would say. She said nothing, waiting for him to fill the gaps. 'She thinks I hang on to the past.'

Alice stayed silent still, but he felt her squeeze his arm.

'I think she may be right.' As Dan said it out loud – said what had previously just been a thought flitting around the periphery of his mind, one he hadn't given too much space to – he found he was hearing the truth of the words. 'You know about Sophie, I think?'

'Yes, I will remember the day you told us about her until the day I die. Your sermon had a real impact. But your grandma isn't suggesting that you forget her, is she?'

'No, no she's not. She was very fond of Sophie and was heartbroken when we lost her. But I don't think it's Sophie she wanted me to talk about. Sophie wasn't my first loss.'

'Okay.' One word. A simple word, no judgement made.

'I don't really remember the details, but I do remember the feelings, so I'm going to tell you as best as I can, but I may get things a bit muddled.'

'Go on.'

'I moved to live with my grandmother; as far as I was aware it was just something she and my mum and dad agreed, although now and with a little more knowledge I expect social services would have been involved. I had just started Mrs Ashby's class, Year One I think they call it now, so I must have been about six. My parents struggled, they really did. They struggled with their illness and they struggled with everyday life. I don't know which came first, but I suppose it doesn't really change the outcome.' As he spoke, he kept his eyes down, on his hands, not willing to look Alice in the eye, not prepared to see her reaction to his words. 'My understanding was that when they first had me they managed to get and stay clean. They were addicts you see, although obviously I didn't know or understand then as much as I do now. They both signed up to methadone and I don't know if or how many times they slipped up but largely they managed to get and stay clean, on and off, throughout the pregnancy and after I was born. For a short while.' He shifted his gaze to the window, looking out at the falling snow.

'Their intentions were good, but their will was a little weaker. That's the nature of addiction I guess. It gets its claws in and there's a reason people struggle to shake it.' He felt his voice take on a faraway tone, as if he were discussing someone else, and yet at the same time he was somehow shot back to being that small boy, the boy who had been picked up from school one day by his grandma and was told that from now on, for a short while he would be staying at Granny Annie's house, just until Mummy and Daddy were well and then they would come and get him and all live back in their house together again and visit Granny every weekend. He liked spending time at his grandmother's, she always had treats for him and gave him dinners he really enjoyed.

He continued telling Alice his story, lost a little in the past as he did so. He told her how time went by, he grew up month by month, year by year, and was settled and happy at home, in Annie's home. He knew she loved him and she treated him as she always had done, as if he was the centre of her world. Unlike school, who had suddenly started acting strangely with him, checking in all the time, making special allowances as if he were somehow different from the others, as if he were pitied – not that he could identify that at the time but like everything else, he could remember how it had felt. As if he needed bloody forest school every year so he could talk about his feelings as they sat around the fire. As an adult he knew they had meant well, had been looking after him the best way they could for the time. It had just lacked any finesse and instead of making him feel secure and important it had made him feel different. Small.

He saw his parents periodically but knew – even to his child's eye – that they seemed to be looking less healthy rather than more so. They weren't going away and getting better as they'd promised; even Granny Annie had stopped saying that was happening quite some time ago. Their skin was increasingly grey, their bodies dropping weight. Their animation when they saw him not quite real, and yet also overwhelming, all-encompassing, suffocating. He may not have known to identify these specifics, but he knew the emotions triggered by seeing his mum and dad when they turned up unannounced. School had done a lot of work with flashcards about emotions.

Their presence made him worried and unable to explain or understand why; guilty for feeling like he just wanted them to leave as they showered him in affection and attention, knowing he was meant to enjoy it; sad that they seemed in pain and he didn't know how to help. Even sadder that Annie's face would take on a frail, resigned look that she only wore when she saw Dan's parents. A look that said she was powerless, hurting and stuck.

The visits were sporadic, spontaneous, always coming as a surprise to him and Annie. When he was due to do something and then they would turn up, his plans had to be cancelled even as they told him to go ahead, but somehow he knew he couldn't, that he had to stay and see them just in case this was the last one for a while. Or there would be flurries of visits, his parents popping in to see him, making a fuss of him, giving him things they had found that they thought he might like, listening as he read to them, trying to eat the meal that Annie would give them, Dan and Annie having to watch them from the other side of the kitchen table as they moved food around their plates.

And then periods of nothing.

One day, just before his eighth birthday, Annie came and picked him up from school and he could see she had been crying. Her usual *How was your day? What did you do? What was the best bit?* questions that accompanied every pickup lacked their normal sparkle. She took him home and pulled him to her lap, on the old brown sofa that she'd had since forever – until he had replaced it with his first pay cheque as a vicar – and she had held him tight and explained that Mummy hadn't got better, that Mummy wouldn't be able to visit any more but that she would always, always be watching him, her heart glowing with pride and with love.

She drew a picture of his mother floating around on a cloud in heaven, a benevolent God looking after her as she smiled down on Dan, witnessing his every move. Annie didn't mention his father but he didn't visit again for many, many years. Arriving instead as Dan was bereaved again, as a young adult, the one time in his life he didn't want to see his father, didn't want to hear about his father's pain about losing his mother, or deal with the anger that understanding and adolescence had brought to him. As he lost Sophie, he needed to concentrate upon his own pain not witness his father's.

Dan pulled himself back into the room, sent the young child back to the past and grimaced at Alice, who was still sitting leaning against him, her eyes full and round and on him, a tear welled up at the bottom of each eye. Yet she hadn't cried, hadn't spoken, hadn't gasped or asked for clarification or made this about her in anyway. She had simply listened as he talked, hearing him and absorbing the knowledge that he was sharing. As he looked at her he felt the need to clarify exactly what had happened, to make sure she knew, wasn't sidelined by any of his words that masked the real facts. He didn't want any misunderstanding, any miscommunication. He wanted her to understand that his parents had been ill through addiction, not some sanitised disease where they spent their time away from him in a clean, fresh hospital ward.

No, this was an illness that accompanied them, drove them into the dark rooms, hidden public spaces, rundown buildings in which they sought their sanctuary and looked for their medicine. A medicine necessary for them to get their heads clear so they could contemplate getting clean again, if only for an instant and as if good intention was all it took.

He wanted her to know that what shaped them, compelled them, their genes that made them more susceptible, they were what made him too. They were the genes that had shaped who he was and what could be in his future. What he, if he wasn't really, *really* careful every bloody day, could potentially become.

'My parents were heroin addicts, it made them sick and it claimed their all. My mother died and my father has spent the rest of his life mourning her and has given up any attempt to become clean again. The truth is, I don't think he could cope if he did give it up now. His physical health may improve but his mental health… I don't think he could cope with where his life has taken him. So that, I guess, is what Annie wanted me to tell you. And she was right, you are perfect, and I am so far from it. But now you know the genes that made me.'

'Yes, yes I do. But I also know the genes that nurtured you, the woman who loves you so much and has so much faith in you that she has forced you into a room with me and made us eat shellfish. You are not making the choices that your parents made, you are neither your mum, nor your dad, nor Annie but you are you and the you I see in front of me is a man who has lived through devastating loss, and a man who stands strong for the people around him; the man who has, and it's a presumption, but a man who has channelled his grief, unendurable grief, into making sure he is always there as a support for others. Your mum and dad's addiction will always shape you, but *you* define you, no one and nothing else. And I like you. I think you're pretty next level amazing and I consider myself extremely lucky to have you as my friend.' She scrunched her face up and nodded her head as she issued her last pronouncement and right there and then, in that moment he knew he loved her. He loved her but despite listening intently, she hadn't really heard him.

Chapter Eighteen

Alice really hoped that the sentence that she had just uttered wouldn't be considered flippant. She had heard every word Dan had been trying to say and her whole inside had melted. The sadness she had seen fill his eyes as he recalled being young stung her sharply, yet she knew it couldn't be a fraction of the amount that he was hurting. What he had seemed to not understand though – despite his wan smile as she had spoken – when she had told him that she liked him and thought he was amazing, was how much she admired him. How the respect she had always held for him now ran even deeper.

'Next level amazing, huh?' Dan looked down at her and as Alice turned her head up to face him she felt something shift. She had known they were sitting closely, for goodness' sake she had just had her head on his shoulder, but now their proximity was enhanced. The snow was falling outside, the fire was flickering flames not yet down to embers and Dan's story of loss, his open vulnerability had made Alice feel like a lioness, in an I-want-to-protect-this-man-from-any-more-hurt way rather than I-could-rip-a-gazelle-limb-from-limb style.

How could she make him understand and see how special he was? She was so overwhelmed with love, admiration, everything for him and as she looked into his deep blue eyes, she knew she wanted to be by his side, batting hurt out of his path as if she were Wonder Woman with her magical weaponised bronze cuffs. She wanted him to know everything was going to be okay now.

'Next level.' She smiled back, but her words did not break the tension in the room. A tension that had built in seconds, despite being months, years in the making. She didn't move. Frozen as Dan was looking back at her with an intensity that she was sure was also bounding off her, the room practically throbbing with a mixture of emotions. The wish to nurture him was translated into a wish to love him, every part of him and in all manner of ways.

At this moment she saw the adult that was sitting next to her; the little lost boy was no longer on her mind but the man very much was. Alice felt a pooling of lust within her tummy, overwhelming and flowing into the rest of her, making her feel weak, light-headed and resolute.

This man, this one right here was who she wanted to be with and she was fed up with admonishing herself for having a crush on him. Yes, he was clergy but he was also a man and her whole self was screaming out for him to lower his head, brush his lips against her and show her that he felt the same.

Although why should it be him? Why should she not make that first move? Why not respond to what her body was telling her, screaming at her to do? *Because, you fool, you slightly predatory, gross, selfish fool, the man has just opened up about the death of his parents – as well as briefly mentioning the dead love of his life – and you're sitting here slavering for a kiss and a bit of a fumble. You're a disgrace.*

Her old default setting came into play and the short-lived determination to follow her heart – and that very definite physical part of her – was squashed down, put in its place by common sense and decency. However, she was still having trouble taking her eyes from his and…

Dan dipped his head down and tenderly, tentatively, claimed her lips. A slow, measured kiss, a kiss that asked if she too wanted this. She did. She responded, letting her lips furl into his, a gentle but clear yes.

He pulled back and looked at her again and she nodded slightly, still caught by those dark deep eyes, her heart beating so fast she thought it may come out of her chest and her mind struggling to compute what was happening. Right now, she didn't need her mind complicating things.

She reached up, just a smidge and Dan met her as she did so, kissing her again. Not soft this time, but deep, searching. His arms encircled her and pulled her so close that there was not a millimetre between them. She could feel his heart now as she could feel hers, both of them running fast and hard. She found herself holding onto Dan, her hands in his hair, pulling him closer, deeper in, showing him how she wanted this. The kiss became urgent, frantic and she started to pull on his jumper. He lifted his arms, allowing her to wriggle it up and off, and then he reached behind her and started to undo the zip of her dress. He did it firmly, with intent and she felt desire spilling over her, racing through her, the intensity of what she was feeling all-consuming.

He leant back a little, breaking off their kiss and staring at her. The appreciation clear in his face, love or lust shining out. She wasn't sure which it was, but it was definitely one of them. She sat up straight and allowed herself to hold his eyes. She felt so bold, she had never been this confident before, had always been so conscious of her body, the weight she carried, how she didn't feel good enough. But today was different, she felt confident here with Dan, as if this was the right thing for the both of them and that he wanted her for her, not for some airbrushed version of womanhood. This was about him and her specifically and she was loving it. This was meant to be.

But then something flickered across his face and in that second she knew she had lost him. The sense of the room changed and he moved himself back a few centimetres, regret in his eyes as he did so.

Suddenly she felt exposed, bare. Flustered, she tried to pull up her dress then arched her hands around to the zip at the back, unable to ask him to help.

Unable to say anything.

What had just happened? It had been a split second and everything had changed.

'I'm so sorry,' Dan said to her, *at* her, to make sure she understood he was apologising.

She did, but that didn't make a difference, didn't help her feel suddenly okay about what had just happened. What she did know though was that her self-worth had just plummeted from a zillion to zero.

'That's okay.' She shrugged her shoulders and pretended that it didn't matter, whatever the reason he had for changing his mind, and she was aware there could be many. But she couldn't help the fear that it was that he had been repulsed when he realised what was happening, when he *saw* her, and who could blame him? She didn't like to look at herself naked most days – even the good ones – so why should she expect him to?

Her eyes caught sight of the *It's a Wonderful Life* DVD on the floor next to them and she realised that as lovely as the evening had been, it was time to head home. She didn't want to sit here and listen as Dan was forced to explain why he had changed his mind.

'Perhaps we can watch this another time.' She pointed at the DVD. 'I've had a fabulous evening, I really have. But I've got such a long day tomorrow what with the ch— um, with Christmas coming up and I think I should probably get myself to bed. It's all right, no panic, I meant alone.' She giggled as she delivered that last sentence to make sure he knew she understood that this was not to happen again, self-deprecation her default setting for covering up embarrassment.

'I'll walk you back. The fire looks like it'll die out.'

'Honestly, its fine.' She was up on her feet now, making her way to the kitchen to grab her coat and get herself out of here. 'Oh, the plates.'

'If you wait a second, I'll do them then we can both lock up and head back.'

'Really, I'll be fine to walk back if you're okay to lock up.' She knew her voice sounded flustered, but she didn't know what to do with herself. Or what she had been thinking? Writhing around on the floor with the Reverend Dan Daniels was not how this evening was supposed to turn out, and now she had shown what she felt for him and he had decided against it.

They were in the kitchen now, she was pulling on her coat and making the quickest getaway she could, her hand moved towards the door handle ready to leave.

'Hang on, I'll only be a min...' Dan was rinsing the dishes and she avoided his eyes. She didn't need to seem *them* right at this second. She shot an empty-looking smile across at him, avoiding eye contact completely and opened the door.

'Thank you for a lovely evening, I'll see you on Sunday if not before,' Alice said in an attempt to keep things normal and show she didn't mind being rejected. And then she shut the door and cursed herself as she began her walk home.

Chapter Nineteen

Dan had never washed up so quickly in his life, pulling the dishes through the water at the speed of light. He wasn't sure how any of that had happened. Okay, so he knew exactly *how* that had happened and he knew he also *had* to stop it. The relief at having spoken to someone about his parents, and to have that person look at him and not judge him was massive. As he had sat there looking at her he was so full of love for this amazing woman who had listened to him, although her innate good nature had meant that she didn't really understand what he was saying. Hadn't seen the darkness he was trying to allude to.

But he couldn't blame her for that. *He* didn't understand what he was saying. He knew that he was warning her that he was damaged goods, not good enough for her. He knew that he was saying that he was scared, that he didn't want to get more emotionally invested than he already was, that he wasn't the man you chose to settle down and have a family with. And right now, he knew that she was scurrying down the road as quickly as she could to escape him.

As she had sat listening to him and responded as she had – *you define you, no one and nothing else. And I like you* – he had become tired of fighting his attraction to her, tired of keeping walls up and tired of always doing the right thing.

So, he had leant in to kiss her and that act, that act had lit a fire within him, an acknowledgement that he wanted Alice, he wanted to be in her life, he wanted to support her in her choices and he wanted to be in her bed.

Wanting to love Alice didn't diminish his love for Sophie, and wanting to be with Alice didn't stop him having fear for his future and who he could become, but it did feel right. It felt more than right, it felt necessary, and so, so good. As if he were coming home. He belonged.

But his good sense had kicked in.

And Alice had walked out.

He pulled his arms into his coat and shut the back door behind him. Urgency and speed still his priority. He couldn't let, didn't want, Alice to be walking home by herself right now. Not because she was unsafe, Penmenna was as safe as villages came, but because he didn't want them to leave like this. Her forced gaiety hadn't deceived him for a minute and he was determined that she saw it was he who was at fault, not Alice.

Unfortunately, though, Ethel's back door didn't seem to understand his urgency, the key refusing to turn with ease, and as he took it out to try again, he dropped it on the floor and was left scrabbling around on the ground in an ironic repeat of earlier, before he had put a nuclear bomb under his friendship with Alice.

The door finally locked, he started to jog down the path and out onto Fore Street, rushing from one end of the village to the other. The snow was still falling and there by the street light in front of the church, the same one that had lit Alice's tumble on the ice a few weeks ago, he could see her. She was walking quickly in the direction of her house. Her hair undulating down her back, almost as if it was waving goodbye at him, reminding him of what he could have had, had his head not jumped in and messed everything up.

Now was not the time to get caught up in the romantic or fanciful. He wanted to catch her before she went in, say goodnight and make sure things were left without confusion. Dan sped up and called out her name, her head turning sharply on the third call. She stopped and looked at him then took another pace or two before shaking her head and waiting again, the street light shining down on her as she rubbed her eyes on her sleeve in that way people do when they've had a little cry in the cinema and don't want anyone to see.

He approached her and stood with her under the street light. He hadn't been wrong, she had been crying a little. Her eyes weren't red and swollen but a smidge of pink hinted the truth.

'Hey.'

'Hey...'

He wanted to tell her that he was sorry, that he hadn't meant to kiss her, to lead her on, that he didn't want her getting entangled with him because he knew things could only end badly.

'Alice...' he started but the words wouldn't come. Instead he found himself looking at an eyelash upon her pink cheek, leaning in, his finger ever so gently – so as not to disturb her – collecting it. He held it up to her, for her to blow off and make a wish even though he suspected that her wish would involve him sodding off.

She looked back at him and he saw a flash of hurt, hurt that he had caused, and he wanted to do nothing more than to put the smile back on her face.

'Make a wish,' he said.

She leant down and blew the eyelash from his finger and looked up at him. The corners of her lips quirked upwards tentatively, as if she were reluctant to trust him and yet her good nature wouldn't allow her to be cross or punish him. He found himself desperate to reclaim her lips, to make up for earlier and to show her that it was all right, that they could work it out.

Here, under the lamplight and with the snow falling, once more he gave in to himself and the romance of the setting and took a step closer before ducking his head down an inch or two to kiss her.

He wasn't prepared for the speed of her response. But this time instead of arching herself into him, kissing him back with the same ferocity and intensity as he was showing her, she stepped back, bringing her hands up to push him away. And leaving them raised so that he could not step into her space again.

'You've got to be joking me!' Sweet, demure, wouldn't-hurt-a-fly Alice had disappeared and now the woman standing in front of him was a different woman altogether, a woman he hadn't seen before, but clearly one with a backbone of steel.

'I've had enough of this. You can't do this to me twice in one evening. It's ridiculous. I'm not prepared to play games with you, Dan. I'm too old for that sort of nonsense and I will not engage. Now step back, and think about what it is you want, think about whether that is actually a wise thing and you're in the right place for it in your life and then take action. But do not play with me.' She fixed him with a gaze so fierce, so determined and so thoroughly right in what she was saying that he felt utterly admonished.

He took a step back and bowed his head, this was not the message he wanted to give her. He had wanted to make her see that his behaviour in front of the fire, him backing off and stopping them from the natural progression, from kissing by the sofa to full on love-making in Ethel's living room hadn't been because he didn't want her but because he was trying to do the right thing. And now he had messed it up again.

Although he guessed from this point on she was at least walking away confident in the knowledge that he was the weak link, the one that couldn't be trusted and that she was not at fault at all.

'Alice, I'm sorry. You're ri—'

'Stop. I think we've both established that tonight was lovely but then something went wrong and repeating it isn't going to help either you or me. Now as romantic as this snow is, especially bathed in this orange light' – she put her hands out to catch the snow as it fell – 'it's also bloody cold, I've had a very long day and I need to get home. So thank you for a lovely evening, let's chalk it up to experience and leave it right there. There's no need for either of us to repeat it, or' – she arched her eyebrow at him as she said the next bit – 'beat ourselves up over what could be, should be or is. Now I'm going home so good night, Dan, and I'll see you in church on Sunday.'

She spun on her heel and started the short walk back to her house, whilst Dan stood there knowing that she spoke a wisdom he could only wish that he had.

Chapter Twenty

It took all of Alice's determination and self-control to turn up to choir practice the next day. She had spent the whole day afraid, afraid that someone from Penmenna had seen her crying – just a little – on her walk home last night. Afraid that someone had seen Dan try to kiss her under the lamplight as she stepped back and tried to do the right thing for the both of them.

She had returned home and found herself picking up the phone to Sylvie. She knew that before Sylvie and Alex had been together they had been best friends, and that Sylvie understood the agony of crushing on someone you were already super close to better than anyone else. She also knew Sylvie wouldn't be tempted to interfere, would gently support her without wanting to dream up six different and desperate schemes to win Alice the man, as Pippa would and indeed had when it came to her and Kam.

It had done her good; Sylvie had come around, despite the late hour, and sat with her as Alice explained her humiliation, had a little sob and wondered why she had been fool enough to think Dan liked her in the first place. Her friend reassured her, comforting her that she was a remarkable, beautiful woman that anyone would be proud to have as a partner, that no one would have seen them under the lamplight and known what was going on and managed to say all of that without bad-mouthing Dan. Sylvie had skills.

And so far had been proved right, for Alice had reached the end of the school day and no one had said a word. It was her own world which had been exploded, upended and whirled about last night, causing her to feel almost every emotion under the sun ranging from desire to anger, from ecstasy to grief. And no one else had noticed.

This was a good thing, and a great relief, but now she had the choir coming in and she was worried about what might be said. Whilst the children had all been in bed – or should have been – the adults in a village were also particularly good at noticing what went on outside the curtains of their cosy homes of an evening and were quite happy to chat about it. She walked into the hall and opened the lid of the piano with a great big swirl of trepidation in her tummy.

Ethel would be here for a start, and it was quite possible she would be bringing Annie, so even if the improbable occurred and no neighbour had noticed the sobbing and the attempted kissing, she would still have to face the disappointment in Ethel and Annie's faces as she declared their evening a dismal, heart-breaking failure. Although, of course, she wouldn't word it like that!

As her first practice tinkle on the piano keys rang out Rosy came racing into the hall.

'Hello, am I…? Oh, brilliant, no one's here yet. In that case I'm just going to whizz back into my office and finish up what I was doing, I shouldn't be more than ten minutes max, Matt is on his way with Chase.'

'Go, I'm all good here. I expect it'll take a while for everyone to float in.'

'Well we're here, although Polly isn't back from uni yet, but she's a bright girl so she can pick it all up at the end.' Pippa's mum walked in along with one of the stalwarts of the church and the existing choir.

'Hi, Mrs Parkin and Mrs Talbot, thank you so much.'

'We'll put the chairs out whilst we're waiting for everyone else.'

Which is exactly what they did before taking their seats in the front row and talking about village matters as Sarah Fielding drifted in, happy to be back in Penmenna School's hall so soon after her retirement. She was swiftly followed all at once by a whole host of others. Chase, a tall blond Viking-like American who had settled in the village and had fallen in love with Matt Masters' celebrity sister, Angelina, immediately perched on a chair next to Jan Parkin and pinched one of her orange and cardamom biscuits shaped like a musical note. Matt Masters, Rosy's boyfriend and local TV star, followed him in a few seconds later and also attacked the biscuit tub.

'Tra-la-la-la.' Dave, Lynne's husband and a fan of medieval music came strolling in, singing a choral refrain with Jane and Jenny from the PTA following behind and, as predicted, Ethel and Annie.

Alice's phone buzzed in her pocket and she pulled it out and saw it was her mum again. She'd return it this evening after choir practice. She'd had missed a call yesterday and it was most unlike her mother to be so tenacious about calling her. Normally she only called to tell Alice how wonderful her life was and how her life choices were superior to Alice's in every way. Last month, she had spoken for a whole half an hour about how difficult it was choosing which set of gold taps to have in their new apartment. It wasn't a problem Alice could relate to.

Alice put her phone back in her pocket and let the others all talk amongst themselves for a few minutes to see if there were any more last-minute stragglers. As Ethel and Annie bowled in through the heavy hall door she headed to talk to them. She thought it may be sensible to get to them first before they shouted anything about last night across the hall for all to hear.

'Wow, look at you two. You both look magnificent.' Annie was a pure colour explosion in a bright yellow cotton blouse with a ginormous bow, wide-legged scarlet trousers and a purple jacquard jacket. Ethel was in her usual uniform of lacy blouse and sensible skirt but had, presumably, been persuaded into a captain's hat and a maritime jacket, complete with braiding and epaulettes.

Ethel tipped her hat and Annie curtsied.

'We've been to Truro to that TK Maxx place and then found the perfect hidden-away second-hand shop, they call it vintage nowadays don't they? But it was fab, quirky and they were very kind to us in there. They had a Biba dress in there that I had myself when I was young, but I couldn't get into this one. We tried didn't we, Ethel, I bent over, I lay on the floor and Ethel and the dear lad working there tried everything to get that blasted zip up, but I just have to accept that I'll never be as skinny as I was at twenty and that's okay. I'm going to make up for it with colour. I was so bored of my everyday clothes and its Ethel's birthday soon so we thought if you can't get a bit experimental in your seventies—'

'Eighties,' Ethel interrupted.

'Seventies and eighties' – Annie nodded at Ethel – 'then, when can you? I think we look fabulous.'

'Oh you do, no doubt about it. I'm so glad you've come and I wanted to say a big thank you for last night. I had a lovely evening, it was so carefully planned, I can't thank you enough.'

She gave them a big grin as she said this; every word was truth – there was no need to add that she had been rejected just as she had allowed herself to open up to the possibility of being with Dan. Rejected and with her bosoms flapping around on display as he did so. She didn't think she'd ever get over the indignity.

'We're glad to hear it, aren't we?' Ethel answered, including Annie in her statement.

'Yes, we are and did you… um… you know…' Annie nodded knowingly and gave Alice a wink.

Alice quickly cast around the hall to see who was watching but everyone seemed to be in animated conversation so didn't appear to have heard. 'The food was so delicious, I really can't thank you enough.' She decided to slide past the specifics that Annie was asking about.

'Yes but did you, you know. And?' Annie gave a graphic hand signal, with one hand forming a tunnel and the other pointing in and out of it. Alice hadn't seen that since she was at school herself and could feel the colour flush up her face as Ethel started to giggle. Polite ladylike giggles that made her shoulders shake whilst not emitting much noise.

'We've been in The Smuggler's Curse for a bit as well, it's been a jam-packed day. So, *did you*?' Annie wasn't letting it slide.

Being honest was clearly going to be the quickest way to escape this inquisition, otherwise it would drag out and Alice could imagine Annie getting louder and louder until everyone in the room knew what she and Dan had, or had not, got up to the evening before.

'No, no we did not. He's my vicar and that is never going to happen between us. I'm sorry. I know you really wanted us to get together but we're just not compatible,' Alice fiercely whispered. She couldn't quite go full truth – that when he saw her half naked he realised he could do a lot better. She didn't want her mind going there right now. She had a duty to this hotchpotch group of people standing chatting in the hall.

'You are compatible,' Ethel said mutinously, 'you're perfect for each other.'

'Apparently not,' Alice heard herself say with a little hint of bitterness.

Eek, that was a bit too close to the bone. She wondered how she was going to explain her tone just as the hall door opened again and in walked Rafe Marksharp, Marion's oldest child who had moved up to secondary school in the September.

'Oh, is that the boy you were telling me about?' Annie hissed to Ethel, their focus immediately off Alice and firmly on the pre-teen who had just wandered him, still wearing his school uniform. 'He looks like the one, you said all tall and gangly with a shock of blond hair. Look, he looks charming and thoroughly untrustworthy, like you said.'

'Yup, it's him sure as eggs is eggs.'

'Right. You, you, young man…'

Rafe bestowed a golden smile on them as if that were sufficient answer and turned to Alice as he spoke. 'Hello, Miss Pentire, nice to see you.'

'Hello, Rafe, how are you?' replied Alice, aware that Ethel and Annie were muttering furiously and shooting foul looks at the boy.

'I'm well thank you. Mum asked me to nip in rather than just send a text to say that she can't make choir after all, she's really sorry but she said she's sure you'll do a grand job without her.'

'Did she indeed?' muttered Pippa's mum, Jan, who although all the way across the hall still apparently had ears that would hear planes taking off in France.

'That's very kind of her. Are you staying to sing?'

'No, you know, Miss, I can't sing, I sound like a decapitated frog.' Alice didn't know for certain what a decapitated frog sounded like and was a little concerned that Rafe actually might do. 'I'm heading down to Whispering Pines, I like to sit with some of the residents,' he continued and gave her a great big Marksharp grin that in that moment reminded Alice of a fox about to enter the henhouse, and he headed towards the door just as Rosy was walking in, accompanied by Mr Greenleaf and Denise, chattering ten to the dozen about the filming going on down the road.

'You keep away from Reg, young man, or I'm coming for you,' Annie shouted after him. 'Your friend is called Reg, isn't he?' she asked Ethel quickly whilst Rafe failed to respond, even with Annie loudly adding, 'I'll chop those hands of yours off with a rusty machete, do you hear me?' as the door shut behind him.

'Ethel, what's Rafe doing to Reg?' Alice turned to ask, not unaware that Rosy had broken off conversation for a second to look askance at Annie but had not, as yet, moved towards them to find out what was going on.

'He's been down there pretending to be all good and kind playing cards with them and fleecing them all! At least that's what Ethel reckons.'

Alice thought about this and figured Ethel should know; it was a well-known fact that you didn't engage Ethel in cards for money unless you were happy to lose a small fortune. Anyone who knew anything would only play her for coppers and still accept it would be an expensive night.

'Is this true?' Alice asked Ethel directly.

'Yes, he's very good at it, the staff and the residents think he's a good boy coming down in his school blazer and playing cards with the old folks, but I know his game. My Derek taught me a lot.' She nodded sagely and Alice was very glad that Dan wasn't in the room because despite the embarrassment of last night, she knew he would find that as funny as she did. 'Rafe's been losing for a while and is now improving his game, looking like he doesn't know what he's doing, but I'm telling you he's sharpening up for the kill. At the moments he's only taking a fiver here, a tenner here and with everyone saying how kind he is, so good at conversation, tra-la-la. But you mark my words, he's going to be taking a lot more and very soon.'

'I'm sure that can't be the case, Ethel.' Alice knew as she said it that it was more than likely that Ethel was right. The Marksharp boys were shockingly clever and even more devious. They looked like angels and yet if there was ever any trouble anywhere, you could be guaranteed that they would more than likely be involved and most probably be the ringleaders. Maybe she should have a word with Marion. The woman would hear no ill about her boys, but Alice had long suspected that Marion was much more aware of their naughtiness than she let on.

But now was not the time to worry about the Mark-sharps; right now she was here for the choir. With Sheila running in, all flustered at being late, Alice headed to the piano, gave a quick welcome, a thank you speech and started playing the opening bars of 'Silent Night'.

Chapter Twenty-One

The school bell rang the next day to mark the end of school and Alice raced down the granite steps and out of the school gates towards Marion's house. Last night had revealed many disconcerting things:

1) That the choir was going to need an awful lot of work. Whilst the intention was there they did sound a lot like tone-deaf marauding pirates after a gallon or two of rum rather than a joyful chorus of earthly angels.

2) Annie and Ethel were determined not to take no for an answer and had pretended to back off whilst clearly having no intention of doing so.

3) Rafe Marksharp may be running a racket as a card sharp, targeting the elderly inhabitants of the care home in the village.

4) Her mother was determined that Alice move out to the United Arab Emirates to be closer to her (Alice suspected this may be more to do with her mother's recent diagnosis of arthritis than actual maternal love) and had secured her an interview at the English School in Dubai. Somewhere Alice didn't really want to work. It wasn't that she was averse to year-round sunshine or a salary that would make her eyes water but she didn't think she wanted to leave Penmenna. It was only very recent events that meant she was even vaguely considering it.

The only practical thing she could do now though was to try and tackle the Rafe issue. Her mother would take time to sort out and the choir would need a few more rehearsals. As for Annie and Ethel, that was clearly going to take a strict talking-to and Alice wasn't feeling brave enough at the moment to take them both on herself, and she was certainly too embarrassed to get Dan to help her.

So consequently, she was now on her way to Marion's house to brave the lioness in her den. The woman hadn't been in school for a couple of days and Alice hadn't seen her pick up the boys either. So as soon as she had whizzed around the classroom and got everything ready for the next morning, she was free to go and knock for Marion. She knew there was no guarantee that she'd be in, but she also knew the boys were doing after-school badminton with Kam Choudhury at Roscarrock Leisure Centre so she may get a chance to speak to her and with no children or indeed any other witnesses present.

Alice couldn't decide if that was a good thing or bad. She figured if she washed up on Penmenna Beach tomorrow then it would have been the latter.

Standing on the doorstep she knocked hard on the door and took a couple of deep breaths to prepare herself for the hell that Marion may unleash. Having seen the state of her in the stationery cupboard just two days ago – how had that only been two days ago? Her whole world seemed to have crashed and burned since then – she knew she was right to be here. Not just to rat out Rafe but also to see how Marion was coping.

'Yes?' Marion opened the door very quickly – barely before Alice's hand had a chance to rest again at her side – and stood on the doorstep glaring at the teaching assistant.

The snap in her tone didn't indicate that she was at all pleased to see Alice, quite the opposite.

Marion was dressed in jeans and a jumper, no print or tightly fitted dress in sight, and certainly lacking the heels she liked to wear — always handy to have an additional weapon, in case one's tongue wasn't quite up to it — and was the most dressed down Alice had ever seen her. However, her trademark fuchsia lipstick was in place and her hair was immaculate. Alice couldn't help but wonder if she slept with it sprayed into position so it would always be perfect in the morning, or if she just got up and it was so scared of the woman it sat upon that it hopped into place obediently to save itself from being pulled about ferociously until it capitulated, which is what Alice had to do with hers.

'I just thought I'd drop by and see how you were doing. You were missed at choir practice last night but it was nice to see Rafe briefly.'

As ever, mention of Marion's sons made her — if only for a couple of seconds — slightly softer, malleable. She almost managed to squeeze out a smile, but in truth looked more like a cat with something stuck in its teeth.

Alice stepped up her advantage. 'He was looking so grown up and smart in his new uniform. You must be ridiculously proud.'

Marion opened the door a little wider. 'You'd better come in then. Quick, quick, I have to pick the boys up in a bit.' Not the most welcoming invitation Alice had ever received but it was a start.

'Thank you.'

Alice had only ever been inside the Marksharp house before at parties — when it was filled to bursting, a throng of people jam-packed inside – so seeing it today, empty, was a new experience. It was as immaculate as she would have expected. It was all open-plan and everything was so achingly stylish it would have fitted in beautifully to a home interiors magazine, but then Alice supposed that was the look Marion was going for. White and pale blue and Cornish seaside slate meets Christmas at Selfridges. The decorations were up and twinkling, a white and gold colour theme dominated, even the dog bed – complete with sleeping, glossy Weimaraner – had white gossamer snowflakes wound around it; everything looked as if she had hired the most expensive set-dressers money could buy. It was breathtaking. Alice wouldn't be surprised if the Queen popped around to film her Christmas message from here.

Alice hadn't put up her Christmas tree yet, although she had managed to drag the box of decorations out of the attic in preparation. Her couple of bits of gaudy tinsel and the baubles she had had since childhood would not have fared well in Marion's house. But then Alice's home was a little more lived in, or 'crammed full of old junk and completely lacking in style', as her mother would say. Did say. Her heart fell as she thought of her mother; that was something she would have to deal with later. Focus on one thing at a time.

'Now you're here I suppose I should make you some tea.' It seemed that Marion was further thawed by Alice's awe-filled silence as she looked around the ground floor of Marion's home.

'This is so beautiful, Marion. You really are talented. We should get you in to do the flowers in church.' Marion arched her eyebrow and gave Alice a 'really' look. Alice backtracked. 'Right, yes, of course. Tea would be lovely. Thank you.'

'Well, sit there then and don't touch anything.' Marion pointed to a chair that Alice would swear she had seen in a magazine that Lynne had left in the staffroom and cost the equivalent of a small island's GDP.

'Okay.' Alice tentatively lowered herself into it, whilst hoping that she didn't have any paint or icky things from school hiding on her anywhere. It wouldn't be the first time she had left work with paint smudges on her skirt. Right now, it would be a miracle if she wasn't leaking glitter from every possible orifice.

It didn't take long until Marion was back in the room, carrying an ornate and rather beautiful Japanese iron teapot and matching cups.

'Now, I've not made you proper tea because I'm very aware that you're watching your figure and we both know that left to your own devices you'll pile it full of sugar, so there's liquorice tea in there. Very sweet but terribly good for you. Maybe it will help with your bloating. Here.' Alice sat and watched as Marion poured her the tea and then sat back and took a slurp. To be fair it was delicious and she'd take any help she could get on the weight front, regardless of how it was delivered. As she lifted her eyes above the cup she found Marion's hawk-like eyes upon her.

'So...?' The word was drawn out.

'So, I wanted to nip around to see you for a couple of reasons, the first was to briefly talk about Rafe.'

'Such a clever dear boy.'

'Yes, absolutely.' Alice knew agreement here was the only way forward. 'It's just I heard something that made me a little uneasy and knowing what a fabulous mother you are, I thought I should probably tell you and leave it to you to resolve things. I thought you would rather know than not.'

Marion looked at her as if she had just dragged ten poorly sealed bags of manure across the white carpets before raising her eyebrows and continuing to stare at her in a very uncomfortable silence.

'Okay, so… um…' Alice was just working out how to phrase *your son is a small-town crook with no moral compass* into something more digestible when Marion, clearly bored of waiting for a reply, jumped in.

'Let's not worry about that. So, how are you any way, dear?'

The 'dear' was alarming. Why was Marion attempting small talk? She never normally bothered. Normally she came straight to the point in the most brutal manner possible. Normally she was very keen to discuss her sons. Unless this was a finely honed distraction technique.

'Yes, fine thank you.'

'And your mother? Still in Dubai with that lovely new husband of hers?'

Ahhh of course, money. Money always attracted Marion, like four-year-olds and glitter. Alice's new step-father – the lovely new husband – was ninety-three and had made a fortune doing something that had never been made entirely clear. There had been murmurs of rug exportation but Alice was never convinced that that in itself was enough to pay for the excessively lavish lifestyle. Unless 'rug' was a code word for automatic weaponry or artillery.

'Yes, busy decorating I think. But really, Marion, I did want to talk about Ra—'

'Oh, how charming. And have you spoken to her recently?'

Alice's innate politeness meant that she couldn't shout *let's cut the bullshit* and instead had to resort to, 'Yes, she's very keen for me to go and settle over there. She's even arranged me a job interview in one of the English schools there after Christmas but I've n—' Alice was interrupted by the rattle of the letterbox being opened, the dog lifting his head as it did so, and a gentle thud onto the door mat.

It was way too late in the day for the postman, who would smoke a rollie at the bottom of the village as the church clock rang out for noon and then laboriously walk from door to door huffing and wheezing, only to finish up by Rosy's house at the other end of the village as the church bells chimed one, whereupon he'd celebrate with another cigarette before walking back to his van. His routine could be relied upon. It had been for thirty years. And right now, there was a letter on the mat and it was four o'clock.

She looked at Marion; the woman had frozen, her attention no longer on Alice but on the door and its accompanying mat at the far side of the room.

'Do you want to get that?' Alice indicated the envelope with a nod of her head, grateful that the conversation had moved on from her mother when the realisation of what she was looking at hit her.

Marion finally stopped looking at the door mat as if she were in a state of paralysis and shook her head. 'No, no, absolutely fine. Now what were we talking about? In fact, why *are* you here?'

'Marion, is that another letter? You know, like the last one you showed me.'

'No, no. I'm sure it's not.' There was a silence; both women knew she was lying and Alice wasn't quite sure what to say or do.

'Okay,' was the best she could come up with after a pause. If that was a letter, should she really be piling the pressure on Marion with regards to Rafe? She was just working out how to approach it tactfully when Marion got to her feet and walked zombie-like to the mat. Then with a flash of Marion's usual vigour she pulled the door open and arched her head around it, as if she had some kind of special neck that enabled her head to swivel 180 degrees at speed, looking right to left to see if she could see who'd posted the envelope. Presumably she had no luck, as she closed the door with a sigh and picked up the envelope.

'I suppose seeing that you already know about it, I can tell you. Yes, I suspect it's another bloody letter.' She sat back in her chair and ripped open the envelope, barely bothering to peer inside before handing it to Alice. 'Here, you can have the joy of seeing what this one has to say.'

Alice took the envelope, her brow furrowing as she did so. She didn't like this one iota. Marion may be a bit of a nightmare but these letters were bullying of the highest order and bullying that pervaded her home as well. If your home couldn't be a safe space then something was seriously wrong. This needed to be dealt with.

She pulled the letter from the envelope and unfolded it, and there once again in black and white cut-out letters was another message: *Someone needs to concentrate on your home – your husband clearly isn't*. Alice read it to herself, but didn't want to read it out aloud. Who would do something so vile?

Marion's eyes scanned the note as it was held aloft and sighed then shrugged her shoulders at Alice, her whole posture showing, just for a second, total resignation. 'What can I say or do? Maybe it's true. This one feels pretty true.'

'Oh Marion, I'm sure it's not, but either way you can't allow this to go unchecked. This is malicious and like I said, I'm pretty sure there are laws against this sort of thing.'

'What's your point?'

'You should ring the police?'

'Ring the police. Ha!' Marion's tone was back. 'I don't think my husband cheating on me is something the police can do anything about.'

'You don't *know* that Richard is cheating, do you?' Alice would be surprised; Marion's husband was head of governors at Penmenna School and although he was frequently absent, especially in the last year or so, he was pretty devoted when he was home. So devoted that it had turned the stomachs of pretty much every member of staff at some point. The couple had an alarming habit of demonstrating their affection in places people would prefer not to see it. Whilst Alice had never told anybody, she had once seen them doing things that she was fairly sure may be illegal in several American states in one of the hidden coves along the coast path. That was only last summer, during half term.

'These letters seem pretty convinced.'

'Yes, but no one knows a marriage like the people involved in it. What do *you* think? What does your instinct tell you?'

Marion looked at her as if she was completely batty at this point. 'Instinct, what's it got to do with instinct? I think it's always best to deal in facts, don't you, dear?'

'Okay, well what do the facts tell you?'

'The *facts*, dear, tell me that my husband has been absent for quite some time because of so-called pressures of work and that whoever is sending me these messages presumably has some *facts* that I don't possess.'

'How many letters – is this not the second?'

Alice witnessed a battle going on. Marion was never one skilled at hiding what she was thinking and right now Alice could see the struggle taking place, a desire to keep the wall up and maintain the status quo and the very human emotion of wanting someone you could share things with, be honest about whatever current trauma you are living. It seemed the desire to have someone to confide in triumphed as Marion, somewhat shamefacedly and very quietly admitted, 'This is the sixth.'

'The sixth? But you only got that first one a couple of days ago.' Alice knew the surprise shaped her tone, but six!

'There's been two a day.'

'Oh Marion.' Alice got up and walked across to the blonde woman sitting opposite her and leant down and gave her a cuddle.

It was like hugging a skeleton, the ones they have in school labs up and down the country. Or at least so Alice imagined; the nearest thing she could equate to it not in human form was a cat she had rescued from the side of the road last winter, all emaciated and poorly, huddled and shivering from the cold. Despite several trips to the vets, it didn't last the week. Marion would not appreciate the comparison.

'I'm fine.' Marion batted her off but not until after she had leaned into the hug, albeit only for a nanosecond, and taken a deep breath. This woman really needed some friends.

'What did they say, were they all in this same vein?' Alice used her gentlest voice, the one that worked when very young children had shut down and didn't want to confide anything.

Marion shrugged her shoulders, faking insouciance and fooling no one.

'Yes, more or less. More actually, thinking about it.' She accompanied her words with a fake, shriller than usual giggle. 'Here, I'll show you. I did think about burning them but decided I would keep them, they may come in handy one day.'

Alice nodded as Marion pulled herself up from her seat and went and opened an old-fashioned bureau in the corner, a piece of furniture a little at odds with the room, but that somehow blended in seamlessly.

'Here.' Marion thrust a small sheaf of letters into Alice's hand, before sitting back down again and letting the teeniest sigh escape from her lips as she did so.

The one on top was the first one that Alice had seen, but as she flipped through she knew her face would be telling a story. This was unbelievable. The level of malice was off the scale and Alice flicked a glance at Marion. It was hard to see how she was coping, holding it all together whilst bringing up the boys practically by herself, her fiefdom of the school being challenged and pure poison seeping through her letterbox and into her home twice a day.

Alice sat in her chair and made eye contact, determined to be as fierce as it took. 'We can't allow this to continue, we need to report it. Get it stopped. It's malicious harassment.'

'I'm hardly going to bother the police at Christmas because someone is saying mean things about Richard and I. Besides…' She stopped and Alice could only imagine what she had planned to say. All of her guesses involved Marion worrying that the police may not just catch the culprit but also reveal truths she did not want to know.

'Marion…' Alice started, but it turned out she was wrong, that was not what Marion intended at all. What Marion intended suddenly poured out of her, a torrent of words flooding the room, the swift change of mood taking Alice by surprise.

'No, don't sit in my house *Marion*-ing me. Do you know how much I've got on at the moment? It's not just that we have non-uniform day on Friday to collect for the jar stall, that's two days away, with only nine days to the Christmas Fayre. Or Winter bloody Fayre as it's now apparently called. Not to mention the trip to Truro for the pantomime, the Christmas postboxes that need to be collected every day and handed out into the children's trays, there's the staff Secret Santa to oversee, the school is a base for the Christmas charity boxes for the vulnerable in Penmenna and surrounding villages—'

'I run that.' Alice couldn't help herself, but that was one responsibility Marion definitely didn't have.

'And who do you think moves the boxes and stops them piling up in the hall at the drop point? I hate to tell you, dear, but elves aren't real you know, not even in December. That's my girls and I tirelessly looking after the school for no appreciation, no depth of understanding of how much goes into keeping it all going smoothly. I'm not even going to mention that woman, that upstart baggage who thinks it's all right to start messing with that which has taken years to fine-tune. And look at this house' – she spread her arms wide to encompass the open-plan living space – 'it's a nightmare to keep clean, I have three boys, a dog the size of a rhino, and my cleaner, the selfish cow, is in hospital with pneumonia, with no thought as to organising a replacement for me. And quite frankly the boys are a little off the rails at the moment...' She sighed.

At the *moment*? Alice managed to keep her eyebrows under control.

'Rafe is gambling, possibly fleecing the whole elderly community in the village which I imagine is what you were so coyly alluding to earlier and I'm tired, I'm so tired, I just grin and say what dear boys they are. Rupert has been showing Rufus all sorts of unsightly things on the Internet and I think has taught him how to download content illegally and the upshot of all that is Rufus has decided when he's at home he won't use his words any more. He just snarls, and bites. Bites! It's not even as if he's two or three or four, he's *six*! He knows better and he does it anyway. It amuses him. I know for a fact he manages to communicate properly at school. And Richard, the person supposed to help me with all of this, Richard is never bloody here! So, do I have time, do I have the energy, to report this minor irritation to the police? Do I, hell!'

'I don't—'

'You don't know what to say, no of course you don't, dear, because everyone thinks my life is perfect. But guess what, I'm as human as the next person, and sometimes things just go to shit.'

Alice had never heard bad language from Marion before, and couldn't help but know that she spoke truth, that everyone did think she had some kind of idyllic existence with her perfect family in her perfect house.

'Marion, I can't argue with any of that. But if you let me...' Was she going to get her head bitten off? The woman in front of her remained silent, which was an indicator to continue. Had she suddenly spouted many snarling heads atop long weaving necks then Alice may have stopped. 'If you let me, I might be able to help a little. I will definitely take charge of the community boxes and can get someone to step in and arrange the Secret Santa. I can't do it myself as I have a whole week taken up with class rehearsals for the nativity this week, and then it will be whole school rehearsals, which as you know take some engineering. I do think the best thing to do is to see if we can make some kind of peace with Serena. It's not good having this sort of rivalry brewing in a school, or anywhere, and it's definitely not helping you right now. Perhaps we could...'

'I am not asking that woman for help.'

'Listen to me, what I'm suggesting is that...' Alice weighed up how to make her choice of words more Marion. '...is that she wants to help, but *you* know what needs doing and the best way to do it. Use her. Get her to do what you need doing. It won't take much. We can nip around for a cup of tea and see how the land lies, use her to your advantage, call a ceasefire for now and then if you have to, once you're recharged and Christmas is out of the way, you can go back to being mortal enemies. Although obviously I wouldn't advise it, but you could. What do you reckon?'

'Go to that woman's house and drink tea…' Marion's eyes lit up. Alice *knew* it would work; Marion did love having a nose around everyone's houses. 'Hmm. I suppose so, in the name of a temporary truce, and Christmas of course. She could do the panto lists, with Jenny's support.'

'Of course. I think maybe we should go tomorrow, that way we can get her on board before Friday's non-uniform day. That's always pretty hectic,' Alice suggested, taking a last slurp of tea. 'Now, about the boys—'

'Tomorrow works, we could go after school.' Marion nodded before changing her tone and adding, as she held Alice's eye, in her most intimidating fashion, 'There's nothing wrong with my boys.'

'I know, I was just thinking, you know, um… the biting. How I could help? Would you like me to take him aside at school and have a quick word?'

'I don't know what you're talking about…'

'But you just said—'

'I did not!' Marion's eyes were practically out on stalks.

'Right, well then, Rafe, that is who I came to talk about. Rafe and Whispering Pines.'

'He's helping the elderly, very admirable.'

'The cards, Marion. The money.'

'He is spending time with the elderly and engaged in traditional pursuits that they enjoy; if you're suggesting that my boy is profiting…'

'I am, Marion, yes. And so did you a minute ago.' Alice was loath to be so upfront but the woman had admitted it a few short minutes ago and now was in full-out brazen denial.

'Well, I suggest you stop. And I certainly did not. No little words in school, please, no judgements about what they do in their leisure time. Leave the raising of my boys to myself and my husband.'

'Right. Okay.' One of the advantages of being raised by her mother was that she knew when to throw in the towel, lose the battle to win the war.

'Good. I would never recommend interfering somewhere you're not wanted.' That told Alice. 'But I do agree to your idea about using that hideous woman – can you set that up?' Marion said, as she stood up and whisked the cups and teapot from the side table and smiled. 'Excellent, now no need to outstay a welcome. So, if you'd let me get on with my day.'

Chapter Twenty-Two

Over the course of the week the children had been practising their nativity songs and parts within their class-rooms. Yesterday Alice had spent the afternoon with Classes One and Two, who were largely angels, stars, sheep and other barn animals. They had a lot of singing to do but the stage movements and marking were relatively simple. It all seemed to be going to plan. Today she would be with Classes Three and Four and, as they had the main parts, things would be slightly more complex. However, seeing as they were able to pay attention for longer than six minutes and didn't like snorting glitter, licking pine cones or eating the stale popcorn from the tree, things were a lot easier.

Right now the stage hands, Molly and Stefan – the most introverted children of the group, who didn't want a starring role, preferring to dress all in black and hide – were attempting to cover a trike with some grey fun fur using a staple gun and Sellotape, and balance a donkey's head pinched from Penmenna's Players' costume box upon the handlebars whilst 'Mary' perched on it precari-ously and everyone sat around shouting suggestions, with Rupert at the front of the class, thoroughly enjoying his role as director, marshalling them all.

'I don't think this is going to be very safe,' Mary suggested, aka Emily G, as she tried to get off the 'donkey' with some difficulty. 'I think with a long blue dress I'm probably going to fall over and if you think I'm doing that in front of the whole school, you are so wrong! I reckon you might struggle too, Fleur.'

Fleur, the other Mary, nodded in agreement.

'You could wear a short blue dress,' Jake shouted out only to be quashed with a Rupert glare. Jake was quite forward for his age, and normally Rupert would be the first to laugh along with him, though today he clearly felt that Jake's role as assistant director meant he should be less self-serving and toe the line. Jake had had a badly hidden crush on Emily since infants, and she had so far refused all his advances which usually took the shape of teddy bears on Valentine's Day and shy requests to pair up with her on school trips.

'I still don't see why we can't...' Tom shouted out, pausing only as the door to the class creaked open. Alice's heart jumped into her throat and stayed there as she saw Dan's familiar face peering around the wood of the door. She hadn't seen him since Monday, the evening he had decided she was too fat for him and that any interest he may have had dissolved into repulsion once she had started taking her clothes off.

'Hi, Reverend Daniels, come in. We're just trying to solve the problem of the donkey.' Rupert invited him in, as Alice hadn't said anything yet, but merely stood there offering up a quick prayer that she wasn't the same colour as Wise Man Number Two's scarlet robe.

'It's being an ass,' Jake quipped, earning himself another Marksharp glare.

'Ah, donkey's looking a bit wonky, it wheely is,' Dan added with a grin.

The class sniggered, although Alice ungenerously assumed it may be the fact that the vicar had made a joke at all rather than because it was a funny one. But then maybe he was feeling as awkward as she was.

She looked up and gave him a smile of welcome; she could be professional. She knew that things for Dan were far more complex than what she was dwelling upon, deeper than the surface of her hurt. She *knew* that it was his own demons rather than her waistline that had made him stop their embrace. She also knew that the emotion behind rejection was what was governing her behaviours and thoughts at the moment, not the facts. And that was okay, she would get to them when she was ready.

'Come in, this is perfect timing. We're just running through some of the logistics of staging the nativity and problem-solving them.' She hoped he knew that her welcome was genuine; she still liked and respected him, regardless of what had happened between them on Monday.

'Brilliant. I was just picking up some of the Christmas packages to take them over to the church hall ready to start sorting before more come in next week, and I thought I'd pop my head in and say hi, see how things are going. I know I'm due next week to help with the whole school rehearsals, but I thought I'd see if you need a hand before then. You were working out a donkey dilemma?'

'Yes, and I was saying that I still don't see why we can't have a real donkey. My nan has one in the paddock with her horses and she says she doesn't mind us borrowing him as long as we're careful.' Tom spoke up again, continuing what he was saying before the door opened. It was a point he made often. Alice didn't need to concentrate too much on Tom's words, they were quite predictable.

Which was just as well as Dan met her eyes above the class and mouthed 'Are we all right?' above the heads of the children and her tummy squirmed a little at the hope and the concern upon his face.

'Of course we are,' she mouthed back, and knew they would be. She could be friends; Dan had had so much strife in his life and did so much good that she wasn't ever going to contribute to making his life more difficult.

With those words whispered she suddenly felt a lot more at peace; she hated confrontation of any kind and had been dreading seeing him again, assuming it may well not have been until church on Sunday. She wouldn't be such a coward that she wouldn't attend but the thought had crossed her mind. This was much easier, it was done now. They carried on smiling at each other above the children's heads and she could see the relief upon his face too when she realised that she should probably be listening to the children.

'I've had riding lessons since I was six,' Emily seemed to be saying, 'and so has Fleur. I can canter and all sorts so I could easily stay on a donkey.'

'And he's ever so good. Me and my brothers have been riding him ever since we were little. Mind you we have to promise to not tell Mum.'

Rupert was standing at the front of the class, stroking his non-existent beard upon his cherubic eleven-year-old face. 'It does sound like it might be a better plan than *that*.' He nodded at the trike they had pinched from the infant playground and all the children gathered nodded assent whilst casting dismissive glances at the yellow metal contraption, now bedecked in patchy bits of fur.

Joey, the boy who was playing Joseph, nodded in agreement. 'I feel a bit of a twit pulling the trike around, that's for sure.'

'Woah, woah just a minute.' Alice switched herself back on. 'What do you have to keep a secret from your mum? Besides, we can't have a real donkey in the nativity!'

'Why not, Miss? Rupert asked. 'My mum says if you can make someone's day brighter, or happier than we should.'

'*Your* mum said that?' Alice's disbelief bounced around the walls before she realised how rude her words were. But really! Mind you, Rupert seemed not to notice whereas Dan had burrowed his chin and mouth down into his dog collar and when he looked up and met her eye she could see him fighting the laughter. Who thought Mrs Marksharp would be giving such advice. 'Of course, she is quite right. We should.' Alice decided she'd better make good.

'Great, Miss. Thanks. Look how happy you've made Tom.' It was true, Tom was sitting there beaming whilst his friends were clapping him on the back and saying things like *good one, Tom,* or *result.*

'No, no! No! I was not saying we could have a donkey, I was agreeing that we should be kind.'

'What do you think, Reverend Daniels? Surely a real donkey would be better. I mean Mary did ride a donkey not an infant's trike.'

'Well, she did but I would have to agree with Miss Pentire on this. She is the one in charge and it could be difficult managing a donkey in the school hall.'

'Ah but we're not having it in the school hall. Aidan's dad is going to let us borrow one of those domes he rents out during summer, you know like a mini Eden Project. He's going to put it up for us and everything, completely free of charge. We're going to have our nativity in there on the school field, it's going to be covered in stars and it's going to have a real donkey and it's going to be the best nativity ever!' Betsy explained animatedly.

A cheer went up from the children and Alice had a feeling she may have lost this battle.

Chapter Twenty-Three

Dan seemed to enjoy being in the classroom so much that he ended up staying for the whole afternoon. After the donkey they had talked about costuming and, following a voracious argument, Rupert, a benevolent dictator, acquiesced that tradition was tradition for a reason and that tea towels probably were best for the shepherds and that gold tinsel halos would be considerably cheaper than anything else. Rupert also took time to cock his head and raise his eyebrows at Dan in question, to which Dan nodded in unspoken answer.

Alice was a bit worried that as the children practised some of the songs that they may let slip about the secret carol choral practice she had organised, but they managed to keep quiet all the way through, even as she made them wrap up warm once the bell for home had rung. It was bitingly cold out there. It might be dry, but it was one of those afternoons where if you breathed out, your breath turned into billowing puffs.

'That was so much fun. No wonder you love working in a classroom, although I have a feeling that you might now be trapped into having a donkey on stage.'

'Oh, don't! I probably have been. The trouble was that I was trying to give them ownership of the nativity play, really make it theirs, rather than just following the dictates of an adult. So I told the whole class at the start that they were in charge, with the director's team having final say, and I would be here in an advisory capacity to oversee and facilitate. I did wonder if that might come back and bite me on the arse.'

'Ha, yup. But then so might the donkey. They can be unpredictable beasts.'

'As can the children! Thank you for joining in today, you were good with them and strong when it came to sourcing the "myrrh".'

'It was so much fun, although to be honest I can't claim any credit for that. I merely described it to them as best as I could and then we looked up pictures online. It was Rupert's genius idea to go and swipe Sheila's sugar crystals from the staffroom. I don't know how he knew they were there.'

'There's nothing those boys don't know,' Alice said darkly. 'Interesting that only a few minutes with Rupert Marksharp and you're fully involved in theft and deception.'

'Oh, yes. Hadn't thought of it like that. You're right, that boy is going to be a criminal mastermind, equipped with powers that cloak individual thought process and encourage blind obedience.'

'Yup.' Alice smirked as she finished putting the books back on the shelves.

'I was wondering—' Dan began, only to be interrupted by the high-pitched squeak of Marion careering around the corner and into the classroom.

'Coo-ee, just me. And which boy is that, that you're talking about?'

'Oh, um… no one to worry about,' Alice responded although she was pretty sure Marion may have a fair idea. 'I won't be a minute.'

'Okay, but I want to catch that hideous woman before she leaves to pick Josie up from Christmas craft club.'

'Yup, ready now. Just give me a minute. I've got to go, Dan, sorry. What were you saying though?'

'Oh not to worry, I was going to ask if you had a minute to grab a coffee but we can do it another time.'

'Oh nonsense, Vicar, we won't be long. It doesn't take long to make peace, does it? I don't think I've ever done it before.' Marion giggled her tinkly oh-so-fake laugh and added, 'Why don't you come along with us and then you two can have coffee after? It's always nice to get to spend time with you so I'd be very happy if you joined us.' Simper, stare, shoulder shimmy, simper. Alice wondered if she could get away with faux vomiting.

Dan looked at Alice, who stopped making faces and nodded; she could hardly say no. And she supposed this could work out to be a good thing. If she spent some time with him whilst in someone else's company, then it might normalise things a bit and they could get their friendship back on an even keel. Alice didn't want to lose him as a friend, and she was very fond of Catsanova – ooh, she'd try that name next.

As Alice was nodding she noticed that Marion was still looking at Dan the way a cat eyes up a fish bowl. Oh, for goodness' sake! She'd be walking around him in circles next and licking her lips.

How Marion manged to combine ogling with chivvying them along had to be an art form, but she managed. 'Right then, chop, chop, Alice. Let's get this done.'

As the three adults left the school grounds and turned down the street to walk towards the house that Serena had moved into last year, Marion managed to weasel in next to Dan, pushing Alice into the road as she did so, before slipping her arm through his, beaming up at him and asking him what made Christmas time extra special to him.

'Are you okay, Alice?' Dan queried before answering Marion. 'Did you slip?'

'I'm fine,' Alice muttered as she stepped back onto the narrow pavement behind them. Which meant she got to watch Marion and her super thin body coo over Dan all the way up to The Hill. She did at least get to cheer herself up by playing Dragon Breath with the cold air behind, and directly towards, Marion's back.

When Dan asked about Richard, Alice's sympathy returned as Marion's tone faltered – just for a fraction – before she talked about how he wouldn't be back until Christmas Eve and how excited the boys were, and how it would be wonderful to have a few whole days together with nothing to interrupt them.

Alice felt for her, knowing now about the tremendous personal pressure Marion was under with her husband's absences and those vile letters. She no longer wanted to tie her up and force feed her pork pies and cream cakes but wanted instead to reach forward and give the woman a reassuring shoulder squeeze, let her know that Alice was on her team and wishing that she'd have exactly the Christmas she wanted with her family. Although Alice would rather not stumble across them in a cove again.

Winter had its advantages.

They reached Serena's door, and Marion lifted the knocker and then turned around to look at Alice.

'Here goes, but do note, I'm here and willing. This woman had better behave herself— oh hello, Selina.' The door swung open to show its owner standing there, immediately snarling as she spied Marion on her step.

'It's Serena, as you well know, what on earth are you doing— oh hello, Vicar, oh and Miss Pentire. I didn't see you there. You had better come in, it's freezing.'

She stood back, opening the door fully and with a smile that would rival one of Marion's in the falseness stakes and let them into her house.

As Alice stepped over the threshold she began to feel a little inadequate. Was there no one in this village that had anything but a perfect house? What was it with these women? Then she remembered the state of Pippa's car and this cheered her up.

Serena's home was cosy, but immaculate. She led them through to the living room, which was painted all in bright white. Three large dramatic paintings took up the main body of the wall space, all with bold splashes of colour bringing them to life. The remainder of the walls were filled with bookcases, the shelves weighted with some rather intimidating tomes. Alice wasn't sure how *anyone* could have possibly ploughed through all of those and she was a girl who read in every spare moment. There were knick-knacks too, very different from Marion's clean lines in this respect; all were indicators of a well-travelled, cultured family who wanted to advertise exactly how cosmopolitan and intellectual they were. Alice was fairly sure she had just walked past a collection of Pygmy skulls pinned to the wall. Either that or it might be worth getting the police to trawl old cold cases.

'So, how can I help you?' Serena motioned for them to sit down and spoke directly to Dan, giving him a big beam and flicking her hair over her shoulder.

Oh for goodness' sake! Alice knew this happened everywhere that Dan went but it was getting tedious. Did he really not notice it?

Had she really thought that she had a shot?

Dan shrugged his shoulders. 'This is school stuff, I'm here by coincidence. Alice, Mrs Marksharp.' He indicated at them.

Marion beamed approval back at him before focusing her gaze on Serena. 'Lovely home, you must give me a tour.' Serena looked at her as if she would rather saw her own limbs off.

Marion continued, oblivious to the looks she was receiving or perhaps as Alice had long suspected a Mistress of Disguise, masking what she truly felt in order to weave a web around those she was speaking too. 'We, Alice and I, thought we'd just drop in for a cup of tea.' There was a pointed pause as Marion glanced at the coffee table and its noticeable lack of cups. 'And speak to you about the upcoming festivities. It seems you and I may have got off to an awkward start, and that's such a shame. I like to be friends with all my ladies.'

'Well, it might help if you tried remembering their names,' Serena snapped and then glanced at the vicar and continued, 'Although of course at this time of year, we should all remember to be grateful for what we have and look to helping others less fortunate than ourselves.' She faux-grinned at Marion again whilst shooting a quick look at Dan to seek approval.

Alice felt her eyes roll and then wander; she could see the study from here. She assumed it was a study – the door to the room was ajar and she could see a large desk covered with papers. Alice gasped as she noticed an awfully large pile of newspapers and magazines teetering next to the regular printer paper. Surely it was just coincidence?

Unfortunately not everyone in the room was so charitably minded and as Marion heard Alice's gasp, she swivelled her head to follow Alice's gaze and also saw the clutter on the desk. Clutter most out of sync with this house.

Serena was still going on about all the ways in which she liked to help the community at Christmas time as Dan was guilelessly nodding encouragement when Marion leapt from her chair and stormed out into the hall, flinging open the study door fully as she reached it.

'What on earth do—' Serena didn't get a chance to finish her sentence as Marion came roaring back into the living room, waving a clutch of newspapers and armed with scissors.

'You!' The word hissed out of her mouth at speed. 'You! How did I not guess? You like cutting up newspapers? Well, I like cutting evil-tongued spiteful witches who get involved with other people's lives for no reason other than sheer malevolence.' This was quite a speech considering that she was haring towards Serena, scissors raised, as Dan and Alice both jumped to their feet to intervene. Alice hurled herself in front of Serena which, on reflection, may not have been wise and Dan barrelled into Marion and tried to disarm her. The result of which was an awful lot of flailing and not much resolution as Marion kept arching over Dan, despite his height, making jabbing motions towards Serena whilst gurning out facial expressions of such rage that it remined Alice of The Incredible Hulk.

Serena meanwhile wasn't bowing down and meekly apologising. Oh no. Whilst using her arms to try and parry Marion's thrusts she was also taking the opportunity to grab at and pull as much of Marion's hair as possible, the action clearly giving her far more joy than was natural.

'This isn't working,' Dan huffed; for a tall and athletic man he seemed to be having awful trouble containing Marion. Priest school obviously didn't have a practical element on what to do when two of your flock try and kill each other just before Christmas.

On top of which, Alice was having no luck at all with Serena. It was as if the adrenaline, and weeks of mutual hatred, had turned them into mean, lean fighting machines that kept punctuating their squabble with noises you would expect at a female wrestling match.

'Right, I'll be back. Just do your best!' Alice had an idea.

'You can't leave me.'

'You'll be fine, right is on your side,' Alice shouted over her shoulder as she sprinted into the kitchen.

'I don't think right is anywhere near this fight at the moment,' Dan shouted back. 'Will you stop that! Ouch! I swear, Marion, if you get me with those scissors— Oi! That's my jumper, not Marion's dress. Stop pulling!'

'Sorry, Vicar, just get out the way and let me get her.'

'You know I can't do—' The battling suddenly came to a swift and shocking halt as Alice came back out of the kitchen and, running at full pelt, hurled a washing-up bowl full of cold water over the three of them.

'Arggghhhhh!'

'Ahhhhhh. That's freezing!'

'Oh my g—!'

All three voices shouted out at the same time as the wave of tap water hit them with no warning.

'Sorry, Dan,' Alice apologised to him before adding, 'but now you've all stopped for a minute can we get some distance, please? Take a step back, Marion, I mean it, now! And you, Serena. Here, Dan, sorry about that.' She handed a dripping wet Dan a tea towel as she took the scissors out of Marion's hands and gave Serena a look that would have made Genghis Khan cower.

Dan started to laugh, even as he was taking the towel from her. 'I would have never have thought about doing that, Alice Pentire, you're a genius. Perhaps they should fly you around from global hotspot to hotspot sorting out all manner of conflicts.' He rubbed his face and then mussed his hair with the towel and as he did so Alice realised her crush wasn't actually as diminished as she had hoped. She supposed it was a good thing it was winter; had he been in a T-shirt she may well have lost power of speech.

'This isn't over, but can someone get me a towel?' Marion said as she shook herself, like a cat and with a similar expression of distaste.

'I'm not having that woman *touch* one of my towels!' Serena snapped, wringing her hair out onto the wooden floor. 'And how dare you do this to me in my own home?'

'Serena, I dared because it's the best way to separate fighting cats. And what's more seeing as it looks like Marion has just discovered you've been involved in malicious and criminal activity I think it's best if you shush a bit.' Alice wasn't sure where this I-am-woman-hear-me-roar side of her personality was coming from but she liked it. 'And get these guys some proper towels, please. Then we can dry off, sit down and discuss what we do next.'

They heard Serena humphing all the way up the stairs and into the airing cupboard, eventually returning with extra-fluffy towels and a slightly penitent look. She handed the towels out wordlessly as Alice hid the scissors in the garden, just in case.

Chapter Twenty-Four

If Dan had thought the afternoon in class had been eventful, then nothing could have prepared him for the events afterwards. He had no idea that school life was so exciting! He was rather glad he was a vicar; it might mean that people in the villages and surrounding areas thought he was public property and they could come to him any time of day and night, but it was still more restful than involvement in Penmenna School, which seemed to feature one drama after another.

However, right now, he was dry and wearing one of Serena's husband's Christmas jumpers with two Christmas puddings placed roughly where his nipples were. He was fascinated as to which of them had chosen and bought this item of clothing. It was well worth wearing though, simply to see the delight on Alice's face as he followed Serena downstairs. She completely failed to hide her snigger.

He had been feeling a bit all over the place since he had seen Alice last. His attempts to apologise under the street light that night had not gone well, and certainly not the way he had hoped. He knew his grandmother, and apparently Ethel, were both very keen for him to start a relationship with Alice. In their heads they'd be married and popping out babies before the year was out. If they could manage triplets then he had a feeling they would be even more pleased. And in his weaker moments that had an appeal, it really did.

He adored Alice, thought she was one of the best people he had ever met and felt remarkably lucky to know her and have her in his life. He was certainly sexually attracted to her, there was no doubt about that in his mind. In fact since Monday, since he had taken her in his arms, since he had determinedly unzipped her dress, he knew exactly how attracted he was. It played in glorious technicolour whenever he least needed it: as his head hit the pillow at night; as he had tried to make a start on this week's sermon; and as Denise had been wittering at him about getting the Christingle oranges in and ordered and the programmes for the Christmas services printed out.

But it was precisely because of how strongly he felt for Alice that he wasn't prepared to fulfil all of Annie's hopes and dreams. He knew he had some more work to do on himself first, before he was a suitable partner for anybody. How could he possibly even consider starting a family, and give his children the best possible start in life, until he had dealt with his issues with his own parents?

He had hoped that he could make it clear to her today how he respected what she had said under the lamplight that night, and apologise for his behaviour. He also knew bringing it up again was a bit self-indulgent, but he was human, had never claimed to be anything else, and the thought of possible bad feeling between them was eating him up.

On Sunday, if she came to church – and he had to assume she would, she had said so and one of the many things he knew about Alice Pentire was that she was a woman of her word – he didn't want to iron it out in front of the whole church community. Their friendship was so special to him that he wanted to try and get them back on track, make her see that all the fault was his – although what she'd said under the street light did imply she may already be secure in that fact – well before Sunday came around.

What he hadn't expected today was for that to play out as it had, with him now wearing a nipple jumper having watched a full-on fight between two women that involved scissors and a whole heap of water. He hadn't thought he was naive but this afternoon had taught him that an awful lot went on in Penmenna without his knowledge.

Alice was now humming Christmas carols as she wandered around Serena's kitchen making them all a cup of tea and looking for all the world like she hadn't just poured water over the most frightening inhabitant of the village. Whereas he was sitting in the living room with both Marion and Serena, who were drying their hair with towels and snarling at each other, a tower of newspapers piled between them, which looked as if they had words hacked out of the headlines. He wasn't sure what on earth was going on here but he wished he was in charge of tea – he wasn't as confident in his abilities to maintain the peace as Alice was.

As if she could read minds Alice popped in the door, beaming, with a tea tray in her hands and a packet of mini stollen next to the steaming teapot.

'I hope you don't mind, but I had a rifle in the cupboards. I'll replace them but I thought we could all do with a little bit of sugar. Although if you need them put back then do say because it was a little cheeky of me. We haven't got long before the kids' clubs are all finished so we should probably get on with this as quickly as possible, unless you would rather I sent Dan to pick the kids up to give us more time?'

It would seem that Serena and Marion could at least agree on something as they both shook their heads quickly – which was just as well as Dan was fairly certain that he'd return home with the wrong children.

Alice sat on the floor by the table and poured out tea for everyone.

'Now, I'm about to say this as I see it from an objective outsider's view and hope that some of it, any of it, finds some agreement. Then you both tell me what you think, okay?' Both women nodded mulishly. 'Right, then it seems that, Serena, you have taken against Marion and have undermined her at school at every possible oppor- tunity. I don't say this because I have any kind of bias, I say it because I have sat in all the meetings. You have then gone on to send Marion vile poison pen letters, twice a day, in an unmitigated campaign to wear her down. Not only are the things that you have said hurtful and based on no real knowledge of fact—'

'Oh, they're fact!'

'Um, not feeling you understand quite how serious this is. But even if they are based on fact and yes—' She held up her hands as both women started talking at once, in high-pitched fast tones that Dan defied anybody to be able to decode. 'We'll get to the truth of the things you say in the letters in a moment, but Serena, as irritating as you may find Marion, your actions are by far the most egregious and Marion has every right to call the police and have this treated as a criminal matter. Uhuhuhuh!' Alice held up her hand again to stop Serena as her mouth opened to speak. 'I'm still talking. Seeing as you do have amends to make and both of you wish to work towards making the PTA as successful as it can be and ensure Christmas this year is truly special for all at the school and those involved in it, it seems to me that the solution is finding a way for you both to work together, which quite frankly, Marion, if you have her arrested is only going to make it harder. That said, Serena, what you have done is possibly the most malicious thing I have ever witnessed' – and that was saying something when you considered her own mother – 'so you do need to make reparation. Now I'm going to ask you to speak one at a time, not because I enjoy being Queen Bossy but because you clearly both want to pick your children up on time. Marion, you first, what have you got to say?'

Dan was expecting a barrage of abuse to fall from Marion's lips. Whilst he hadn't really had an awful lot of encounters with her, her reputation preceded her, so he was surprised when a more demure Marion took the floor. She looked at Serena with a whole mix of emotions flitting across her face and Dan found it tricky to guess which one was the dominant.

'Firstly, I notice you haven't denied that it was you that did this to me.'

Serena shook her head.

'So I have to ask why? What is it that myself and my husband have done to make you so angry, so determined to ruin our marriage? I would assume you were the one having an affair with him but he's never bloody here, hasn't been for a year, more or less, so I can't see how that would work. So why, why do this? And why be so specific? Is it really just over the fact that I kept calling you Selina and you wanted to run the PTA yourself? It can't be!'

Serena looked up at Marion, her eyes having been downcast whilst the other woman was speaking. 'It wasn't the PTA. I moved to the area coincidentally, already knowing who you were and was determined not to like you. I still don't like you so I was right about that. You're cruel, bossy, judgemental—'

'Serena.' Alice sounded every bit the teaching professional. She managed to fit in a whole load of meaning into one word with her tone alone.

'Okay, I know. I haven't got a leg to stand on. What I did was really bad, really bad.'

'So how did you know me before here? I've never met you, I'm sure of it.'

'No, you haven't. But my best friend knows Richard.'

'Still doesn't make much sense,' Marion answered.

'Maybe if you let me finish,' Serena snapped before she remembered she was meant to be being penitent. 'My best friend is in love with your husband. She's frustrated that he is still coming back to Cornwall and asked me to do this to speed things up. I didn't want to, but I did it. I owe her. And I know how much she is in love with Richard, how she pictures her future with him and is hurting because he remains married to you. So I did it. I knew it was wrong but it was you or her and I've known her my whole life. I had to choose between loyalty to a lifelong friend or doing something mean to someone I barely knew. So, I made them and posted them and' – she let out a reflective little half laugh – 'and I found it so much easier if I hated you.' Serena looked Marion directly in the eye. 'Are you going to ring the police?'

'I think I need some more answers first.'

Dan noticed how Marion had gripped the side of her chair as Serena had explained how another woman was in love with her husband. He knew he wasn't alone, he knew Alice had also noticed the way she had paled and held on, as if by gripping tight she could somehow hold herself together. It was a trick he had used in the past as well; somehow by keeping your body taut, the muscles clenched, you felt that you had more control, that your body wasn't going to disintegrate into a liquid snivelling mess. She was managing well. He was best remaining quiet but was filled with a new respect for Marion that he hadn't seen coming. After this afternoon's performance he half-expected her to lunge at this Serena woman again, but so far she was showing a stoic forbearance that he didn't think he would be able to manage if he found out the person he loved might be cheating. He looked at Alice, who was sitting watching the two women, her keen eyes picking up every detail of what was unravelling, and his heart pinched.

'You say your friend is in love with my husband. Is he...' Marion took an intake of breath and closed her eyes, just for a second, opening them to stare at Serena as she asked directly, 'Is he in love with her?'

'Well, he's not here, is he?'

Ouch.

There was a silence as Marion took a deep breath and looked Serena square in the eye.

'No, no he's not. But that doesn't mean he's in love with your friend, who don't think I haven't noticed, you haven't named yet. It just means it's a Thursday afternoon, nearing four o'clock and he's in work, trying to earn enough to give his family the best chances in life. And I respect him for that; I don't assume that he is sleeping with everything in London just because he happens to be absent. Anyone with half an inch of wit would love my husband, he's a very lovable man. He's handsome, *loyal* and does right by everyone he meets, but that doesn't mean he'd love them back.' Dan noticed her gulp as she said this and he wondered how true her bold words were and how much she believed what she said. 'But as Alice pointed out time is ticking and I have a decision to make.' She gave Serena her trademark Marion look up and down, raised her eyebrow and sniffed. Quite a triumvirate. 'Have you ever done anything like this before?'

'No.' Serena only needed her answer to be one word, and this presumably was the right one; it was certainly firm. Dan hoped it was a truthful one as well.

'Why do you say you owe your friend and who is she?'

'I owe her because she and I have grown up together. She's practically all the family I know. We were both packed up at eight and sent to boarding school, we shared a dorm for ten years and I went back to hers in the holidays, every holiday. That's sisterhood. I *can't* tell you her name.'

'As one woman to another, this is not about retribution, this isn't about police proceedings, this is about my marriage and if you want me to process this in a way that doesn't blow your new life in Penmenna sky high and get you scorned from valley to hilltop, you *will* tell me the name of the woman who you say has her very sharp eye on my husband.'

'I can't.'

'You have no idea the tsunami of horror I am capable of unleashing. You had no qualms about what you did to my family, and I am going to enjoy destroying yours.'

Serena looked like she probably was aware of the horror and gulped again before closing her eyes and sighing deeply. 'Oh for God's sake. You'll find out at some point no doubt, but you do know her quite well – it's Claudia.'

'Well, it's a good job the resistance didn't have you on their side in the war; that took you all of five seconds. I was looking forward to ramping that up a bit more,' Marion snapped. Dan noticed Alice look down at her lap and hide her smile. Marion was quick, he'd give her that. 'Claudia, has a flat in Treporth? Works in the city with *my* husband. The woman who pretended to be my friend and I set up on a date with Alex McKenzie last year?' Marion pressed for clarity.

Serena nodded.

'Right, well I think this is the bit when Alice tells us we need to find a way to make peace whilst Dan agrees with her. I shall listen to what they have to say. But know that I will never be able to forgive you; your words wormed into my home through the letterbox and the damage you have caused could have been considerably worse.' Serena had the grace to look down at the floor as Marion spoke, shame on her face, her fingers fidgeting with the hem of her top. Her obvious remorse wasn't enough to stop Marion. 'Imagine if darling Rufus had found a letter. Or did you not consider the effect that blowing my life apart may have upon the children? No mother's code for you, eh? However' – Marion sat straight up, no longer leaning over as she spoke – 'I believe in putting the needs of the many first, and in this case the school.'

Serena looked less ashamed at this point and remarkably like she wanted to snort but thankfully had the good sense to shut up.

Marion steamrollered on, looking like she was enjoying herself a little too much. 'So I suggest that there is only one way that you can do this and that is by doing exactly as I tell you. First, you need to come on board as my deputy but not as you have been, half-hearted and meddling, currying insurrection with Harmony Rivers and that Alison woman, for goodness' sake! Oh no, you need to proclaim your loyalty to me so loudly that even deaf old Mr Meacher can hear it. You do everything I say, when I say it and you do it happily. No matter what I ask. If I want you in the school loos cleaning them with no more than your toothbrush and a drop of your venomous spit, you're on your knees in seconds. I want you to follow me around as if you worship me – sorry, Vicar. Do you understand?' She didn't look particularly sorry.

'You mean you want me to be another one of your—' Serena was quelled by a look. It seemed vulnerable Marion had done one and traditional Marksharp was back in the room. 'I understand,' Serena mumbled instead.

'Secondly, I like my ladies looking smart; we represent the school, the heart of this village, generations of Penmenna residents so no more jeans in school, please. Jenny will advise you where to shop and you can thank me later for improving your sartorial style considerably. Denim is only appropriate at the weekends and times of crisis.' Marion paused and gave Serena another very pointed look at that bit, clearly referencing the fact that she was currently sitting in jeans herself and Serena was to blame. 'I'm amazed you've got this far in life without learning that. So much for an expensive education. And thirdly...' Marion couldn't help herself but she grinned like the Enormous Crocodile at this point. 'Thirdly, when I open the fayre next week, I want you on the stage with me, dressed in the way I dictate and when I pass you the mic, to cement our new friendship, obviously' – Serena visibly winced – 'I want you to announce the *Christmas* Fayre open. Do you understand? No Winter anything, you'll need to sort those posters out, but a Christmas Fayre.' Marion leant forward again and grabbed Serena by both hands. 'You're mine now, for as long as I see fit. Or this little lot' – she swung her hands to include the newspapers and magazines piled next to them – 'this little lot will find its way into the gossip of everyone from here to Truro. The police will become involved and you will be utterly ostracised. Trust me. Do you trust me, Serena?'

'Yes.'

'Yes, Marion.'

'Yes, Marion.'

'Jolly good, then in that case, dear, I think we're done. Wouldn't want to be late for my darling Rufus and your thing, Josie or whatever you've called her. Thank you, Alice, for facilitating this. I shall miss you when you're working in Dubai.' Marion didn't look like she'd miss her that much.

Then the meaning, the gravity of her words fell into place in Dan's head. Alice was going to Dubai? Since when? How long for? Dan could still hear Marion talking but couldn't quite process the news he had just learnt. Dubai? Why hadn't she told him?

Marion was still speaking. 'And thank you, Vicar, for being a witness. Such a good resolution for the community, don't you think? Oh and Serena, your friend Claudia, you can tell her I'm coming for her. I'm not saying when, but I'm coming.' And with a nod so ferocious that Dan thought it may possibly give him nightmares, but nowhere near as terrifying as the thought that Alice was moving *continents* away, Marion swept from the house, head held high and a triumphant grin on her lips.

Chapter Twenty-Five

Alice and Dan said goodbye to Serena, who needed to leave to get Josie, and watched her as she raced down the road.

'Thank you for coming, Dan. I don't think I could have separated them if I had been on my own. I really appreciate it.' She shook her head, unaware of the torrent of confusion, of loss, that had just been unleashed in Dan's world. He had a niggle in his head that he was being a bit of a selfish twit but right now all he could feel was panic.

Alice carried on in her usual cheerful vein. 'I was so shocked when I found out about the letters, I can't believe it was someone so close, and at the same time I'm kind of glad too, because it's all been resolved so quickly. I can't wait to see what Marion makes her wear at the Christmas Fayre. That's coming up so quickly now. Is that uncharitable? You know, I think I can live with it.'

Dan stopped walking and looked at her. How could she be so normal when his world was being turned upside down? All the familiar feelings of loss came whooshing back with an intensity that surprised him. Alice was moving far away and she hadn't told him. It was hardly comparable to his mum, or to Sophie. It reinforced what he knew: he knew he wasn't meant to have someone just for him – well, apart from Annie, but in this context, and this context only, she didn't really count.

'Do you have time for a coffee now? We could go over to Treporth Bay? Or just keep it simple and go back to mine.' He realised what he had said. 'Um, obviously not go back to mine as in, er, you know... I meant just for coffee.'

Alice smiled at him, her eyes shining with compassion but not necessarily with assent. He knew she always said yes if she could but this time she glanced at her watch and then scrunched up her lips and shrugged her shoulders.

'I'd have liked that, and I know I dragged you along with me just now on the hope of having coffee later but I can't go to Treporth, there's somewhere I have to be at five. Sorry.'

'That's okay, somewhere interesting?'

For a normal question Alice suddenly got shifty, or at least he assumed it was shifty; it certainly wasn't a look he had ever seen on her face before.

'Um, um... I guess.' She obviously wasn't going to tell him. He took a deep breath, not knowing where to go from here. They had been friends ever since he started in the village and now, after Monday, she had started keeping secrets.

That was secrets plural, as in whatever this was and Dubai.

'Oh, okay then. I was hoping to talk to you before Sunday.'

'Yep, that's a good idea, it's just that...' She looked at her watch again. 'Okay, if we go to The Vicarage we can have a super quick drink and you can say what it is that you wanted to say.'

He bowed deferentially, like a butler from a bygone age, and led the way. He'd had it so perfectly in his mind when he had been watching her work at school, all the things he wanted to say to her. Lay out his feelings and his fears, but the news of her move changed everything. He figured he had about three minutes of chit-chat before they got home and he would have to decide again what he was going to say in light of this development. Should he stick to his original plan? Should he find out more about her move from the village? Was it permanent?

'Annie's out for the day, she's visiting friends up in Plymouth. I think she's taken Ethel with her, so we'll have the house to ourselves.'

'Apart from Catsanova, renowned serial killer of the animal world.' She grinned, clearly thinking she had just found the perfect name.

He smiled; she did love his cat. 'Yup, apart from *Dave*, the very embodiment of a perfect pet,' he teased. For a second he felt they were back where they should be. Back to being friends without any of the awkwardness.

He opened the door and led the way into the kitchen, making sure that his first stop was the cake tin.

'Coffee, tea or chocolate? They all take the same time to make.'

'Um… it's nearly Christmas, I *want* chocolate but I should probably have a herbal tea and seriously, you have to stop giving me cake!' She took the plate from him and picked out a cherry, looking at it longingly and popping it into her mouth.

He felt the familiar stirrings of lust and then reminded himself that he was here to put the record straight, not strip her naked. Sometimes he wished he wasn't quite so good.

'Why? If it makes you happy and is doing no harm?'

'Because it is doing harm, it's not good for me. Definitely not my figure.' She patted her tummy and then looked down to the floor, a half smile on her face with a hint of embarrassment. 'Anyway, what is it you want to talk about?'

'First, why the funny look and tummy pat? You do know you're beautiful. It shines from you.'

'Have you met my mother? Body issues are as routine and necessary as childhood vaccinations, trust me. If you had met her you'd understand. I hope. Anyway, it's about health as well.'

'You're healthy, aren't you?'

'There's nothing wrong if that's what you mean, you can stop looking so worried. I could be healthier, though. Seriously, this is what you want to talk about? My weight issues?'

He held out a mug for her filled with hot chocolate, a squeeze of cream and marshmallows. 'I didn't know you had weight issues. Look how good that looks and it is nearly Christmas. And I know it's none of my business and you don't need some man blethering nonsense at you but you appear to be a perfectly normal weight and as I said, in a not completely objective way, I think you look absolutely beautiful.'

'Right.' Alice rolled her eyes, which was something she had never done directly *at* him, but usually *with* him before.

Maybe he should have kept his mouth shut; it wasn't his place to offer an opinion on what was obviously something that bothered her. He hadn't realised Alice had issues around her self-image when she was such an outwardly confident, positive person. Apart from now, she wasn't looking so positive right now. Her mouth wasn't upturned as it was usually, instead making a sort of wavy line – a smidge curled up one side, curled down the other and completely indecipherable in the middle. Was he wrong to have said she was beautiful?

She took a big slurp of her chocolate, the swirl of cream sliding down the side of the mug, and then looked across at him, a fake smile now on her face. 'What was it you wanted to say?'

'I wanted to talk about the other night.'

He could feel her tense, not because she was particularly close to him but because the whole room felt it. It was an inching in of breath and then a metal clanging as a fortress protected itself, portcullis down, walls of stone up.

'I'd rather not.' She gave a half shrug, designed to be a nonchalant hope-that's-okay but also indicating that she had no intention of deep discussion.

'Okay.' He too took a deep draught of his drink and noticed that the kitchen wall clock said it was already ten to five. He didn't have much time. Was it really important that he explained himself if she didn't want to talk? Shouldn't he respect that? He knew the answer was yes, but it was pressing on him; he wanted her to know that Monday was no reflection of her at all. Surely that had to be a good thing? 'But...'

'I knew that was coming.'

'Okay, sorry. I know you want me to shut up...' He knew at that point that was exactly what he should do and yet the words kept coming from his mouth, clearly oblivious to good sense or respect. 'I can feel the resistance thrumming from you but if you would just bear with me, just for five minutes, less, even. Then I'll say what I have to say and you can get to your secret assignation.'

'Hardly a secret assignation,' she retorted and then thought for a second or two before a wry grin crossed her face. 'Actually I suppose that's exactly what it is. Sorry.'

Why was she sorry? Was she sorry because she had someone else she was more interested in and was off to see them? Was she sorry because she had a secret? No, that wouldn't make sense, everyone was allowed secrets – it was part of being human. He may be her friend; that didn't mean he had automatic rights to her diary or her head. It must be the former, someone else, in which case she should hear what he had to say. To make her feel good about moving forward, free.

He took a deep breath, and let it fly.

'Alice, I wanted to talk about Monday because I have a feeling we've miscommunicated and it's important to me that we resolve this with no misunderstandings at all. Ethel and Annie set us up because they thought we were a good match—'

She interrupted him, 'They were well-intentioned but wrong. Honestly, it's fine. I get it.' She shifted slightly in the chair.

'But I'm not convinced you do. I know that sounds patronising as... well, patronising, but please hear me out. I think you are a remarkable woman...' That wasn't much better, he really didn't want to sound like such a conde-scending twit.

Did she just roll her eyes at him again? Never mind, onward bravely...

'I adore you, really I do. No one makes me laugh like you, we have the best fun together, you and I. Then as well as all that, I don't think I have known anyone bring as much to the community as you do. You are good and kind and patient, you lighten people...' These words were met with a curled lip and a low sigh. He really wasn't getting his message across and he was meant to be good with words! 'You are a huge part of my life here and I am grateful every day for it. I would love to have you as my partner, Alice, be by your side day by day. I really would but it's not that simple, it's just not. I have a whole truckload of issues and I cannot, I can't be in a relationship until I've sorted them out. It wouldn't be fair on you. Plus, I know you want children, you would be such an awesome mother, and I can't be a father. Not yet at least. I have a whole lot more work to do and I know I'm in the right place and have the right guidance but I'm not there yet. It would be foolish and selfish to pretend I was. Do you understand what I'm trying to say?' He blurted the words, relieved to have them out but aware they may not have been his most articulate.

'Um, not really cos it's gotten big really quickly. We've gone from too many slices of fruit cake to having children together?' Her eyebrows raised so high he worried that the cat might pop his head through the cat flap after adventuring and think they were birds.

'But I think the core of what you're trying to say is the whole *it's-not-you-it's-me* speech with a sprinkling of *you-think-I'm-perfect-but-you're-just-not-ready*.' She nailed more or less exactly what he was trying to say but doing it in a voice that didn't reflect the tone he was going for, not in the slightest. Her tone made it sound like an age-old cop-out.

She pulled her shoulders up and cocked her head back. 'Honestly Dan, I appreciate this little chat, but it seems to me, I hope you don't mind me being honest and I'm going by behaviour as much as words, but it seems to me that you don't know what you want. And that's okay, we had a kiss and a cuddle and that was it. A kiss and a cuddle at our age, I think we're old enough for it not to be the first or the last and it's all okay. You didn't do anything wrong, or make any false promises and neither did I. Let's not blow it out of proportion. Ethel and Annie set us up with the sweetest intentions. We had lovely food, we probably drank a little too much and you racked up the oysters.'

A picture of her sitting opposite him giggling about how much she didn't like them popped into his head. He didn't have time to dwell on it though, savour it, as she was ploughing firmly ahead.

'It's okay. I understand that you have a lot of things to deal with, and I understand that your faith and your friendships support you in many ways. I am glad to be included amongst your friends. But if you're asking me, and I'm not sure that you are – I think it could be another thing you're not sure about – if you're asking me to wait while you sort your head out, you know I can't promise that. It wouldn't be good for you and honestly, it would be really bad for me. I don't know where life is going to take me, and I won't make a promise I can't keep. So, let's not talk about this any more, I'll buy the *it's-not-you-it's-me* line, even though I'm a bit shocked you pulled that one out and we'll leave everything as it is, sorted and not to be worried about. I'll be your friend, you'll be my friend and everything will be fine. We're best never going past that again. Now, I'm sorry but I really can't be late.'

She pulled herself out of the low-slung seat. 'Give my love to Annie and Dave and tell them – well, Annie – that I'll see her on Sunday.'

She never called the cat Dave. Was she not as cool as she was making out? What was going on here? He had initiated this to make things clear and somehow he was even more confused now than before. Why did he keep messing this up?

'Let me see you out.' He jumped up and walked into the hallway, one last big question playing on his mind. 'You've got a job in Dubai, Marion said. Are you going?'

'Mum's managed to get me an interview and at the moment, Dan' – she stopped by the door, her hand on the handle and looked him full in the eye – 'at the moment, Dan, I just don't know.'

As she walked down the path and turned left for the school, he realised that his panicked foreboding was right, he may well have lost her.

Chapter Twenty-Six

Alice looked around the school hall, her heart swelling with pride as she saw the faces gathered there, all come to sing their little – okay, grown-up – hearts out and be together whilst doing so. Her smile broadened as she saw Matt reach for Rosy's hand as they sang. They really were the sweetest couple, nearly two years on and they still looked at each other as if they were in those very first few weeks of being in love, and secure in love at that. Earlier she had spied Matt twirling Rosy around in her office, pulling her scarf off as he did so and then grabbing a kiss as he whisked some mistletoe out of his pocket and dangled it above her head. It was too cute; Christmas really was a special time of year.

Having said that, Alice had had a crazy couple of weeks and her hopes that life would settle down after the drama of Marion's poison pen letter problems had come to nothing. If anything, the pace had been stepped up even more. At least Marion was looking a bit more together these days; she seemed to have life breathed anew into her, quite remarkable for someone who had just been told there was a strong chance her husband was cheating.

Whilst Alice did not know the truth of that, she did know that Serena was toeing the line and had come into school the morning after their showdown in a fitted, patterned navy number that came straight out of the Marion Marksharp fashion-handbook-for-respectable-motherhood. She had also managed to get all new posters up and dotted around the school by morning break, with the words 'Christmas Fayre' in bold green and red type so that no one could miss them. Her penitence seemed genuine as it accompanied her along the school corridors.

It had been non-uniform day, when all the children brought in jars full of treats for one of the most popular stalls at the fayre and the school had been full of hustle and bustle with Marion walking around wearing a dress dotted with robins and her customary high heels, in weather that was very definitely better suited to boots. Serena trailed after her obediently with a forced beam on her face and Marion looked like the cat that got the cream. She particularly took joy in going in and out of Harmony's class with her new serf in tow. Alice was fairly sure at one point she heard her talking about revolutions that had been successfully quashed.

However, as pleased as Marion seemed to be, Alice was exhausted. She had spent every afternoon this week in rehearsals with the whole cast of the nativity, and even though they had been divided into two groups, it was still an awful lot of children and their moving parts to organise.

Dan had been great and had been in most afternoons to help, but that had brought additional problems for Alice's poor head. Yes, an extra pair of hands was very definitely useful but it was tricky when they were attached to the man whose presence was no longer something to swoon over, but something that brought a little nip of hurt, of disappointment that the tiny grain of hope that accompanies a crush was long gone. Before it was merely his dog collar that had shrieked 'off limits'; after their latest chat she couldn't see him without being reminded that the tattered state of his heart and the misgivings he seemed to have about his soul were the stumbling blocks. Alice didn't mind fighting for what she wanted but she had the sense to only take on the battles she had half a chance of winning.

Neither did it help that despite his words about how beautiful she was, her insecurities meant she was still embarrassed about the flabby bit of tummy and her ludicrously huge breasts. Boobs that reminded her of a cow out to pasture, its udders hanging low, heavy, before it was called in to milk. Not for her those pert little breasts that could be covered in two flimsy triangles. Hers required scaffolding.

To top it off, during the nativity's dress rehearsal that afternoon, everything that could possibly go wrong did go wrong and Dan had laughed so much as the donkey had weed all over the set, practically half filling the cradle, that he had fallen off his small plastic chair. The children had been delighted to see the vicar in such a state of discomposure especially over something as serious, and sacrilegious, as the scene that had unfolded in front of them.

Alice on the other hand had been flurrying around trying to get everything cleaned up and wondering if she would be arrested for animal cruelty if she just didn't let the donkey drink for a couple of hours before the performance actually began. She decided it wasn't worth having it on her conscience; better the odd puddle than being deliberately cruel. But it was tempting. They'd never get the smell off the Tiny Tears if it happened again.

She had wanted to join in the hilarity with the others but she was just so tired. Half of her felt the giggle coming, the other half aware it was something else to add to her list of things to do. For not only was she having full-on whole-school nativity run-throughs every day, but she was also doing this, running the choir rehearsals after school for the adults, a project which had taken on a life of its own.

The word had got around the village about how she was trying to make the Christmas Eve carol services extra special and that with the threat of the church choir dissipating into nothing this service was going to be a swansong to see it out in style. Alice was half hoping that the resurgence of interest would last beyond Christmas itself and would reinject vigour and life back into the choir as people discovered the joy of singing as a group, regardless of religious persuasion. And it did bring joy. Joy alongside the exhaustion every night as her head hit the pillow.

At the start of the choir a couple of weeks ago she had been a little alarmed as everyone had opened their mouths to sing and the cacophony that came out was enough to scare the corpses in the graveyard out of their final resting place. All of the voices individually were melodic enough; it was just that together, well… Alice didn't really have the words to describe the racket. Although 'foxes in a henhouse' may come close. It had taken a lot of practice – a lot of intense practice – and a fair bit of vision.

Yet it was Christmas and a miracle had appeared to happen; they had all accepted that if this was to work then everyone participating had to put some effort in, turning up every evening, pitching in, helping each other and practising like mad until they sounded really special.

They had all worked so hard at hearing everyone else's melodies, trying to find a way to make them flow together that, finally, magic was happening.

As the evenings passed, more and more of the village became interested and would poke their noses around the hall door in the school as Alice played the piano to see if they needed anyone else to join. Their numbers had swollen so much that at one point Roger came over from The Smuggler's Curse to see why he had no customers in the evenings until after nine.

Even his two most regular regulars had abandoned him for an hour or so to come and add their voices to the singing and had brought Flynn the dog – who also frequented the pub – along with them. Flynn liked to accompany the piano every time Alice played a note whereas Mickey – who had a massive dance hit in the early nineties and as far as anyone could tell hadn't worked since – suggested that some synth noises and a little bit of a trance background could only enrich 'O Little Town of Bethlehem'. Luckily everyone had shouted him down. When he added that his celebrity stardust was bound to help and that they should all be a bit nicer, the entire choir pointedly, silently, looked at Matt and Chase and then arched their brows. Alice swore that Flynn had laughed at that point. An arf arf arf bark that filled the hall.

The only person still not in the know was Dan. Annie had confided that when he remarked that the village seemed a bit quiet she had told him it was just Christmas time and everyone was running around trying to get everything sorted for their families. She also mentioned that he was away with the fairies a lot of time at the moment and seemed happy to accept it as an explanation – a bit of a concern for a man usually so on the ball.

Ethel added that Annie was worried about him because although he was throwing himself into the Christmas preparations, organising as much as he could to give the parish a good Christmas, he also seemed to be spending a lot of time online researching Dubai. Annie had no idea what was going on, he hadn't been on holiday for years and she wasn't aware that all that sand and gold was to his taste, but judging by the number of hours he was spending looking it up, an interest in the oil industry could well be his new passion. It made no sense at all.

Alice had gulped when she heard this; she knew she should never have allowed Dan to think she was going to Dubai and made a mental note to talk to him at the first opportunity. However, she also knew she was allowed occasionally to be a bit of an arse and after having to sit through that torturous *it's-not-you-it's-me* speech and *honestly-I-find-you-beautiful-both-inside-and-out-but-I'm-just-not-able-to-commit* nonsense, she was still a bit riled and taking the opportunity to ruffle his feathers had been hard to resist.

The truth was that she *was* allowing it to sink into her mind as she considered it. Going to the United Arab Emirates *did* have an appeal. She had been working at Penmenna School now for seven years, joining when Jordan did in Reception. With him now in his final year, would it not be a good time to move on? Admittedly she hadn't considered doing so but now there was this opportunity, the seed of an idea was being born. It would be an adventure, and surely life was about having adventures? Doing new things, far outside your comfort zone, taught you, broadened you – you learnt new skills as well as a bit more about who *you* were and what you were capable of. She loved Penmenna but she wasn't unaware that there were other places in the world to see, that maybe the time had come to shake things up a bit. The joy of having Penmenna as her home, her soul home, was that she could always come back.

She liked the sunshine, she would earn several times what she did here which she could save and then maybe put towards enabling herself to do some of the Voluntary Service Overseas she had always wanted to do. She would get to spend more time with her mother.

This was a double-sided coin; Alice always felt she should spend more time with her mother – she was her mother for goodness' sake. It was just so very difficult when she did. The fact that her mother didn't appear to like her much didn't help. Alice knew she had always disappointed her: never quite pretty enough, nor slim enough nor tried hard enough to do anything about it. Every time her dad gave her something nice as a child to eat she would hear her mother tut in the background – those were on her more restrained days. On her more emotional ones she would rain torrents of abuse down on Alice about how she was too lazy to make the best of herself.

She was six the first time she heard this.

Her mother had no qualms about potentially fostering an eating disorder, frequently telling her she'd never get a husband if she kept eating cake. The fact that Alice might not want a husband but would rather have the cake seemed to be a point of view that Mrs Pentire was incapable of grasping. Alice felt her mother had enough husbands for the both of them, frequently changing the old one in for a newer, flashier model. She often thought her mother would rather do the same with Alice.

Alice remained her one and only child because as she repeatedly told anyone who would listen – running her hands down her frame, across her tummy, flickering over her hips as she did so – she'd had a lucky escape first time, two children was simply tempting fate.

Yeah, maybe there were downsides to Dubai after all.

However, in the pros list she wouldn't have to see Dan every day and suffer the smart of rejection, although she accepted the sting of that may diminish over time. Lots of time.

The reality would be that one day Dan would find the right woman for him and then all his worries, made up or not, would vanish and – poof – she'd have to watch them walking happily around the village. She may try as hard as she could to be as good as she could but she knew it would sting, so maybe it was better not to be around to witness that. Maybe the smart of her mother's words wouldn't dart as deep as watching Dan fall in love with someone else. Maybe she needed to sleep on it a bit more.

Chapter Twenty-Seven

It was the first evening of nativity performances and Alice raced from the school and across the field, throwing up a little prayer in thanks for a cool, clear crisp day. The directors had decided that it was far better to do the play in the early evening, meaning that although the children had to stay on after school more of the parents would be able to come from work, or at least slide off for the last hour or so of it. This was remarkably considerate although Alice suspected that Rupert's desire to see how his lighting idea would work out with dusk as a backdrop was the more convincing factor.

As well as the donkey urinating freely in the dress rehearsals – she should never have let the children win that argument – *get Miss Pentire to do it* seemed their default answer to any problems and she was getting tired of explaining that is not how problem-solving works.

On top of which there was a horrid cold going around which meant that a third of the cast were missing come dress rehearsal yesterday and whilst Rupert quickly reassigned himself and the other directors to the main roles it hadn't worked out brilliantly. Betsy was too tall and too broad to fit the Mary costume that had been made for Emily, and Alice didn't dare ask Pippa's mum Jan, who had just made all the costumes for the nativity, to make another one, especially as right now she was whirring her way through the gowns for the main part of the choir. Alice and Ethel's secret vestry mission at the start of the month had revealed that there were nowhere near enough robes for the newly formed choir so Jan had volunteered to step into the breach and make sixteen new gowns. Alice felt asking her to whisk up another set of Mary robes on the off chance that Emily didn't make it in seemed pushing her luck a bit.

Having sent Dan to dig out the old nativity costumes and see if there was a spare that fitted meant that he came back with a handful of blue-looking material that smelt so strongly of damp and mildew – the curse of Cornwall's winters – that there was no way she could ask Betsy to wear them, even with twenty hot washes and an outdoor stage.

All this meant that last night she had issued an awful lot of prayers that the children would be well enough to return to school so her direction team could get back to what they were meant to be doing and everyone would be in costumes with no threat of a screeching rip or tear as their elbows broke out. Then she had felt guilty and added her bits about blessing everyone the world over and putting an end to child poverty.

She needn't have worried for, as she stood there now in the opening of the dome with the moon high in the sky and a bite in the air, she was in awe of what was in front of her. The dome was all white and shimmery against the deep blue of the early evening December sky. Parents were milling about and making their way inside to sit on the benches that Matt had managed to secure from the open-air theatre that opened during the spring and summer at

Penmenna Hall, each row of seats lit up by tealights in jam jars. And not a single child had been absent this morning.

'That's his signature move.' Rosy had crept up and was standing next to her, nodding her head towards the jars.

'On our first date, the night we got together, he had made me a romantic path lit by those. He hadn't reckoned with the rain that torrented down putting most of them out.' Alice remembered the detail as Rosy reminisced. Rosy was a very private person but had been so bursting full of love, wonder and possibility as she began her relationship with Matt, it had been impossible to ignore. Alice was one of the first people the headteacher had turned to confide in, testing a toe in safe waters before letting everyone else know.

Rosy had been wary of people in the community discussing her private life, largely because of her role as headteacher but right at this moment, Alice knew exactly how Rosy had felt. She never wanted the community at large to know how attracted she was to Dan; she'd be mortified to know people were gossiping about it, laughing at her or pitying her – she was unsure what was worse – behind her back. It had turned out well for Rosy in the end but Alice wasn't going to get her Happy-Ever-After as her friend had.

'Rain or not, it obviously worked.'

'It certainly did.' Rosy beamed as Matt walked towards the two of them, in conversation with the vicar but Rosy being his clear end goal. 'You were wonderful at the time. I remember being so scared of telling people and yet I knew I could trust you. You were so kind, you made it all feel like it was okay, made me feel brave and able to give it my all. I don't think I've ever told you how much I appreciated that, but it wasn't just Matt that made me feel brave and able to take on anything, you and your reaction did as well. We don't thank the people we care about often enough, so I'm going to do it now. Thank you.'

Alice leant down and gave her friend's hand a squeeze; she was so happy she had found Matt – Rosy truly deserved the world. But as Matt and Dan approached, Alice gulped. It was great that she and Dan were working side by side again without too much obvious weirdness but the truth was she still felt a prick of guilt about the fact she hadn't updated him about her decision over Dubai.

She had given it a lot of thought over the last two weeks. The money would be amazing, she could do so much with a salary like that, it would give her a savings pot and she could use that to do the work overseas that had always appealed. She knew that she would love her charges; children were children wherever they were in the world and she was sure she would fall in love with her class there as deeply as she did here in Cornwall.

But yesterday evening as she had learnt about Dan's current Internet obsession, she had spent the whole night playing things over and over in her mind. With sleep evading her she had made her way to her dressing table and wrote a pros and cons list, the pros column full of all the obvious things – adventure, sunshine, money, being a supportive daughter, new experiences – and yet as she found herself tackling the cons list she wrote one word on it.

HOME.

She had written it in capitals and it had taken up most of the paper, a smile broadening across her face as she looked at it, bold on the page and everything about that word warming her heart. She had stood up from her dressing table to head back to bed and caught a glimpse of the village through a gap in her curtains. The fingers of moonlight dappled the church, the pub, the houses in which her friends lived. She found herself pulling the curtains open, pushing up the sash window and sticking her head out. The cold hit hard but woke her senses, and as well as smelling the tang of salt in the air she could hear the crash of the waves. She lowered her eyelids and breathed in deep and in that moment knew her decision was made.

She wasn't going anywhere.

She had needed to toy with adventure, distract herself from the embarrassment of the other night and her fears of seeing Dan settle with someone else, but the truth was she was heart and soul entrenched in this community and whilst she would love to travel, to have adventures, the thought of signing a contract right now, at this time, that would take her away from Penmenna for a minimum of a year was too much. Her travels would come later, perhaps when she had raised a family here in the security of Penmenna. She may not know when that day was coming but she knew it was here she wanted to be when it did.

She had settled back into her bed, at peace with the feeling that had made her decision for her, and fallen asleep almost immediately. But now standing in this dome, she knew the time had come to tell Dan. She took a deep breath as he and Matt approached. She'd get the nativity out of the way and then drop it into conversation.

'Hey.' Dan smiled as he drew close, and Matt grinned at Rosy, squishing her shoulder in greeting. 'Excited?'

'Terrified,' she admitted.

'Oh, they are going to be brilliant. We all know it, I've seen a lot of nativities in my time and this one is going to be awesome. That's my expert opinion.'

They walked inside the tent together and Marion came running over, a delightedly smug expression on her face, Jenny and the unfortunate Serena standing either side of her, a sulky-looking Rafe a few paces behind.

'Isn't it wonderful, Rupert really has done well, hasn't he? Of course, I always knew he would. It's innate in them, I tell you, my boys are born to be stars.' She was positively bursting with pride, the beam wide across her face before dropping a second as she turned to look at her oldest son. 'Stand here and don't move!' she barked, pointing at the spot upon which she wanted him. It was the first time Alice had ever heard her be sharp with any of her boys, let alone apply one of her famed volte-faces. Rafe grunted mutinously but did as he was told and slid into position a little to the side in front of her. 'Rafe's joining us tonight to celebrate his brother's hard work. He has decided to take time away from supporting the elderly in the community and will be helping me out more at home for the next few weeks, setting a positive role model for his younger brothers. He was very keen to come and support his brother's hard work.' Rafe's face really wasn't encapsulating 'wildly keen', more 'imprisoned and resigned' – remarkably like Serena's. Marion, as ever, had no interest in reading their facial expressions, as she waved her arms around the dome. 'It's really come together perfectly, just look at it.'

'Of course. It was always going to be a triumph with Rupert in charge,' Jenny added. Serena looked like she wanted to roll her eyes but didn't dare and Rafe plastered on a fake smile that proved he was his mother's son.

As Jenny said this, Dan stood to the side of Alice and lightly touched her back in what she had to guess was a gesture of support.

'Everyone has worked really hard,' Dan added, directing his words towards Marion.

'They have. But it was my Rupert's vision, look at it.' She waved her arms around the inside of the tent, the candles flickering atmospherically in the dusky light. It really did look pretty enchanting.

'Rupert has done phenomenally well – nice to see you, Rafe. Will you excuse me so I can go and make sure everybody's ready and I'll see you all afterwards.' Alice was relieved that some action had been taken with regard to Rafe and Whispering Pines and waved hello as Ethel and Annie came into the tent, both dressed in red and green and each the proud owner of sparkly Christmas tree light-up earrings and a tinsel crown.

'Hello, darlings. Ethel and I thought we would join in the spirit of things. After all, death could be imminent for us any minute now so we thought we could get away with looking a little angelic.'

'You're so bad. I think it might take more than a bit of tinsel to secure your places in heaven.' Dan laughed. 'And you both know you're likely to outlast the whole village.'

'Ouch! You mean all those dinners I cooked for you doesn't secure me and my friend's' – she linked arms with Ethel – 'immediate entrance to heaven?'

'No, I think you have to be in with Rupert Marksharp to attain that,' Matt mumbled under his breath as Rosy playfully punched his arm before darting a quick look at Marion to see if she had heard.

She hadn't but Dan roared with laughter as Annie beamed, assuming it was her own naughtiness that was responsible.

'Right, I must go and see to the children. Make yourself comfortable and prepare to be amazed.' Alice gave a theatrical flourish in Annie and Ethel's direction and turned to go and make sure all the cast and crew were ready.

'Go with her!' she heard Annie stage whisper at Dan and then felt a light thud in her back making her stumble forwards as Dan fell into her. As she whipped her head around Ethel and Annie looked as if butter wouldn't melt and Dan was righting himself and looking a bit confused.

'I'm sorry.' He regained his footing and furrowed his brow at her in apology.

'I'm fine, are you okay?' she asked whilst shooting a look at Annie and Ethel, who seemed remarkably unconcerned with Dan's welfare and stood there radiating glee.

'Of course; those two are getting further from heaven with every millisecond,' he joked and nodded his head towards the two women and their Christmas earrings.

'Go with her.' Annie had given up any pretence of discretion.

'Did you want to come? I'm sure they'll be pleased to see you. Or would you rather stay here and get everyone seated?' She glanced at her watch. 'It should be starting soon, as long as everything is going smoothly backstage.'

'I'll come with you. Annie, Ethel, do you want to take your seats so you don't miss anything? And maybe try not to assault anyone else as you do so.' He quirked an eyebrow up as he jested with them.

Surprisingly they nodded acquiescence, presumably happy now Dan appeared to be following Alice backstage.

'We'll get everyone seated and ready out here,' Matt reassured Alice and Dan as they darted out the side of the dome towards the children. Alice could hear Rosy clear her throat and put on her most headmistressy tone as she welcomed everyone into the tent, encouraging any last-minute stragglers to mount the candlelit steps and find their seats.

'Alice. I was really hoping we could have a talk tonight, I was wondering about your pl—'

Alice knew she had to talk to Dan, planned to clear the air but right now she was only concerned about what she would find as she turned the corner. The best-case scenario was that all the children would have risen to their responsibilities and would be ready to start any minute. Experience taught her it may be wise to brace herself just in case.

Yet there were the children all lined up in their character groups, costumes on and spotless as the production team bustled around checking everything.

'Oh wow, they are impressive!'

'They seem to be pretty on it don't they? And Dan, I know I need to speak to you about Dubai, let's do this first and then I'm all yours – not all yours, you know what I mean.'

He nodded in acquiescence and as they stood there taking in the organised scene in front of them, Rupert, who was over by the lighting controls, caught sight of

Alice and the vicar and came bounding over. The enthusiasm for tonight's performance shone all over his face.

'Hello, Miss Pentire, Reverend Daniels, you can see we're all ready to go. We're just waiting for all the adults to be seated.'

'Wow. you have done a phenomenal job. I came to see what help you might need but...'

'Yup, we seem to have it all under control.' Rupert grinned, clearly and deservedly proud of what he and his team had produced. 'Hey, Milly, we're ready in one minute, do you want to get your stars into position?'

'Will do, Ru!' Milly gave him a salute. She was in the year below but her dancing was so fabulous that she had blown Sylvie away when she first joined her class. Alice knew this because Sylvie hadn't been able to stop talking about her in the staffroom. She was hoping to encourage her to apply to dance school when she was older. Right now she was dressed head to toe in gold with a huge star shape attached to her, from her neck to her waist.

'All ready.' Rosy stuck her head around the outside of the dome and waved at them.

'Okay, stars in position, yes. Lights? Ready, guys, you know you're going to smash this. Let's show the world that Miss Pentire was right to put us in charge for a change! Miss Pentire, Reverend Daniels, go and watch. Right, you lot, you've got this and three, two, one, go!'

Chapter Twenty-Eight

Alice and Dan sidled out the front to watch but rather than take a seat Alice wanted to be close enough to be able to dash backstage and help in case it was needed.

The first thing that happened was that the inky black of the sky within the dome was suddenly lit with a projection of twinkly lights causing a wave of 'ahhhs' to ripple across the audience. Then five stars came and cartwheeled across the stage with Milly doing a starlight dance in front of them. She was the only child to do her part on both performance evenings, she was that good. She moved with grace, elegance and such precision that you could hear the appreciative murmur arise again from the audience. As she reached the other side, at exactly the same time as the last cartwheeling baby star, the tent was plunged back into darkness with only the light of the tealights flickering.

The silent darkness was pierced by a large spotlight, revealing Caesar, in purple robes and a garland, standing behind a podium in front of the Roman Senate, with Jordan standing next to him dressed as a tax collector complete with scroll.

'We need to have a census to tally how many people we have within this magnificent empire. Then we can make sure that everyone is paying the right amount of tax,' Caesar bellowed and the tax collector nodded sagely, looking over his glasses at the audience.

'Numbers are very important,' Jordan added.

'Everyone must travel to the place of their birth and register at once.' Caesar's declaration was accompanied by the sound of trumpets blaring out from the speakers, before the dome was plunged into darkness again.

The projection twinkling starlight came back on to show Joseph – played by Joey – leading Mary on the donkey across the stage, with snow lightly falling as they did so. Joseph looked absolutely terrified and had his whole body turned to an awkward angle as he gingerly held the bridle, looking like there was a good chance he would trip and bring both the donkey and Mary crashing down on top of him any second. Meanwhile all the younger children who were dressed as animals or stars for the stable were sitting down, legs crossed, gently singing 'Little Donkey'. Joseph wasn't joining in and neither was Mary, who initially looked as if she was clinging on for dear life but by the end of the procession – three turns around the stage – had relaxed into it and started doing a wave to the audience that rivalled the Queen's in its regalness.

'Is he okay? Joseph looks like he may have preferred the trike,' Dan whispered.

'His brothers have been winding him up about the donkey biting. Apparently, they've been showing him videos of donkeys attacking people; their favourite seems to be one of a cowboy having to leap a paddock after a donkey attacks. They threatened to turn his "inevitable" donkey bite into a GIF the minute it happened. Look, there is his oldest brother recording it all on his phone.'

Alice pointed to a teenage boy in the audience, the antici-patory glee on his face lit by the candles. 'But it was quite sweet listening to Rupert try and talk him down today, warning him that brothers seem to think their job involves winding each other up. He should know, he also added a biting donkey was better than a biting brother, which the Marksharp family appear to be dealing with at the moment, and that Tom's gran's donkey is so old it probably doesn't have teeth, let alone the energy to bite. I'm not sure that Joseph – sorry, Joey – believed him, although he has definitely given Rufus Marksharp a wide berth all day. He now appears more scared of him than he is the donkey.'

'Rupert's brother bites people?' Dan whispered back.

'Oh, it's just a phase, he'll stop soon, I'm sure of it. Oh look!'

The donkey, a still nervous Joseph and the majestic-looking Mary came to a stop outside what looked like the biggest cardboard box known to man, painted to resemble a doorway.

The spotlight came back on and Joseph curled himself in two as he knocked, still trying to avoid the donkey's mouth when a hatch in the door opened and out popped Miles with a huge grin on his face, so wide it threatened to dislodge the long piece of straw he had between his teeth. He beamed at the audience, took the straw out of his mouth momentarily and then turned to address the donkey in his broad Cornish accent, 'Alreet my bewtie, you be doing a grand job. Well done.' He wrinkled his nose up at the donkey in encouragement and the audience tittered, which seemed to remind him of his role on stage.

'Nope, no! No point knocking 'ere. There's no room at the inn.' He held his hands up, to reinforce his point.

'Please, my wife and I have travelled all the way from Galilee for Caesar's census and she is about to have a baby.'

Mary groaned loudly and clutched her tummy.

'No, I can't be magicking up beds for you that don't exist. There's no room at the inn. No!'

Alice snuck a glance at Rupert, who had come to stand with her for a minute, and saw the pride on his face. Deservedly so; agreeing to cast Miles as innkeeper was a stroke of genius – his strong rural accent lent something extra to the role. It had been a risk as Miles rarely participated in anything much in class, preferring instead to spend his days dreaming about the latest John Deere tractor rather than joining in with maths, history or art. Rupert turned as he felt Alice's eyes upon him and gave her a double thumbs up.

'It's going all right, isn't it, Miss?'

'It certainly is, Rupert,' she whispered back. 'Everything okay backstage?

'Clockwork, Miss.' He winked.

The rest of the nativity sped past, complete with the audience's reactions; there were gasps as Mary graphically gave birth in the stable – shades of Harmony's production last year, but thankfully only a smidge – and the animals groaned, baaed, mooed and clucked gently in support, which did at least add a layered effect to Mary's panting. The donkey however looked petrified and Joseph spent far more time nervously glancing at it, although it was now tied and secure, than he spent reassuring his 'wife'.

As the birth scene finished there were oohs and ahhs of delight (and possibly relief) as Milly somersaulted back across the stage before the spotlight fell upon the shepherds, complete with tea towels on heads and accompanied by the smallest children in the school dressed as sheep. The parents tittered as two of the lambs had a brief bout of fisticuffs at the back before a shepherd quickly intervened.

The three kings looked fabulous in the costumes that Jan and Pippa had designed in deep jewel colours – ruby, emerald and sapphire – proudly carrying their gifts aloft as they approached Tiny Tears in the manger.

Alice snuck a look at Dan; it seemed his sugar crystals had made the cut as the myrrh and he glanced back at her, a look shot under his eyelashes, so full of pride for the children that it couldn't help but make her feel warm inside. They were amazing. The whole thing ran smoothly and the carols they were singing were beautiful, absolutely beautiful. She had expected them to plump for some more modern nativity songs, maybe something with a bit more pizzazz, high-energy numbers, but Rupert had led the children in class in a vote and they had chosen to be traditional. It was certainly pleasing the mums, the dads, the grandmas and the granddads in the audience.

Then as the final act concluded and everyone was onstage, the Class One children dressed as a mixture of angels, stars and animals came to the front and sang an a cappella version of 'Away in a Manger'.

There wasn't a dry eye left in the house – or rather the dome – including Alice, who had tears of pride and of joy streaming down both cheeks. Out of the corner of a misty eye she saw Marion push Serena to her feet, who stumbled towards the stage with a mutinous look on her face.

She sensed Dan look at her before wrapping his arm across her shoulder, giving her a squeeze. She wanted to nestle in, take comfort in his arms, let him wipe away her happy tears. She had tried to make her peace with what had occurred between them in Ethel's house but didn't want to get too comfortable. She needed to protect herself and nestling into his frame was not looking after herself, it would be indulging in dangerous and self-destructive fantasy. She moved a little to the left, resulting in him dropping his arm and reinforcing a distance between them. He was not here as her friend, he was here in his capacity as parish vicar and she was here, even though nothing could have kept her away, in her role as educational professional, overseer of the nativity and very proud classroom assistant.

As the children finished their final hymn and started to stand up and prepare to take a bow, Serena approached the stage from a discreet side angle and untied the donkey. Presumably Marion had the sense, or had possibly been directed by Rupert, to get him off the stage before the audience burst into rapturous applause and upset him. She also had the wit not to get Rafe to do it.

Joey flicked her a look of gratitude and just as he did so, the donkey lunged at him, but although his lips were bared it was only to give him an affectionate snicker. Joey's face changed from terror at the initial lunge to a giggle as he, still a little nervously and with his body arched back, patted the donkey in approval.

Serena, clearly anxious to get this over with, tugged on the donkey's bridle to pull him away and lead him from the stage.

He didn't take so kindly to her.

As he gave her a filthy donkey look – who knew they were so expressive – he began to speed up, nudging Serena from the stage, prodding her bottom rather forcefully with his nose and completely reversing their roles, leading to a titter from the audience, who were now starting to clap the children. The hum of their applause crescendoed as they stood to their feet and clapped their hearts out. They were right to do so. The nativity had been absolutely breathtaking, combining the beautiful with the cute, appropriate respect with the perfect hint of humour and all delivered with a seamless efficiency. Alice may have been a little biased but it had proved to be the best nativity she had ever seen.

Dan stood next to her, clapping so hard and standing so straight that she felt a little whoosh of her previous adoration come back. She may not be prepared to repeat that mistake but he was a good man. He really was.

'That was awesome, you should be so proud of what you've achieved.'

'It was all them, they were outstanding, weren't they?' She looked up at him, trying not to get caught in the blue of his eyes, highlighted by the lighting in the tent, radiating from his face.

It was a good job she had iron self-will.

'They were, and you're right, they do deserve the credit, but you facilitated this, you went against Mrs Adams' reservations and stood firm to support the class's choice of directing team and look, it's been a resounding success.'

'Thank you. You helped too.'

'I'm not sure turning up a few times and helping paint bits of cardboard counts. It looked amazing, though, I didn't expect it to look as good as it did.'

'But where on earth did Rupert get a snow machine from? I don't know anyone in the village with one.' She looked at Dan, who was looking rather smug and most unlike his usual self. 'You! That's what you and him kept whispering in corners about!'

'Hardly in corners, but yes, he enlisted my help back on that very first day. But that aside, Rupert knows what he's doing. Tonight was faultless.'

'He does, doesn't he. Marion has a point, he is pretty amazing. And you did more than painting a bit of cardboard and sourcing snow, you've listened to me rant on at length over my worries about this.'

'And that's my point: you were anxious about how it could pan out but you didn't vocalise that to the children, you trusted them and they respected the fact that you trusted them. By letting them more or less run this and just keeping a guiding eye you've taught these kids a lot about themselves and done wonders for their self-esteem. It seems to be a habit you have.'

Alice looked at him sharply. Her wonders for others' self-esteem didn't seem to have had much of an impact upon him. He caught her look – she imagined it was hard to ignore.

'You should have more faith in yourself,' he responded to the expression on her face. 'But I also wanted to ask you about Dubai; it was a bit of a bombshell you dropped the other day. Have you thought any more about it?'

'Marion dropped the bombshell, not me. But no, I'm not going to Dubai.' She said it clearly, necessarily loud because of the applause still reverberating around the dome tent. Yet she kept her eyes at her feet, slightly ashamed, knowing her love for Penmenna meant that though she may have dallied with it as an escape, it was never seriously, not really. She had her whole life wrapped up in this community and didn't want to leave it. She could still have adventures, just ones that were slightly less binding. She glanced up and saw his happiness all across his face; he looked like a little boy who had just been given the best Christmas present ever.

Chapter Twenty-Nine

Dan had wanted to double-check what Alice had said but knew that was just insecurity. Her words had been clear. She wasn't going to Dubai. By default, he assumed that meant she was staying in Penmenna. He hoped so. It had taken all his self-control not to pick her up and whirl her around in a circle, letting the Christmas tree-themed skirt she was wearing fly out as he did so. He had really wanted to but figured she may not appreciate it. She had been pretty clear about physical contact under the street lamp light that night and lifting a body up and around was generally considered quite a lot of physical contact.

He didn't get the chance to say much after that as Rosy, with Marion as her backing band – typically louder and more expressive than any backing group should ever be – gave a thank you speech to the children and dragged Alice up onto the stage. That was it, she was caught up in a whirl of post-show talk from families, friends and pupils and he knew he had to step back and let her celebrate with her class. He was chatting to Matt when he spied Annie helping Ethel gingerly down the steps.

Dashing over he could see how tired Ethel was so, with Annie, he helped her out of the dome and back to her house. Listening to her and his grandmother was hilarious; they bickered like an old married couple, full of love with a relationship built on affectionate teasing. However, Ethel point blank refused to let them put her to bed – she threatened to take Annie's knees out if she tried – and said she was staying up for a sherry and a bit of an ogle at that nice man on the telly. She shooed them out and Dan and Annie walked back along Fore Street to The Vicarage.

'It was a smashing show, um, nativity, wasn't it? They've certainly come a long way from when you were a child, and your mum as well, where it would take place in a freezing cold church and you'd hope they were quick about it. It was like a professional production. You helped the lovely Alice with it, didn't you?'

'Annie, you are a toe-rag, you know you loved the nativities I did as a kid, you're just saying that to be naughty. As to helping, I nipped into school a few times but I didn't do much to be honest.'

'That doesn't sound like you.'

'Well, the kids pretty much had it under control. They gave their all; it was impressive how well they rose to the occasion.'

'And what's Alice doing now? Why she's not here with us?'

'Because she's back at school with her friends from work and we were getting Ethel home.' Dan knew his answer was a little sharp.

'Little bit snappy there boy, but true, of course she is and we were. Look, it takes no time at all, does it, from Ethel's to yours.'

'Are you happy in Penmenna then, Annie? Have you given any more thought to staying after Christmas?' He flashed her a grin, partly to make up for his tone. She knew full well he wanted her to stay and she grinned back.

'I do like it here, it's a nice community. I like going in the pub and I love the fact that I've found a friend in Ethel – there's a lot more to that woman than people realise.'

'Oh, yes,' Dan reassured her, his tone knowing. 'So, you staying?'

He unlocked the door, they headed into the kitchen and Annie batted Dave from the pink chair.

'Honestly? I'm not missing the city as much as I thought I would. I always thought villages were sleepy and dull but that couldn't be further from the truth, could it? It's alive here, people always stop to chat, although some of them you wish wouldn't. I met that Bill fellow the other day, my goodness he does go on. I'd have slipped something in his tea some time ago if I were his wife. No surprise he's single. But yes, I like it here. Am I going to change my views on living in this beautiful old house with you?' She waved her arms around the kitchen with such verve that her Christmas earrings jangled and her halo, remarkably still perched atop her head, fell a smidge making it lopsided. 'No, I'm not. I stand by what I say. You should have this house to yourself so you can find a partner, and now I've met Alice I know who I think that should be. I'm not sure why it's taking so long to happen. It's rare to find anyone as good as you, and as sweet as Alice, both single, same values and in the same village. It's meant to be.'

'Annie, I love you but you're wrong. Alice doesn't want anything to do with me.'

'Well, that's nonsense.'

'No, it's not. We had a lovely evening at Ethel's.' They had and he didn't want Annie to think they hadn't appreciated the effort she had gone to. 'But Alice recognises I'm not ready to settle down and have children. I'm not, and neither am I prepared to hold her back. She can't sit around waiting for me to be ready.'

'Damn right she can't, but my God, boy, you talk some horseshit. And no, I'm not apologising for blaspheming or swearing. If God wants to do something about it, he can knock me down right here.' She paused and looked up. 'See, he's not going to. Because he knows I'm right, and you're an idiot.'

Dan couldn't help but laugh at the passion in her voice. Not because she was wrong but because he bloody loved this woman.

'No, don't you go laughing at me. I am a woman of the world and so is Ethel!'

'Oh, I know it.'

'Good, so listen to our wisdom. Alice is one of the best women I have ever met and I can sniff them out a mile away, trust me.'

'I do.'

'Stop standing there and blindly nodding and agreeing, boy, I need you to listen. To listen, process what I'm saying and then agree because you *know* that I'm right. You're obviously in the middle of an episode of such extreme stupidity it's award-winning. And don't raise your brows at me. I'm serious. Now what was it that you said?'

'Um… I don't know now.'

'Seriously! Well, try to remember. And you can make me some cocoa whilst you're at it.'

'Okay, will you be a bit nicer if I do?'

'No. Now what were the reasons you just gave me for not pursuing things with Alice, because you will never convince me that that girl is not keen. She is. You can see it. It's written all over her beautiful face. But unlike every other damn fool in this world she loves you for *you*, not those pretty eyes you were born with and that floppy fringe that I've been itching to cut. The shallow surface stuff, that's not what's pulling her in, it's the core of who you are that has won her heart and hers has won mine, and I don't understand why she is not here with you now. Why you're faffing about playing silly beggars instead of sealing the deal.' She paused and motioned at the mug. 'And you can put a dollop of cream on the top there as well when that's done.'

'I'm not disputing that Alice is great.' Dan moved to the fridge and hid his face behind the door as he vocalised that which he had not dared to before. 'I'll admit to being more than a little besotted by her; she's often the last thing on my mind as I fall asleep and the first when I wake up. I see her and my heart speeds up as if I've run ten miles and I want to tell her everything, always, but, and it's a huge but, that doesn't mean I'm right for her. It means that because I care about her I'm going to keep her safe and protect her, not follow my own selfish wishes. You should know better than anyone that I've got quite a lot to deal with on a personal level, I need to work through stuff and the truth is I'm not there yet. I'm sorry. I'm not going to risk Alice's future happiness by going to her when I'm far from feeling whole.'

Annie got up from the chair and came to the fridge, pushing the door slightly so he had to move out of the way as it closed.

'And that, my child, is exactly what I mean.' Her voice was softer now and she grabbed hold of one of his hands and reached for the other so they were both standing clasping hands as she looked him straight in the eye. 'No one is saying you haven't had massive loss in your life, of course you have. Losing your mother was devastating and then the next time you dared give your heart away there was that horrible accident. No one could blame you for being reluctant to give your heart again. But you have to break the pattern at some time; you can't refuse to love again because you're scared of losing the person you love, or you will run the risk of missing out on one of the greatest joys life has to offer. The human race would have died out centuries ago if that was the stance people took. Yes, love brings loss and hurt, of course it does, because at some point one of you will outlive the other, but that is no excuse not to grasp hold of life and feel, revel in, the joy of loving someone and being loved. Not everyone has that opportunity so be a bit respectful of that if you do. Do not allow your losses to destroy the rest of your life, do not sit, or stand here and believe that your mother, or Sophie, would be happy that you are making these choices. It's wallowing, and wallowing doesn't help anyone if it goes on for too long. It's okay for a bit but then you have to stand up and get on, and both those women would be the first to say so.'

Dan broke eye contact and looked down; he hadn't expected Annie to respond to his openness with a telling-off, gentle and well-intentioned as it was. He could feel her eyes burning into him and she stroked his hand, forcing him to look back up at her whereupon she carried on speaking, gently but with her characteristic firmness.

'You had no control over the loss of those two but if you let Alice slip away from you because you're too scared to stand up and speak out, which is not something I would ever have thought I'd have to say to you, then you will be an idiot. It will be a loss in your life that you could have stopped and yet you will be fully responsible for it. Waiting for you to fully heal and become perfect before you commit, that is a fool's choice, a naive one. It's by moving on, by committing again that you start to properly heal, you foolish child. Otherwise you remain stuck in limbo never going forward. I'll have some marshmallows too whilst you're at it.'

Dan took a deep breath as his grandmother finished what she had to say. He had such huge respect for her and had only known her to be wise and kind. These words didn't feel very kind but he knew full well that she was probably being very wise; if he could only explain why he was reluctant, that it wasn't as simple as she thought.

He took her mug from the microwave and scattered it with cream and marshmallows exactly as he had for Alice recently whilst she had stood in the same spot. Then he carried it to the table and popped it down, pulling out a chair for Annie and one for himself.

He hadn't planned to discuss any of this this evening but seeing as she was clearly determined to, he needed to take the opportunity to explain his position.

'If I agree with what you say, that to miss out on the chance of love and all of the hope that comes with it is both a selfish and a stupid act, then will you agree with me?'

Annie took a marshmallow off the top and popped it into her mouth.

'That depends if you're about to talk sense or not. So far, the only sensible thing I've heard you say is your admission of your feeling for Alice and the recognition of what sort of person she is. And my opinion is that once that has been said, acknowledged, there's not much left to say, is there? Action however does need to be taken.'

'It's not that simple. Alice wants children.'

'Your generation do like to overcomplicate things. So, have children, what's wrong with that? You'd make a perfect father and I'd get to be a great-grandma which would be fabulous. I think you should probably just hurry up and get on with it.'

Dan reached across and touched her hand; he needed her to listen to him, not just spout her opinions.

'I'm…' How could he say this without insulting her as well? He tried again. 'I'm scared. This is no reflection upon you, I need you to understand that, you have been a strong and wonderf—'

'Yes, yes, dear. Just cut to the core of what you want to say.'

'Okay, it's just that… well… um… If I have a child then I run the risk of passing my genes on.'

'Yes, that's what happens. Our children are a combination of our genes. And any child you have with Alice will have a beautiful soul and be good and clever.'

'But what if, what if it has the addictive genes, they're double in me. Both Mum and Dad. That's a lot to put onto a child, that's a lot to put onto Alice.'

'Boy, what are you talking about?'

'If both my mum and my dad suffered with addiction then there is a good chance that I have the same genes. With both of them being addicts surely that makes the genes in me like squared, double? I would say there's a one hundred per cent chance that I then pass that on.' He scrunched his face up as he looked at his grandmother; he loved her so much he hated to say things that reminded her of past hurt. 'I have seen how it tore you to bits having your child become an addict, watch the chaos take over their life and be powerless to do anything about it, to never know if the decisions you were making were helping, hindering, enabling. You kept so much hidden from me and I love you for that, but it doesn't mean I was unaware of the everyday pain you were going through only to lose your daughter at the end after years of battling to help her stay alive and trying to get her well. I cannot give Alice a future with that possibility in it. And I cannot go through that again with my child, as I had to when I was a child with my parents. I cannot put you through it and I will not put Alice through it. I'm sorry but my mind is made up.' He finished his speech and felt a relief almost wash over him, relief that he had managed to say what he felt, put the truth out there.

He took a deep breath, squeezed Annie's hand still in his and looked up to see her cheeks awash with tears. 'Annie, Annie, it's okay, I'm sorry, I didn't mean to hurt you. I've had a wonderful life, and it's all down to you, I wouldn't change any of it because then you and I, we may not be here now as we are, doing what we do. But I just wanted you to understand, I'm not pursuing Alice because I don't care, I'm leaving her well alone because I *do*. And I'm sorry if I've upset you with the talk of Mum but we've always been honest about it and always talked openly.'

Annie snorted as she wiped her arm along her nose, a snort so loud it would have scared a herd of elephants. Her lopsided halo was completely at odds with the emotion of the moment. She looked at him through her tears and squished his hands back, but so tight he wondered if she had superpowers.

'You poor, poor silly boy. Is that's what's been stopping you all these years? I thought it was that you were too scared to love again.'

'Ha! No, you taught me so much about love, about how it's the greatest gift we can give and the best one to receive. I *have* been wary of offering my heart, it felt disloyal for a long time. But as you said the other day, I know that Sophie would not want me being alone for the rest of my life. We were eighteen for goodness' sake. So no, I'm not scared to love because you have taught me the truth of its power and that's partly why I spend my days as I do, trying to help others with God's love, and my own.'

'And you do an amazing job. I am so very proud of the man you have become. But your gene argument, it's not true or fair.'

'Eh?' Dan knew his face was the picture of perplexity, but how could she argue with stone-cold hard facts? 'My mum and my dad were both heroin addicts, we know what happened to Mum and neither of us have a clue about where my father is now and what he's doing, if he's even alive. How can you dispute that addiction will be in my genes?'

'It's not me disputing it, dear, dear boy. It's your entire existence. If our paths, or the paths of your children are defined, pre-destined from before they take their first steps then explain *you*. If your genes dictate that your children will struggle with addiction then explain *you*. You are here, sitting with me now; we have had a wonderful evening with our friends and people we care about greatly. As far as I'm aware neither you nor I have spent the evening trying to escape from the tent in a frenzy of determination to seek out and use drugs, or any other addictive behaviour. I'm assuming you don't have a bottle of whisky stashed in your pants or a gambling habit I know nothing of?' Dan shook his head, a muted chuckle escaping his lips. Annie wasn't stopping though. 'If that predilection is so strong, how are you now a vicar, well-respected, loved in this parish and community? How, by the age you are now, have those genes not started to reveal themselves as you lose control of your finances and make reckless decision after reckless decision with compulsion rather than consequence ruling your decision-making process?'

Dan looked at Annie with fresh eyes. Her tears had dried now, having been brushed out of the way as the energy in her argument had gathered pace.

'I guess—'

'I haven't finished, but yes, you've guessed. You haven't tied your argument to logic or the realities of life. I brought up both you and your mother, I didn't do anything particularly different with either of you. I kept you fed, watered, clothed and sheltered and loved you the very best that I could. Laura became an addict, you became a vicar.' She shrugged her shoulders to emphasise her point; Dan nodded, his face serious, as he acknowledged that what she said was true. 'So don't sit here talking about how things are a hundred blooming per cent. Things are not that simple. Your child isn't guaranteed to become an addict; what is fairly certain is that any child you have, whether with Alice or not, will be well-loved and looked after to the very best of your ability, which I happen to know is a high bar. Look how well you look after me.' She broke her hands away to brandish her mug of cocoa, now somewhat depleted, at him and wave her hand over to her sewing basket full to bursting with embroidery threads he had ordered for her online the other day. 'So, if you have any gifts to give this Christmas make sure that one is for yourself. Promise me, *promise* me now that you will re-examine this belief you seem to hold, that is tethered to nothing but fear, concern and misinformation. You are a darling boy and you will have darling children that you will love and equip as best as you can to thrive in the world we live in. If you have concerns about addiction then address them as you raise your children, educate them, talk openly and honestly about them, tell them about Laura, about your mum, but don't deny them life. Don't deny yourself that joy and don't rob me of my great grandchildren. For goodness' sake, man, what do you think I'm hanging on for?'

Chapter Thirty

It was Christmas Eve and as Dan walked from The Vicarage to the church he had a lot to think about. His grandmother's words from the night of the nativity, five days ago, had had an impact and he realised that her way of looking at things, so very different from the view he had held for years, had a great deal of merit. It hadn't been an immediate Damascene moment, but he had seen how strongly Annie believed what she said and as he gave his mind time to work through it all over the last few days, he realised that she had a very good point.

He was the child of two addicts and he hadn't developed issues of dependence – not so far anyway and he couldn't see it happening, not with the love of Annie and his faith to anchor him. With all the soul-searching he had done he couldn't believe he hadn't considered himself as evidence; not that he wasn't flawed, he was human after all, but he certainly didn't have a predilection for hard drug use. It had been ridiculously short-sighted of him, and maybe a little self-indulgent to hang on to this 'I'm-doing-the-world-a-favour' view he had developed. The more the thought sat with him, the more he remembered friends he had met throughout his life who had had parents who gambled or drank to such high levels that it was detrimental to their family life and yet his friends hadn't developed the same issues; they had made sure not to. He had also come across countless parents whose children had fallen by the wayside, exactly like Annie and his mum, despite them never having set such an example or there being any apparent trigger. The uneasy possibility that he had constructed this unconsciously as an argument to stop him fully committing his heart to anyone again had settled in him in the middle of the afternoon yesterday and he didn't like it. He didn't like who it made him. He also had to accept it wasn't just a possibility, it was the reality.

It seemed that since his heartfelt talk with Annie, more and more examples that undermined his 'I-shouldn't-have-kids' theory were popping into his head at random times throughout the day, embedding his grandma's message, highlighting the weakness of his own worries. He had spent the last few days beginning to consider the possibility of children in his life without the fears that had always accompanied it. It wasn't just his conscious thought that was considering this, his subconscious was working overtime as well. His nights were filled with dreams of him and Alice in this house, living a life full of happiness and three, sometimes two, sometimes four, children running around the apple trees in the garden, or painting at the kitchen table. He'd had one very vivid dream, where he had seen this possible future family icing biscuits in the likeness of their happy little brood, just as Alice and Annie had done with his and the cake on the night Alice had fallen over. Alice, Annie and he were all about ten years older in this dream, Alice's thick chocolate hair greying a little at the temples, laughter lines around her and his eyes.

He needed to see Alice and hopefully would this afternoon. All the introspection that had occurred after

Annie's pep talk meant that his new realisation led to the feeling that a weight had lifted from his shoulders. With his fears diminishing – it was a process, they weren't gone overnight but he was definitely now able to consider his future, fatherhood, without that feeling of inevitable doom and loss – then all sorts of options for his future had opened up. He knew he wanted Alice to be a strong part of it.

If she would have him.

But Alice had been notably absent over the last few days. Last year she had been far more involved in the collecting of gifts and foodstuffs for the community; this year she had flown in and out, done what needed to be done – nothing was neglected – but there had been no stopping to chat over a cup of tea, no giggling over boxes and certainly no pulling up of chairs and putting the world to rights. Instead she was distracted, her mind clearly elsewhere and her body shooting out of the door at the earliest opportunity. On top of which her phone appeared to be off in the evenings and so far she hadn't returned any of his calls, merely sent texts to check there was no emergency and after that was ascertained, she didn't reply further. Half of him wished he was naughty enough to fake some imagined trauma – drape himself over the table after a faked Dave attack, for example – to see if that would result in her running over to help but he was adult enough to have learnt that she had enough manipulation in her life without him adding to it. Plus, he didn't fancy facing her fury when she belted over only to realise it was a trick.

He knew Alice had a life outside of the parish and that she must have many commitments at this time of year, but something was off. She seemed to be shifty – the literal definition, eyes darting left to right, a flicker of panic if someone approached him to talk, as if they were going to give up secrets. She was hiding something; there was something she didn't want him to know.

Which made it almost unbearable.

He wanted to confront her and get her to spill all her secrets so this constant wondering could end: this wondering if she had someone else; this wondering if despite not going to Dubai she had her heart set on moving from Penmenna; this wondering how she would respond if he admitted he had been an idiot and could he please, *please* have a second chance?

Maybe he could ask her after the service today? It was Christingle this afternoon and then Midnight Mass late this evening. Last year the church had been full to the rafters for both services; families had come from all the surrounding villages for the children's service and the entire village plus some extras had fallen into the pews straight from The Smuggler's Curse in time for the carols in the evening.

He unlocked the heavy church door and gave it a hefty push open to be greeted by an empty, cold church. With only half an hour before he could expect people to start turning up he knew that it would soon be filled with the hum of Christmas excitement and the warmth that emanates from a crowd. But still, it was odd it was empty; normally at least Mrs Talbot, Denise and sometimes Bill would be pottering around, here early and ready to help.

Regardless of that, though, and despite the cold, the church looked absolutely fabulous, covered from tip to toe in greenery, the vibrant holly and ivy snuggled against the cool grey granite of the building itself. A woollen nativity scene nestled on one of the windowsills, knitted by Ethel and given to him on his first Christmas here; the metal nativity scene painted in bright blues, reds, browns and yellow took pride of place at the front. It had belonged to Penmenna church for decades, with generations of children picking it up to play with, and was something of an institution.

He walked around lighting some of the candles in their tall metal stands and others in their sconces as he waited for his regulars and then the extras to pour in through the door. He smiled as he passed the small bunches of mistletoe he had popped up here and there, despite Denise's shock when he first suggested it. Apparently, Reverend Howells hadn't been fond of such pagan nonsense filling his place of worship. Dan said he liked it; for him it represented a whole host of traditions coming together in one big ball that ultimately symbolised enduring love. That won her over.

The minutes flew past and before he knew it he was standing in the porch with his best vicar face on, welcoming people into the church. It was almost full to bursting already but still none of his regular congregation had appeared. The Christingle programmes had all been laid out in the pews already with a big stack of spares by him at the door and the red-ribboned oranges, bedecked with their Christingle bits, were all laid out in boxes by the pulpit. But there was no sign of the faces he expected to be there. Those that were there most weeks regardless of the festivities – Annie, Alice, Ethel, Mrs Talbot – were nowhere to be seen. Bill Meacher was coming in now; at last, some semblance of normality. And there was Gladys sliding into her place behind the organ, wearing a scarlet, sequinned knee-length dress, a string of multi-coloured Christmas lights wound across her torso and around her waist, the string flashing furiously. She was also sporting novelty Christmas glasses that would put Elton John to shame. He loved the verve with which Gladys threw herself into everything. He should have known she'd bring the sparkle.

Still no sign of Alice, Annie or Ethel for that matter; he couldn't imagine any of them wanting to miss Christingle. Suddenly, a flash of realisation hit – of course! Alice had mentioned she was going to see if she could get a couple more members to join the choir for today and he hadn't heard anything about it since; maybe that's where they were. Maybe he should stop fretting and relax and trust in Alice – if she had been rustling up a choir then he would be so grateful. Choirs and Christmas just went together. All he had to do at this point was make sure everyone was welcomed, begin the service and pray that Alice had this one covered.

Once everyone had settled, the throng of people along-side the candlelight and the decorations made the church feel so special, so Christmassy that he felt invigorated. He really was looking forward to this service, always the busiest of the year. He cast his eyes over the trays of Christ-ingle oranges waiting to be delivered into little hands, gave his welcome speech and was preparing to launch into the first hymn when suddenly Gladys started to play 'O Little Town of Bethlehem'. He knew the order of service like the back of his hand – he was sure the first carol scheduled was 'Once in Royal David's City'. He glanced at Gladys, who winked at him and carried on the tune, her glasses wobbling as she banged the organ ferociously. At least the organ was behaving today. He would just have to start singing and hope the congregation joined in with verve.

Apart from the fact his mind was a complete blank. The change in order had thrown him and he couldn't remember the second line at all, not a single blooming word. How could he have forgotten this? He'd been singing it every year of his life! What could he do? Start the first line and hope his brain kicked in and just followed on seamlessly? Failing that he'd just admit he was clueless and grab a pamphlet.

He could really do with a choir now to back him up.

He heard the door creak open at the other end of the church and all of a sudden came the sound of voices, of many voices, singing 'O Little Town of Bethlehem' and doing so with perfect pitch, confidently ringing through the church. Before he could compute what was happening, a procession of people walked up the aisle, the rest of the congregation turning to watch them, a respectful silence having descended upon the pews as they came past.

At the front of the procession was Mr Greenleaf, followed by Ethel and Annie. He couldn't believe it as so many familiar faces filed down the aisle – the regulars along with many others swelling the choir's ranks – their voices clear and loud. They were all dressed in deep red choral robes, a splash of white around the neck, and each chorister was carrying a long candle. Where had they got those outfits from? He knew there was a huge beam across his face as they all walked past him and took up their seats in the choral stalls behind him. He wasn't just beaming, he was so happy he wanted to cry. They were amazing. And there, at end of the procession was Alice, his Alice, grinning as wildly as he was, as she took up the final place in the stalls.

She looked as if she had delivered Christmas, and at this moment it felt as if that was exactly what she had done. He had expected her to maybe manage a couple of extra people to bolster the choir but there must have been nearly twenty people sitting in the chancel. Their voices rose as they sang the last verse, finishing in a rousing 'Our Lord Emmanuel'. The whole carol from beginning to end sent shivers all down his body and as he stood in front of the Christmas Choir, a choir he'd had no idea existed, he felt the warmth of friendship course all through him. How on earth had they pulled this off without him knowing?

He turned to look at them one more time before launching into his first reading and caught Annie's eye. She was a minx; she must have known about this all along. This was why everyone had been suddenly absent from the pub the evenings he'd nipped in for his game of cards with the mysteriously disappeared Ethel, and his grandmother had kept telling him not to fuss and that people were always busy at this time of year.

As the Christingle service flew by, Alice left the stalls to come and join him as he handed out the Christingle oranges. It felt right. He didn't have any words more sophisticated than that to use as they worked together in tandem, making sure each child had an orange, the queue initially stretching to the church door itself. There was no more eye avoidance, no more shiftiness; things had magically returned to how they used to be and he could feel the warmth of her support bathe him as he stood and explained the symbolism of the oranges the children held in their hands: the fruit representing the world; the candle a symbol of the light of Jesus Christ; the red ribbon his blood and the dolly mixtures and dried fruit representations of the fruits of the earth and the four seasons.

With each one doled out, lessons read and carols sung, the choir finishing off with 'O Come All Ye Faithful', the service was about to come to an end when Alice stepped forward and touched his sleeve just before he was about to launch into his goodbyes.

The church doors were pushed open again, only this time a group of about twenty children from Penmenna School, all dressed in their nativity costumes, walked down the nave, with Pippa Parkin guiding them. They gathered at the front of the church, by Dan and Alice, and several flashed grins at the two of them. Then as Pippa knelt down in front of them and started to mouth the words, all of the children started to sing 'Away in a Manger', just as they had at the school nativity play.

Dan was practically broken and he saw tears spring to the eyes of several people in the pews – and deservedly so. The children's voices were innocent, melodic and full of the promise of life.

It had been the best Christingle ever.

Chapter Thirty-One

Dan stood in the porch as the attendees poured back out into the cold mizzle of Christmas Eve. As the last person departed, he turned to find the choir helping themselves to Mrs Parkin's mince pies and Ethel's mulled wine, carried in army-sized thermos flasks. He remembered the wine from last year, so as he joined them he poured himself just a quarter of a plastic cup full, otherwise he'd be on the floor before the hour was out and either snoring or dancing or both during the late-night service.

'You are amazing. I can't thank you enough, that was magical, really magical.' He addressed all of them as he took a teeny sip. Although his words were meant for them all, everyone turned to look at Alice when he spoke, colour flushing her cheeks as she realised everyone expected her to answer on their behalf.

Everyone that was bar Gladys, who only five minutes in was giggling, wiggling her candy cane-decorated glasses and pouring herself a second cup.

'We wanted you to have a surprise, I'm sorry we had to keep it secret. It felt really odd doing it all behind your back.'

'It wouldn't have had the impact had you known, your face as we all walked down the aisle was a picture, and, well that's the first time I've ever worn a dress.' Matt spoke up, making the assembled group giggle as he explained why they had all chosen to keep it top secret. Annie pointed out that he looked mighty fine in his robes and Gladys gave him a wink of solidarity. 'I didn't expect to enjoy myself as much as I have. It started out as a favour to Rosy; when I say favour it was more fear-for-my-life sort of thing. She looked as if she may make me sleep in the garden because I didn't jump up shouting *yes, can I?* when she initially suggested it. But it was so good, it felt a shame to have it come to an end. I've learnt that something truly special happens when you all sing together, it's bonding,' Matt added.

'We did think we'd struggle to find enough altos let alone a bass, so when Rosy... um...' Alice stole a quick look at her boss, who was grinning like a wild thing. 'When Rosy persuaded Matt to join our ranks, and he brought Chase I was relieved. Although obviously we were lucky to already have Mr Greenleaf on board and Dave with all his experience. Then we never expected Mickey and Andy to bring their... ahem... celebrity stardust.'

Mickey nodded in acknowledgement and then necked his wine, pouring both him and Andy another.

'I'm hoping we might be able to persuade Bill back now the numbers are up.' She shot an anxious look at Bill, who had stayed behind with the others and had hemmed Gladys in to discuss his winter cabbages as she drank rather quickly, nodding in agreement and telepathically begging for someone to bring her the flask. 'And Matt, don't feel it has to end – that's phase two of my clever plan. I know most of you aren't church-going Christians and you lead crazily busy lives but if anyone wants to, I would love to turn this into a community choir; we could perhaps do one church service a month for Dan but otherwise just get together for the pure joy of singing. What do you think?'

There was a murmur of consent as most people agreed that that was something they would like to keep doing.

'Can I pop in and out?' Polly asked. 'I'm at uni in term time but would love to pitch in during the holidays.' Her mum's look of pride was adorable, although not apparently to Polly, who automatically ducked as her mum tried to ruffle her recently bleached hair. As she escaped she added in a high-pitched squeak, 'Plus, someone needs to cover up for Pippa, honestly I don't know how you dared lead those children with that squeaky voice you have! If Alice wasn't so lovely she would have never let you. Perhaps you could join if you promised to mime!'

'Oi! What I may not have in talent, I make up for in enthusiasm and Alice knows I can't sing but it doesn't stop me loving it. Plus, I mouthed the words to the kids' carol as well you know!' Pippa elbowed her sister in the ribs and with no warning they started tickling each other as if they were both six years old, only stopping when Jan walloped them both with her rolled-up Christingle programme.

'Sorry, Vicar.' Jan looked sheepishly at Dan.

'Very wise use of it, I'd say.' Dan winked at them and Polly went bright red and started shuffling on the spot.

'Of course you can, Polly. We would feel very lucky to have you! And your sister brings a vitality that makes a huge difference so would be very welcome to join us, but good point about the miming. I'll definitely make her do that if she does come along.' Alice addressed the two sisters and Dan felt proud to call her his friend as he stood so close to her. His mind slipped back to his recent dreams and wondered if today could be the day that he dared admit he had been a bit of a prat and push for more. Their very closeness, seeing her beaming with pride and the magic of pulling together a choir and rehearsing them until they were as good, as professional as they sounded made him want to pull her in and never let her go, to never mess up again, to confide how wrong he had been. And then see if there was any hope, any hope at all that she would now feel, despite everything he had said and done, that he was ready to try and face the future alongside her? Could he ask her tonight? Could he be that brave?

'How long have you all been practising? It can't have been long. And you sound so polished!' he asked instead. Not infused with the spirit of fearlessness then.

'Only a few weeks, since I said we'd try and pull together a choir for you.'

'You should have heard us at the start though, I didn't know how the poor girl was going to do it. None of us had any idea what we were doing... Oh sorry, apart from Dave and the original choir.' Annie spoke nineteen to the dozen as she approached them, waving one of Ethel's rapidly emptying flasks. 'And we had people who are now altos thinking they were sopranos and sopranos thinking they were descants. That's right isn't it?' She shot a glance at Alice, her smile widening as she checked her terminology and Alice nodded her head at her words whilst surreptitiously placing her hand over the cup she was holding. A very wise move, Dan thought. 'Well, we'd all like to have some of the things we had at twenty but it didn't half make "O Little Town of Bethlehem" a bit tricky. Me and Ethel had had plans to whip them all into shape, didn't we, dear?' Ethel responded by making a whip-cracking sign complete with the noise to accompany it. Dan found his eyes immediately drawn to Alice's and watched as she burst out laughing. 'But luckily we didn't need to. Alice's gentle way worked wonders.'

'And we're all back in again tonight. I'm excited, I used to love Midnight Mass when I was little, all shivery and beautiful, haunting and yet reassuring at the same time. Although now of course I'm dead glad it's not midnight any more, I like my bed too much to be up that late!' Jan, Pippa's mum chimed in.

'Right, shall we all adjourn to The Smuggler's Curse for Christmas Eve drinks? I'm meeting Kam in there,' Pippa added.

Alice pulled her friend and colleague towards her and plopped a kiss on her nose. 'Go see Kam, I'll come and join you in a minute. I'm just going to help Dan sort out the carol sheets for later and then I'll join you all.'

The residents of Penmenna filed out of the church with a flurry of 'See you later', 'That was awesome', 'I really enjoyed myself', 'Oooh, I quite like the thought of joining the community choir', leaving Dan alone with Alice in the church.

'I don't know what to say. I don't know where to start. That was a beautiful thing you did. I was worried when I couldn't see you come into church and then it struck me that you might have a couple of people for the choir, but I didn't expect that! You all looked and sounded amazing.'

'That was all Jan, I don't know how she does it – not only did she make the nativity costumes but she whipped those robes up too. She must have elves that power that sewing machine at night. Matt was funny, he was dancing around excited about never having worn anything like it and how freeing it was. Rosy was teasing him when Mr Greenleaf got very cross, started to mutter about respect for tradition and before you knew it Matt and Rosy were subjected to twenty minutes on the subject. I've never seen Rosy look like a naughty schoolgirl before, she's always so grown up and professional, but her face was a picture. I thought she was going to explode into giggles at any moment and Matt was just as bad. They're so well-suited, such a cute couple!'

'*We* would be so well-suited, we'd make *the* cutest couple and I'm an idiot for not making it clear sooner.'

'Sorry, what did you say?' Alice showed her surprise.

Way to go, Dan, so smooth. After all this worrying about what he was going to say, now the most ridiculous slip of the tongue had meant he just blurted out what he was thinking, with no planning whatsoever. This was not how he had intended to make his declaration.

'Nothing, honestly. Just a slip of the tongue. Ignore it.'

Alice looked at him, measuring up his words as she tilted her head slightly to one side.

'Oh no, I don't think I'm going to ignore it. But just for clarity, do you want to run that past me one more time?'

Chapter Thirty-Two

One minute Alice had been sipping Ethel's mulled wine, giggling at the memories of last year as she cast her eyes over the church they were all in. A church that smelt strongly of Christmas with mulled wine spices mixing with the scent of pine from all the greenery. Ethel's brew packed such a serious punch that it had had Bill Meacher attempting to Elvis dance down the aisle last year – very definitely 'All Shook Up' – as he chased Mrs Talbot and promised her the moon if she would consider his hand in marriage. Luckily Mrs Talbot was a Very Sensible Woman who cordially informed him that it would take a bit more than a gyrating pelvis to persuade her to give up her hard-won independence. Although if he was available for the evening and promised to be silent then a one-off arrangement may be possible.

The next minute everyone had left, she was alone with Dan and needed to take a gulp as she realised what he had just said to her. At least what she *thought* she had heard him say. She asked him to repeat it, just so she could be sure. He was now shuffling his feet on the floor and not meeting her eye. She crossed her arms and waited, her head still tilted to one side. She wanted to play it cool, but she couldn't believe her ears. Was he joking? Should she be cross? Or was some magical romantic moment – of which she had spent *far* too much time daydreaming – about to come true?

Pah, she had been fool enough to think that before!

It might be Christmas but she was not going to be messed about again. If what she thought she had heard was right, then she needed to hear Dan say it again and say it clearly, so it would be completely unmistakeable. She was not going to raise her hopes and then have them dashed again as cruelly as at the start of the month. But what she thought she had heard was something along the lines of that they were well-suited, they would make a great couple and that he was an idiot.

She couldn't help but believe all three were true.

She just couldn't quite believe he was here, in front of her, saying it. She tried to make her eyes glare a bit more. It worked and Dan looked straight at her before speaking.

'Oh, please don't make me. It was painful the first time. I've got a better idea. I've got a present for you. Are you in a hurry?'

'No, not particularly. The only place I really have to be is for the service and seeing as I'm already here…' She smiled, a smile of compromise because it was Christmas and she knew what it was like to feel embarrassed and he was clearly in a bit of a kerfuffle, which was most unusual. She supposed she could let him off the hook for now, but she'd definitely be coming back to this later.

'I had hoped to see you today, so I brought your presents with me, they're in the vestry. But maybe I should wait for tomorrow… You're coming for lunch tomorrow, aren't you?' Dan sounded nervous, keen to have her confirm.

'Yes, I loved our waif and strays Christmas last year.' And she did, although the romance of working alongside Dan in his kitchen, as if she belonged there, hadn't helped her crush at the time. 'You've got quite a lot coming this year I think. Annie's asked me to bring some extra chairs to fit around your huge table.'

'It will be a bit of a squeeze but I think if we can I'd rather keep it in the kitchen; the church hall is much bigger but it loses that homely feel, do you know what I mean?'

'Absolutely. The kitchen is looking stunning, I love Annie's old school paper snowflakes on the windows and with the hearth and Picatso purring, and the smells coming from the cooker – I can't wait. It's much better in your kitchen. Do you remember Bill gazing moonily at Mrs Talbot and her telling him firmly a one-off was a one-off and not to get any ideas and ruin Christmas lunch for everyone?'

'I felt so sorry for him! I didn't know everyone so well back then. Do you reckon Bill might get lucky again this year?'

'I don't know. She did give him a *very* friendly look earlier. When we were all putting the Christingle leaflets out this morning, she seemed to bend over in front of him in a kind of suggestive, old-time glamour puss way. Perhaps it could become Christmas tradition. I think she'd be much more willing if he just didn't talk so much, so endlessly, about the same thing time and time again.'

'I'll see if Ethel can lend her a gag. Then both their romantic dreams could come true.'

The laughter erupted from Alice's mouth. He was so bad! Standing there in his robe looking as if butter wouldn't melt. How could she be cross with him? Yes, the rejection had hurt her, but he had tried so hard to explain why he had done so, and it had all been tied up with fear, fear of the past repeating, fear of what the future may bring and very little to do with her at all.

'So, can I give you your present now? This may be the quietest moment we get and possibly the only one with just us two.' His voice was no longer naughty schoolboy but quiet and hopeful.

'Okay. Who doesn't like presents? And you're right, tomorrow is going to be packed, with your services and lunch, and then are you up at Whispering Pines in the afternoon?'

'Yes, I'll go up and have some cake with them, and maybe play a couple of hands of cards.'

'Ooh, be careful Rafe Marksharp isn't up there. Ethel's convinced he's out to fleece them all. Mind you, Marion seems to have grounded Rafe so you should be okay. I think Richard was due back today; I do hope they have a good Christmas.'

'Me too, that was all a bit horrid. As to Ethel, she's got a cheek! I remember when I first moved to the parish, I thought what a sweet woman she was and happily joined her for a sherry in the pub. I thought I was setting out brilliantly in my first parish duties, and she had fifty quid off me before the night was out. And then she winked, suggested we could play strip poker sometime and added that she had been born lucky!'

'Haha! I do love Ethel!'

'I suspect her bank manager does as well. But rather luckily so does Annie. I haven't had the chance to tell you yet, but Annie has decided to stay in Penmenna and move in with Ethel. She says it's for Ethel's sake because she's worried she's lonely and I have pretended to believe her. Those two became such good friends in such a short space of time, I think it's rather wonderful.'

'So do I. They're so good for each other. This is fabulous news, no wonder you're grinning like a lunatic.'

'Ah, that's because you're still here which I'm hoping means I haven't messed up really badly yet. Now, let me get you your present.'

'Okay, let's do presents, but do you mind if I run home and grab yours? Then we can both swap and it'll be all Christmassy.'

'Deal.'

'I'll be back in five minutes, don't go anywhere.'

'I won't. Promise.'

Alice walked down the aisle, past the great stone font – the sparkle in the granite something she had loved ever since she was a child – out of the porch and home. And she couldn't stop smiling to herself because it felt like she had her best friend back and that he was finally, possibly, speaking sense.

Chapter Thirty-Three

Alice dashed into the house and grabbed Dan's present. She felt guilty as it was pretty rubbish but she had been so busy this year. Christmas was normally a crazy whirl but with the nativity and the secret choir she hadn't had time to breathe. She liked to be personal with her presents, find something that the other person would value, something that said you knew and cared for the person for whom you bought the gift. This year was a bit of a fail.

She found that once she had located Dan's present and locked the house again that her tummy was churning, her palms oddly clammy. Was she coming down with something? She slowed her pace, tried to regulate her breathing. All her old feelings of nerves, that tummy-tingling, slightly sick swooshiness that she used to get before she'd see Dan had come raging back and yet she thought she had got that on track. She *had* got everything on track; this should just be a gift-giving moment between two friends. But as cross as she had been with Dan, hearing him saying those words, blurting out that he thought they were well-matched was having the strangest physical effect.

Ridiculous.

She was walking back to the church as snow started to fall. She stopped for a minute to appreciate the beauty of it as it gently drifted down, the perfect weather for tonight. Then she picked up her pace once more and marched through the lychgate and down the path that twisted through the graveyard towards the entrance of the church.

She heard some bells – a light tinkle – and hummed in contentment. Christmas Eve – it really had been a special sort of day. As she got a bit closer to the church, the bells rang again and she couldn't help but look up to see if she could spot a sleigh tripping across the night sky. Then, from nowhere a dark, shadowy figure emerged from a bush, looming, tall and jangling. Her Christmas dreams smashed as she realised that the shape in front of her resembled a villain from a black and white movie, complete with evil bad-guy cape. She heard a loud scream break through the drizzly evening. What was *that*?

It took a moment before she realised the terrified shrieking was coming from her.

Please God, she begged, *don't let me be murdered in the churchyard on Christmas Eve, especially not with Dan's gift in my hands.*

'Hey, hey, hey. Are you okay?' Dan stepped forward, revealing that it was he who had been lurking in the bushes. High cheekbones made for a terrifying villain in silhouette. Her breath was loud and fast as he approached; her brain knew she was safe now but her body seemed to have trouble keeping up. For the second time this evening she had to try and slow her breathing down and calm her heart. Dan would be racing for the defibrillator on the wall outside The Smuggler's Curse if she didn't sort herself out soon.

'You scared the living daylights out of me. The last thing I expected to see tonight was someone lurking in the graveyard.' Her huge sense of relief seemed to come out all shouty.

'I'm sorry, I really didn't mean to scare you. Are you okay?' He dropped a child's handbell to the ground, its semi-circular form making a ding as it hit the tarmac path, and he took one of her hands in his. He used his other hand to wipe her cheek, the melted snow having turned into a fine film.

Exactly as she used to, she felt spikes of lust as they stood here together, his hand still touching her skin. Dear God, her heart wasn't going to keep up with the extremes of emotion in her this evening. However, this very definitely was not to be a repeat of the nonsense that occurred *that* night… she'd be keeping her clothes firmly on and her guard up until she had definite proof that he was committed this time. She wasn't making a fool of herself twice. But it would really help if he stopped touching her.

'I'm fine, although my heart was in my mouth for a second. I can't believe I screamed.'

Thankfully he bent to pick up the bell, meaning his hands were back at his side as they started to walk through into the church, making it much easier to get herself back to a normal state of being. Dan closed the big door behind them and as they headed towards the vestry, he placed his hand low on the small of her back as they walked down the nave. Half of her wondered if she should ask him to move it, her equilibrium only just restored, but the truth was she liked the feel of it there, intimate, warm. It felt as if it belonged. It *was* Christmas; perhaps she should just relax into it. Stop fretting and just embrace Christmas Eve and all of its magic.

However, she still had a question or two.

'What on earth were you doing out there?'

He stopped walking for a second and shrugged. 'Once you left to get the gift I was... I don't know. Excited, scared? Not of you but... well, I didn't really know what to do with myself so I came and waited in the porch. I remembered how Emily had told you about her mum ringing bells pretending Santa was on his way and I thought that was sweet. It occurred to me I could do the same thing for you so I grabbed the jingle bells from the Sunday School box and went and hid in a bush to ting-a-ling wildly, but it didn't quite conjure up the result I had hoped. The last thing I wanted to do was scare you.' He gave her a half smile with his shoulders ever so slightly hunched. It was an expression she was more than familiar with, it was just that it was normally on her face. She didn't want to embarrass him further.

'It's okay, it was a sweet gesture. It was dark out there this evening. I'll forgive you. Mind you I didn't know I could scream that loud!' She breathed in deeply, deciding to change the subject. 'Oh it is lovely in here, Denise and Mrs Talbot have done an amazing job. It really is such a picture. And I see you managed to sneak some mistletoe in.' What was she doing wittering on about mistletoe? As they reached the door to the vestry, she tried again, 'This has been such a special season, I can't tell you how it felt walking down there with my candle, behind so many people.'

'I don't know how you managed to organise that alongside the nativity; you're incredible, you must be so proud of yourself.'

'I'm proud of the children doing a brilliant job and I'm proud of everyone coming together,' Alice said.

'I didn't mean… look, I seem to be making a right hash of all I want to say around you at the moment so can I just give you a Christmas present instead, and then offer my apologies? I think I'm just nervous.'

She didn't know what he had to be nervous about, standing there in front of her, the bewitching blue of his eyes luminous, highlighted by the richest robes his faith had to offer; a man who should be secure and confident as the heart of the community he had joined.

'Right, gifts!' Alice said brightly but secretly she hoped he hadn't got her something special – she loved giving presents but found receiving them a little over-whelming.

'That is music to my ears. Okay, so here we go.' He opened the door, walked across to an old wooden desk, pulled open a deep drawer and took out a gift bag, handing it to her as she sat on the vestry's stone bench.

If she had felt inadequate about her gift before, once she peeked into the bag she felt dreadful. For inside there was not one gift, nor two but four beautifully wrapped presents, accompanied by a card, the envelope of which Dan had illustrated with Christmas pictures: holly and trees and a stable with a star over it. The illustrations were firmly done, in a bold stroke that showed he had confi-dence in his drawing. As he should have. It was beautiful. Her mind flitted to the other things his hands were good at; she had had a taster that night and now she was blushing all over again.

She looked up at him, gratitude radiating from her face. This had taken time and thought and she was touched that he had made such an effort.

'This envelope is amazing, I don't even want to open it. It seems wrong to tear it.'

'It's fine, it's just a card.'

'And these presents! Honestly, when you see yours you'll understand why I feel dreadful now.'

'Oh, that wasn't the intention. I don't want you to feel bad, I'm just so happy we're getting to spend this small amount of time together. And... um... and it's not just the presents I want you alone for.'

Alice turned bright red as all sorts of thoughts flashed through her mind. What else was he going to do? Was this actually going to be a re-run of Ethel's but with a far better result? Dan looked at her face and smiled.

'I know, I'm bright red, can I blame the alcohol for that as well?' she jumped in before he had a chance to comment.

'You can, and your blushing is cute, rosy-cheeked rather than fire-engine red. Mind you, I'm more than a little biased.' Cue the fire-red engine red. 'I amazed I'm not the one blushing because this evening, it's not just the presents but I have... um... I want to make... argh, oh dear, let me try again... as well as presents I have some things to say, some apologies to make to you. Only if you're don't mind, of course.' He sat down next to her, looking nervous but ready to continue.

'Okay.' Alice drew out the word; she did hope this wasn't another *it's-not-you* speech.

'You told me a long time ago that you were fed up of Lost Boys, the boys that could never grow up, take responsibility for how they were, their actions and the decisions that they took. And I agree with you, you deserve a man, a full-grown man able to nurture you, protect you and love you without his own selfishness getting in the way. And I am sorry.'

Alice was confused; she couldn't disagree with him – a man would be rather nice but she wanted to enjoy Christmas without all this harking back to what had been and what now was not. He really didn't need to keep beating himself up. She proffered her gift in the hope it might change the direction of the conversation.

But he continued, 'And I want to apologise for not realising I was a Lost Boy too. I thought I had everything together, all mapped out but in truth I was scared of making decisions, arrogant enough to think I had some kind of self-awareness and my own fears meant that I messed up something that could be beautiful. I had no idea I had so much growing up to do, but now I do.'

'Okay.' She was reluctant to say much else; she wasn't sure how he wanted her to respond and more importantly she wasn't sure how *she* wanted to respond. It was a good thing, undoubtedly, that he had found some kind of peace, and accepting that he fell into the category of Lost Boy was progress, but it still wasn't a full-blown declaration of wanting to be with her. She couldn't afford to read more into this, could she? She wasn't going to superimpose her feelings onto this situation and assume they were his, not again.

'The night of the nativity I spoke to Annie and I was… I was honest with her about my fears for the future and she tore me to shreds.' Alice couldn't help as the laughter burbled over her lips at the image. 'It was a good thing, I needed to hear it and having thought about what she said I realised I need to stop being such an idiot. I was scared I had lost you. So, I've bought you some presents for Christmas but also to say I'm sorry and I have been an absolute fool. I really hope you like them...'

She didn't know what to say; was he scared he had lost her? She couldn't find the words to respond so instead put the gift bag down to open it and pulled out the first present, squishy and by far the biggest. As she did so she saw that the second was also squishy and the third much smaller, slender, rectangular. The fourth, nestling underneath them all, was wrapped in a great froth of dark green paper and netting, tied with the most delicate pale silver ribbon. It took her breath away. She couldn't cope with that at all. She closed the bag and took a deep breath.

'Dan, you haven't lost me, trust me. But on a more superficial note, I feel really bad now. Could you open your gift first so we can get the embarrassment out of the way?' She handed Dan the gift she'd set aside.

'Don't be daft, you just walked a full-blown choir down my aisle and you're bringing them back again tonight. You are amazing, Alice Pentire, and' – he pulled the wrapping off and laughed – 'there's not a man in the world that doesn't always need more socks. These are great, thank you.'

'I can't believe I bought you socks!' Alice peeked in the bag he had given her again before bringing her hand to her forehead and groaning. 'Socks! And you've given me a whole bag!'

'Three seemed a fitting number initially, you know, with the whole gold, frankincense and myrrh thing, three wise men, the Trinity. There was so much I wanted to get you but I thought I'd start with three. Then I got a bit carried away.' He looked so cute she wanted to wrap him in her arms there and then. She wouldn't but she wanted to.

'Okay, here goes.' She pulled the wrapping from the first gift and a set of gloves fell out, alongside a hat, a scarf and some kneepads. The woollen set was decorated with a happy elf and had a bell hidden within the bobble on the hat. The kneepads were black and sturdy looking.

'I thought the pads were a sensible idea, and when you said you had lost your gloves I went and hunted some down for you, although I really wanted to give them to you before now. When I saw the elves, how could I not get them?'

'These are fab, the kneepads are hilarious and the gloves, the gloves are so soft.' She burrowed her face into the scarf, hat and gloves. 'Thank you so much, it's a really thoughtful present.'

'You're welcome, I'm glad you like them.'

'I really do. Okay, what's this?' She pulled out a present that felt like a DVD – she hadn't had one of those in years.

'I know it's a bit outdated but I figured it might be nice to have a hard copy,' he said as she pulled *It's a Wonderful Life* from the tissue paper. 'I'm so sorry about that night. Can I squeeze in another apology here? I feel awful because you were so excited to watch this movie and I managed to mess that up as well. Now you can watch it any time you like. I feel, it feels, um… it just feels right being with you, Alice, I've known that for a very long time and I guess I panicked and pushed you away. I couldn't believe you seemed to feel the same as I did and then all my old insecurities came flooding back and I messed up, I'm sorry. I went straight back to my default setting – being alone is comfortable somehow.' He then changed tone, from sombre, honest to fun-filled and teasing. 'Now quick, open the next one, this one makes me laugh.'

'Okay, but look, that night didn't go quite the way I hoped, and no, we didn't get to see the movie and I was upset. I didn't realise at the time what you were feeling and it triggered all my insecurities too. I thought you had pushed me away because of my size.' Dan's eyes grew wide and he opened his mouth to interject. 'No, no please don't say anything. I'm embarrassed about it… and I do know what it's like when our heads take over and pour nonsense in our ears, it's just it never occurred to me that you had to deal with that too. I was guilty of thinking everything was so easy for you because you were born beautiful. I shouldn't have been so shallow and I'm sorry. Let's not say any more. Let's stop apologising and just embrace Christmas. Now let me open this next present.'

Dan looked at her as if he were bursting but held his tongue whilst she pulled off the Sellotape.

'I know you may think you're too grown up for cuddly toys and you are very grown up, Miss Pentire, but it seems to me you have a bit of a problem so this is an aid to help.'

'A problem?' she queried, now laughing as she held a soft, squishy ginger cat in her arms. It was as she turned it that she saw that Dan had made one or two changes to the toy.

'Is this red stuff you've painted around his mouth meant to be blood? And you've stuck feathers to him! That's brilliant. Horrific but brilliant!'

'Yes, I wanted to make it realistic. You'll also notice that he has a placard around his neck.'

'Yes! With the name Dave on.'

'Because Dave gets very distressed when you call him those ridiculous names. He feels they're not manly.'

'Casanova and Genghis Khan were the very epitome of being manly during their time, maybe not so much now. I don't know what he's talking about. I've been saving Santa Paws all year especially for tomorrow and now you're telling me he's not going to appreciate it.' She giggled.

'He feels if you are going to spend a lot of time at our house, or if I abandon him for yours, then you need to get it right.'

'Now, why would I spend more time at your house than I do already? Especially as Annie's moving out.' She winked.

'I shall make it a Christmas wish.'

'Well, if you're going to make it a Christmas wish…' She wanted to lean forward. He was a hypnotist.

'Yes…' He came closer to her.

'Then shouldn't you make it' – she deliberately drew out the pause, little temptress that she had suddenly become – 'world peace?' She enjoyed the way she felt; she couldn't help but tease and yet at the same time she knew it was a defence mechanism, because she was scared. Of what would happen if she were to lean towards him without trying to be funny.

At the same time, though, the way he was looking at her was making her feel all confident, all woman, her insecurities fallen by the wayside. He had never not wanted her, he had just been scared of wanting her. That was something she could understand.

'I should.' He held her gaze, prolonging her joke. 'But I could be wildly selfish.'

'I think maybe it's time that you were.'

'What do you think I should wish for?'

She looked at him – she wasn't quite bold enough to shout *me* or even mouth it so she sent a strong telepathic message. He seemed to receive it as he grinned back at her without breaking eye contact. They were mere millimetres apart. She dug deep – after all, he had been brave with his apology. She could find the courage to answer his question honestly.

'I think you should wish for what you truly want.' Her voice a whisper.

'That, I am happy to do. But I think you need to make a wish too, just to make it fair.'

'Okay. I can do that.' She squinted up her eyes and wished as hard as she could.

She heard a laugh escape his lips so she half opened an eye and saw that he was beaming at her, with the brightness and intensity of Penderry Lighthouse.

'I wish I could read your mind right now,' he said.

'Surely you have a pretty good idea? I'm pretty transparent.'

'I have a hope but I'm not sure. Look, you've one more gift. Do you want to unwrap it and see if it's something that will help?'

No! She wanted him to kiss her, or to be bold enough to kiss *him*.

'Of course, one more gift. I feel so spoilt!' She pulled herself away from him; it felt a little like bursting from a magnetic forcefield.

She rifled down into the bag and brought out the last present with the delicate bow.

'I'm almost loath to unwrap it, it's so beautiful. Here, help me.' She held the gift out.

'I'll hold it, but you must undo the ribbon,' Dan suggested as he moved closer along the bench, their thighs, their sides, now touching and Alice felt a surge of lust course through her. But this time it was desire without so much doubt. His honesty from earlier – making her proud she had spoken up all those weeks ago – showed that he knew she wouldn't be messed around.

She nodded and passed the gift to him. Once secure in his palm, she tugged at the ribbon, her fingers brushing against his hand as she let it go. As the tissue paper fell open to reveal the gift, a shiver wriggled from the tip of her head, along the curve of her spine and all the way down.

She heard an 'Oh' fly from her throat. Other than that, she didn't know what to say. For there, amidst a mound of ribbon, tissue and little white snowflakes was a snow globe. Carefully crafted from copper, nestled inside was a replica of Truro Cathedral. It was just like the one she'd had as a child. She looked up at him, eyes wide with surprise, joy and gratitude. This man. To have done this.

'I… I don't know what to say.' She spoke clearly whilst looking straight at him, the rush of emotion coursing through her veins as she did so.

'It's up to you, but you could make your wish again; someone very wise told me that if you wish upon a snow globe then you never know what may happen.'

She shook the globe, her eyes captivated by the falling snow inside the dome. She looked up to see him watching her, so she squashed her eyes tight shut and made her wish, moving her lips but not actually making a sound as she did so. She took a deep breath and revelled in the moment of having a snow globe in her hands again, a snow globe sought out for her by the best man she had ever met. The man who had faced his fears and admitted his weaknesses and was now sitting so close to her that she could feel the very rhythm of his breathing, imagine the beat of his heart. She never wanted this moment to end.

But sitting there with her eyes closed couldn't last forever. Apart from anything there was another service soon. She opened her eyes tentatively, the smile slowly spreading across her face as she felt her heart fill with love for the man next to her, this man who was so clearly happy that his gift had brought her joy.

'I don't know what to say, Dan, I love it. I just love it and…'

'And?'

'And…' She wanted to say *and you, I love you* and be done with it. Roll the dice and see where they fell. Surely tonight, surely the things he had said, the thought he had put into her gifts, meant he felt the same? 'And I can't thank you enough. You are the best friend in the whole world.' She fixed her eyes on his as she spoke, willing him to understand the deeper meaning.

'Best friend is a pretty good start; do you think, would you still…'

'Do I still want more?'

'Yes. I want that to be a yes so badly. I want us to be there for each other forever, to be family.'

She saw the look in his eyes and knew it to be true. He was ready to take the next step; it was what his words said, and it was what his gifts and his actions said. Should she risk making a fool of herself again? Surely there was no risk now? Should she lean in, confirm what she hop—

She didn't have a chance to continue the thought for as her head was racing, Dan leant forward and carefully pressed his lips to hers, moving his body closer as she began to kiss him back. Their embrace deepened as the kiss did, until they were wrapped around each other, no care for anything but losing themselves in one another. This was happening, actually happening.

They paused for breath and locked eyes, checking that the other was as happy. But Alice had spent enough time staring at this man; she leant in to kiss him again and as they drew themselves together once more the silence was shattered by one long drawn-out note of approval from the organ.

Epilogue

It was Christmas morning and Alice and Dan had woken up deliberately early so they could have a long, slow start to their day – one they had both dreamed of for a long time. But Christmas was the busiest day in Dan's calendar and thus they had had to get up and on even though it was Alice's (and she hoped Dan's) fervent wish that they could stay at home, just the two of them, forever.

Despite that, she was inordinately happy right now and with the morning services over, they were sitting at the long wooden table in Dan's kitchen, Dave strategically eyeing the feast from the pink chair, whilst a hubbub of laughter filled The Vicarage.

Mrs Talbot was sending coy smiles Bill Meacher's way and he was looking at her adoringly, in between falling asleep every now and again – his napkin tucked in his jumper and a paper crown perched atop his head, his snoring almost making the gravy sway in its boat. Denise was picking chestnuts out of the sprouts and muttering about faffs and folderols, whilst shooting black looks at Annie, who had taken over the cooking this year. Sheila was there, reminding Alice of Mrs Claus, but a Mrs Claus who had lost an elf or two, set fire to the stockings and accidentally used an entire bottle of brandy in the cake. There were other members of the parish who had come to share lunch too, wolfing down pigs in blankets and pulling crackers enthusiastically. Then, of course, there were Annie and Ethel, both of whom hadn't stopped grinning at Dan and Alice and giving them thumbs up.

'Could you pass the cranberry sauce?' Thumbs up.

'Alice, I don't know what you've done to this turkey but it's the best I've ever had, isn't it, everyone? Hmm, she's a keeper for sure.' And another thumbs up.

'You did the turkey, Annie, you refused to let me help and forced me into the bath by trying to scratch me with Dave. Dan, you should have seen her. She was using that cat as a weapon, terrifying. Normally I'd suggest it was cruel to brandish a paw about wildly and in threat but *Dave*' – Alice emphasised his name – 'seemed to be enjoying himself. Then she brought me a glass of champagne, lit some candles and locked me in the bathroom!'

Annie, clearly proud of herself, gave them both another thumbs up.

'Annie, you are so naughty, I do love you. But you seem to be having some kind of hand seizure. Your thumbs are behaving very oddly. Maybe amputation would help?'

'That is no way to talk to your grandmother, young man! You should be extra happy today.' This time she winked before sneaking a thumbs up at Ethel, who was doing her silent chuckle whilst inhaling the contents of an entire sherry bottle.

Alice closed her eyes for a second and breathed it all in. This Christmas had been so special, and now sitting with what felt like family, her chosen family, she couldn't remember being happier. She felt Dan slide his hand over the top of hers. Opening her eyes again she smiled at him and he leant over and gave her a kiss.

The whole table cheered.

Alice blushed.

Dan took a bow.

Once the pudding had been eaten, the cheeseboard demolished and the mince pies waved away, everyone was slumped at the table or dreaming of lying on the sofa. Dan and Alice excused themselves, wrapped up warm against the bite of the December air and snuck out of the front door of The Vicarage to head towards Penmenna Beach. Their hands found each other, wordlessly, as they walked along his garden path. Wandering down Fore Street, they kept glancing across at each other as if reassuring themselves that this was real. This was happening.

There were others taking the traditional post-Christmas dinner walk, all waving or nodding at Dan and Alice as they made their way through the village. Alice spotted Marion hand in hand with Richard as he dragged their huge dog along the pavement, the boys trailing behind them chattering as they headed home from the beach, no sign of marital strife present.

The Smuggler's Curse was now open and the Parkin family and Kam were heading in en masse, laughing amongst themselves and full of Christmas cheer.

'Oh my God! Oh my God! Ooh sorry, Dan. Wow, though, that's okay isn't it? You two!' Pippa spotted them from across the road and started jumping up and down in the air with excitement. 'I told you, I *told* you!' she crowed triumphantly at Kam and then ran across the road without checking for cars – there were none, it was Christmas Day in a village – and high-fiving Alice.

As usual Alice blushed; what was unusual was that she didn't mind in the slightest. She high-fived Pippa back and allowed Pippa to twirl her around in a circle, kiss both her cheeks, holler again and give Dan a great big hug whilst muttering something about time taken before shouting 'Merry Christmas' and whirling back over the road, practically falling in the door of The Smuggler's Curse as Kam looked on in amusement.

It felt so right strolling through the village, hand in hand with Dan. In fact it had all felt right, from exchanging presents yesterday evening, kissing in the vestry — well, that felt a little naughty but also very, very nice — and coming home. They had sung their hearts out at the Midnight Mass and then fallen into bed and stayed there for hours and hours, exploring, playing until they were both sated. The chemistry between them that evening in Ethel's house had exploded last night, and Alice could truly say she had never ever had a night like it. Judging from the grin on Dan's face as he had gently woken her this morning, he hadn't either. Everything seemed right, as if it were meant to be, and Alice couldn't remember ever feeling more content.

Dan pulled her hand up to his mouth as they turned from the beach and up on to the path that led along the cliffs. They chatted about the events of the last few days as they walked, giggling at the state of Bill Meacher at lunch this afternoon, at Annie and Ethel's excesses and at Annie's face when a tousled, red-cheeked Alice had come down the stairs with Dan this morning. Christmas Eve had brought about a change for the better in both their lives and they were over-spilling with happiness.

As they reached their destination, a cove just off the track, they began to clamber down the rocky path — it was really only suitable for mountain goats and the truly committed. Dan – who had been holding her hand and helping her down – suddenly stopped and held up his other hand. Alice stopped her chatter and looked across at where he was pointing. There in front of them were two very familiar figures, two friends. One was on his knees with the words *Marry Me?* spelt out large in stones on the beach.

Dan and Alice exchanged a smile and silently headed back up to the coast path, hand in hand.

-

Rosy was loving life and so far her Christmas holidays had been utter bliss. She had enjoyed being part of the choir but other than that she and Matt had tried to give themselves up to nothing other than resting, relaxing and revelling in the two weeks' holiday.

Matt had cooked Christmas lunch and the two had lolled around in the house in their pyjamas until Matt and Scramble had dashed out on a mysterious mission, leaving Rosy at home eating her weight in chocolate and watching Christmas movies. It wasn't long before he had come back in, wellies on and moulting sand, still a little out of breath.

He had persuaded Rosy to get dressed and come with him to the beach. Being one of her favourite things to do on a wintry afternoon, and seeing the beam on his face, it didn't take long for her to comply and follow him out of the door to her favourite cove.

Which is where she was standing now.

Speechless.

For there in front of her were the words *Marry Me?* spelt out in rocks laid upon the sand. They had caught her eye as she saw them from the coast path and she'd thought of what a lovely way to propose it was.

What she hadn't realised once she had got down to the beach was that the man she loved with all her heart, his dark curls whipping around his head, had stepped in front of her and dropped to one knee next to the stones.

Rosy's breath caught in her throat as she stood frozen to the spot, Scramble madly overexcited as Matt knelt on the sand and looked up at her, his hands proffering something that he had pulled from his coat pocket.

Oh wow. This couldn't be. Rosy couldn't believe her eyes.

When Matt had moved in next door, she had done everything she could to keep a distance between them. Little had she known back then that this was the man with whom she would fall in love, a man who would cherish her, make her feel safe and help heal the hurt that she had carried. Matt had taught her so much, given her so much and now he was kneeling in front of her on Christmas Day with what looked suspiciously like a ring box.

She needed to breathe. Falling over as she suffocated herself was not the romantic ending she presumed Matt was hoping for. At least, she hoped not. She managed to gulp for air as Matt mirrored the action, taking a deep breath before he spoke.

'Rosy Winter. What can I say? You are the most remarkable woman I have ever met, you have made me feel things I didn't think were possible and every morning I wake up to see your hair spread out on *my* pillow and I know that all is right with the world. We have lived together for nearly two years – okay, just over a year, and not only have you not killed me, you've made each day brighter, and made me happy knowing I have you to come home to, to curl up with in our bed at the end of every evening. You're a miracle worker and I love you with all my heart. So, I'm kneeling down here, in a bit of a gale' – she had been so focused on him, she hadn't even noticed that the breeze coming off the sea was pretty fierce – 'asking you if you would make me the happiest man in the world. Rosy Winter, will you marry me?'

His eyes were round as they gazed up at her, as were Scramble's, who was now sitting next to his master and giving Rosie his best pleading eyes too. Rosy wiped a tear away, scrunched her mouth up and inhaled deeply. This proposal in her favourite place by her favourite person, surely this was the best Christmas present anyone could have? To be told how loved she was by the person who had shaped her life for the better, enriched it, the person with whom she wanted to spend every day of her life, asking if she minded if he did that exact thing.

She gave him a smile and then walked towards him; she was overflowing with love and with so much happiness that she had tears streaming down her face. He slowly stood to his feet as she approached, the box still proffered, his grin matching hers.

She threw her arms around his neck, hearing the words 'Yes, yes, of course it's a yes. I love you so much!' And the two clung to each other, breathing each other in as deeply as they could, feeling safe and loved and joyful. They pulled apart and Matt lifted the ring – an old-fashioned one with an emerald in the middle to match her eyes, tiny diamonds clustered all around it – out of its box and slid it on her finger. She sought his mouth with hers and the two of them stood there on the beach as the wind whistled around them, knowing that the love they had for each other would last forever.

Acknowledgements

First of all, I have to sing to the skies about the huge love and respect I have for my agent, the wonderful Hayley Steed. To have you in my corner, listening to me when I get a little ranty (we both know it happens and that I enjoy it far too much), putting up with my constant anecdotes and never failing to advise me wisely and well means the world. I can't believe I got so lucky. Thank you.

Emily Bedford, my editor at Canelo, you have been an absolute joy to work with. I am really looking forward to working with you again on the next book, we're going to have so much fun.

For this book I had to ask a series of inane questions in the name of research to make sure I didn't mess up too badly in my portrayal of Dan and his profession. For this I'm indebted to Immi and Phil for their kindness as well as the vicar and parishioners of my local church, St Anne's, for their welcome and their patience as I bombarded them with my queries. Any mistakes or inaccuracies are quite obviously my own.

My SisterScribes, that is my dearest writing buddies, thank you so much for the constant support and encouragement: the daily word count check-ins; the lengthy emails as we discuss all and everything; the in-person catch-ups (I believe we are due another soon) and of course, the flowers and the chocolates. I really like the flowers and the chocolates.

Nicky – my other dearest writing buddy – let's make 2020 our year of doing everything!

And finally, my family – my partner, my children, my parents. A constant source of amusement, pride, support and full-out adoration. You're awesome.

Happy Christmas, everyone x

Cornish Village School series